"If Jane Austen had been born about two centuries later, gone to Smith, then palled around with Fran Lebowitz, chances are she'd have written like Elinor Lipman. . . ."
—*Chicago Tribune*

National acclaim for Elinor Lipman and . . .

THEN SHE FOUND ME

"A bright, lively, and funny look at an eccentric mother-daughter relationship."
—*The New York Times Book Review*

"An enchanting tale. . . . Full of charm, humor, and unsentimental wisdom."
—*Publishers Weekly*

"Funny and poignant. . . . *THEN SHE FOUND ME* is a truly happy book."
—*New Orleans Times-Picayune*

"Winningly wry and dry-eyed. . . . Funny, moving, and very wise in the ways of life."
—*Kirkus Reviews*

"Keenly expressed insights. . . . Charming."
—*Vogue*

THE WAY MEN ACT

"Part of the joy of this wise and charming novel . . . is in the writing. The rest is in the thinking—smart, offbeat, funny. What a pleasure."

—*Cosmopolitan*

"Fresh romance blooms on every page, as . . . characters reveal unexpected depths of emotion and capacities for deception."

—*Los Angeles Times Book Review*

"Elinor Lipman's eye for social geography instantly infatuates. . . ."

—*Glamour*

"The ideal novel to read in one stretch."

—*The New York Times Book Review*

"[A] stylish, witty, entertaining concoction."

—*West Coast Review of Books*

ISABEL'S BED

"By about page ten of this novel, the reader gets a . . . grin on his face, and that grin doesn't really stop for about a week."

—*The Washington Post Book World*

"Delightful. . . . Engaging. . . . The perfect companion. . . . After a short while, these characters become more vivid than one's own friends."

—*San Francisco Chronicle*

"Deft and funny. . . . Sit back [and] enjoy."

—*Entertainment Weekly*

Also by Elinor Lipman

My Latest Grievance
The Pursuit of Alice Thrift
The Dearly Departed
The Ladies' Man
The Inn at Lake Devine
Isabel's Bed
The Way Men Act
Into Love and Out Again

Elinor Lipman

Then She Found Me

WASHINGTON SQUARE PRESS
New York   London   Toronto   Sydney

Grateful acknowledgment is made for permission to reprint an excerpt from THE BEST OF DAYTRIPPING AND DINING by Betsy Wittemann and Nancy Webster. Copyright © 1985 by Betsy Wittemann and Nancy Webster. Reprinted by permission of Wood Pond Press, West Hartford, Connecticut.

A Washington Square Press Publication
1230 Avenue of the Americas, New York, NY 10020

Lipman, Elinor.
   Then she found me / Elinor Lipman.
      p.   cm.
   ISBN-13: 978-0-671-68615-4
   ISBN-10:   0-671-68615-1
   I. Title.
[PS3562.I577T47   1991]
813'.54—dc20   90-26437
                                                  CIP

First Washington Square Press trade paperback printing April 1991

20   19   18   17

For information regarding special discounts for bulk purchases,
please contact Simon & Schuster Special Sales at 1-800-456-6798
or business@simonandschuster.com

Cover design by Jeanne M. Lee
Front cover illustration by Coco Masuda
Woodcut by Charles Casey Martin

Printed in the U.S.A.

FOR BOB AND BEN

Special thanks to Henry Dutcher,
Grace Scanlan McDermott,
Atty. James C. Orenstein and Susan Z. Lynn for their
cheerful help in matters of
library science, Latin, law, and adoption, respectively.

Very special thanks to Lizzie Grossman,
dear and faithful agent,
and to Stacy Schiff, ideal editor.

Then She Found Me

ONE

My biological mother was seventeen when she had me in 1952, and even that was more than I wanted to know about her. I had no romantic notions about the coupling that had produced me, not about her being cheerleader to his football captain or au pair to his Rockefeller. When I thought about it at all, this is what I imagined: two faceless and cheap teenagers doing it listlessly in the unfinished basement where they jitterbugged unchaperoned.

"Adopted" was never a label that made me flinch. Its meaning within our family was "hand-selected," "star-crossed," "precious." I loved the story of my parents' first glimpse of me at the agency, how I solemnly studied their faces—hers, his, back to hers—then grinned. I was raised to be glad that the unlucky teenage girl couldn't keep me; the last thing I wanted was some stranger for a mother. Still, I slept with a light on in my bedroom until I was twelve, afraid she'd exercise her rights.

Later it annoyed me. The teenage girl annoyed me, nothing more. Could she ever have worn real maternity clothes or taken a single prenatal vitamin on my behalf? Here is where I remember to feel relief and gratitude and say, no matter. I am healthy, happy, better off. It is a lucky thing she didn't keep me. I'd barely have finished high school. I'd have become a beautician or a licensed practical nurse, and I would think I had a glamorous career. The grittier I made it the more righteous I felt. I invented these jitterbugging teenagers when I was in junior high school, as my adoptive parents began to look old. I voted against the irresponsible kids, emphatically for the Epners. My story suited me and I grew to believe it. I did not attend support groups for adoptees and I did not search for anyone.

Then she found me.

TWO

A Boston Globe staff photographer took the picture on a sunny Sunday. "One more time," read the headline. "April Epner, 3 1/2, makes her displeasure known as swan boat ride—first of the season—ends. Parents Gertrude and Julius Epner of Providence promise another." In ponytails and clutching a miniature pocketbook to my chest, I howl adorably. Trude and Julius smile at each other over my barretted head, the smile of doting parents whose Sunday outing has succeeded beyond their fondest hopes. Wire services picked up the Globe photo and sent it out on the national wire with a new headline: "Make way for ducts." It was used by newspapers all over New England and in odd spots where harbinger-of-spring photos were in short supply. Julius wrote to the Globe's photo librarian expressing his interest in a glossy print, which he matted and framed alongside its grainy, newsprint twin.

* * *

In downtown Boston, Bernice Graverman passed the brass plaque that read "Florence Cohn Agency" on a lunch-hour excursion. She thought, It's fate that made me get off the trolley at Boylston. I didn't mean to, but now that I'm here I must go up. She was pleased with the way she looked that day in her camel's-hair coat from the store's Washington's Birthday sale, and she had good news. She checked her brown pageboy, her lipstick, and the seams in her stockings before taking the elevator to the fourth floor. "Is Mrs. Prince here?" she asked the receptionist.

"There's no one here by that name," she was told.

"Yes, there is," said Bernice. "She was my social worker and it wasn't that long ago." She touched her stomach. One hundred sit-ups a day. As flat as ever.

The receptionist frowned and retreated, "You mean Mrs. Price."

"Isn't that what I said?"

"She's no longer here."

"Did she get fired?" the girl asked.

The receptionist pursed her lips and asked for Bernice's name at the time of her association with the Florence Cohn Agency. She opened a dark wood door and passed through into inner offices. After several minutes, an impeccable-looking woman in cream-colored wool followed the receptionist back to the waiting room. The woman offered her hand, introduced herself as Mrs. Mazur. Bernice rose eagerly to take it and made a mental note about the effects of gold accessories against cream-colored wool.

"Why don't we go into my office," said Mrs. Mazur.

"Love to," said Bernice.

It was Mrs. Price's office, she noticed. Same sappy photographs of well-adjusted children on the walls; same repeating medallions on the green wallpaper. Mrs. Mazur sat behind her desk; Bernice took the visitor's chair.

"I bet you wonder what I'm doing here," she said.

"Would you like to tell me?"

"I was just passing by and I said to myself, Maybe they like to see what happens to their mothers. See how they're doing and how they're adjusting. If they're happy, and stuff like that."

Mrs. Mazur's clasped hands rested on the girl's manila folder. Bernice saw her name typed on a label; she saw the itch in the social worker's fingers. She knew their need to read words on paper, to perform evaluations, to study folders well before the client sat down to talk. "Mrs. Prince always made notes when we talked, too," said Bernice. "I guess anything you'd want to know about me is in there."

Mrs. Mazur's fingers grazed the edges of the folder.

"Go ahead," said Bernice. "How else are you going to know how well I'm doing?"

Mrs. Mazur hesitated—agency policy—then opened the file and scanned.

"I'm doing great," Bernice continued. "I'm starting Northeastern in January and I'm going to study merchandising."

Mrs. Mazur murmured her approval while she read.

"I've gotten three raises in two years at Jordan Marsh and everyone says I'm management material."

Mrs. Mazur looked up, smiled anew, and closed the folder. "I'm so glad. I see it's only been five months since the adoption."

"It's going to be work-study, so I'll be earning my tuition practically at the same time." She sat up straighter. Her navy voile blouse had tucks on the bodice; she wanted this nicely dressed Mrs. Mazur to appreciate its workmanship and notice the navy taffeta slip underneath. "I figured you like to know these things . . . write them down in your official records."

"We certainly do," said Mrs. Mazur automatically. She wrote nothing in the folder. Bernice hated this one too.

"Can you tell Mrs. Prince I came in, and about my getting into college? And that I'm fine? I know she'd remember me."

A buzz from the phone. The manila folder sat unattended on the desk blotter. Bernice stood and smiled, pretending to have been dismissed. In a second she slipped the folder toward her; she had opened and closed it even before the social worker lunged to its rescue. "Sorry," Bernice said, flipping it back.

But she had seen the name—on a white card stapled to the inside of the file, first thing a person saw. How stupid could they be?

Her daughter's name was now Epner. Her daughter was with the Epners.

"Don't get excited," said Bernice. "I didn't see a thing."

There were no Epners in the Boston phone book. The operator said no, there did *not* have to be anyone by that name in the city, no matter how much the young lady insisted, and would she like to talk to her supervisor?

"It's not as if I want to call them or anything," answered Bernice.

Two years later Bernice Graverman found her daughter in the *Globe*. There was that name, Epner, and this little girl, just the right age. It was clear to Bernice that this fair and Polish-looking couple could not have given birth to this dark, sharp-faced little girl. "April," they had named her, of all things. Awful. Bernice cut out the picture, which she folded lengthwise, put in an envelope, and placed in the bottom of her jewelry box. She called information in Providence and got a phone number and address for Julius Epner. She added this to her jewelry box.

She had no plan. She was twenty years old and no more interested in unwed motherhood than she had been three years before. Semiannual phone calls to Providence—polite requests for phony names, apologies for a wrong number, in which she learned that the parents had German accents and the little girl answered eagerly a step ahead of them—were all Bernice Graverman did about her daughter, her only child, for thirty-three years.

THREE

You've seen "60 Minutes"—the airport reunion between the child she gave up twenty-five, thirty years before and the hand-wringing biological mother. Who are these people who invite the television cameras? There's the husband—not the biological father but the guy who married the young mother subsequently and understands her quest. There's their legitimate family, two or three sons. They look like their father, lumpish. The arriving daughter, dressed smartly, is the perfect image of her biological mother, who has bought a black leather trench coat for the occasion and has tied a bandanna around her neck for a touch of the rodeo. They must be getting paid to do this on national television, you think. What we see must be a restaging of what took place minutes before.

But maybe not. The mother is crying, and so is the new daughter. So is the stepfather. So are we.

I met the woman who said she was my biological mother in a diner ten minutes south of Boston. A friend of hers arranged the meeting after a day of laughable surveillance, trailing me nervously in her black BMW. None of it was necessary: my name and address were listed in the phone book; all this friend had to do—since she looked about as dangerous as a buyer for Saks shopping undercover at Bonwit's—was ask me if I was April Epner and I would have said, "Yes, sure." But she had to be a gumshoe; she had to put on sunglasses and follow my old Corolla to my high-rise apartment building. She had to catch up with me in the lobby as I was approaching my mailbox, key extended, and stop me with a tap on my arm. Close up, I could see her lips had been enlarged with lip liner and painted in with a creamy pink. "Were you born April first, nineteen fifty-two?" they said.

I blinked and didn't answer. I thought: This is one of those contests I didn't even enter, a piece of junk mail I threw out.

She tried again: "I represent someone in your past who's looking for an April Epner with that birth date."

I knew then. It had to be her, the woman who gave birth to me; the other mother, the one I had successfully buried. I must have said something filial because the woman asked briskly, "Would that be welcome news?"

"I don't know," I said. "I don't know, I just . . . My mother died."

"I'm talking about your real mother," she said. "Your biological mother."

"It's you, isn't it?" I asked after a few moments of measuring myself against this pancaked face, these monogrammed sunglasses, the sweater set and ropey pearls.

"No," said the woman. "But I'm a friend of hers. A dear, dear friend."

No, I thought. You can't be. You're not right. You can't be a dear, dear friend of the ragged teenage mother who couldn't take care of me even though she loved me.

"Where is she?" I looked toward the woman's car, half expecting to see a pregnant seventeen-year-old watching and sniffling.

"In Boston. She's a celebrity. She had a baby girl thirty-six years ago on your birthday and gave her up for adoption." The woman wore a gigantic square-cut amethyst where a wedding ring might be. I thought: a club of rich single celebrities searching for each other's babies.

"Oh, my God," I said. "What kind of celebrity?"

She pressed her lips together. "Did I say 'celebrity'? I wasn't supposed to reveal that yet. I'm just supposed to make the contact and the evaluation."

"Evaluation?"

"Not an evaluation. Just this, our conversation. I'm sure you understand."

"No," I said. "I'm sure I don't."

"Let me put it this way: my friend needs . . . certain parameters."

I asked what that meant, "parameters"?

She appraised my plain tan trench coat, my corduroy shoulder bag, then smiled tersely. "Bernice is not a social worker by nature. She wants to meet her daughter, but she's cautious. Anyone would be."

Bernice—that was the celebrity's name, a telling slip if only I could think of a single famous Bernice. "And what are you going to tell this Bernice? That I'm suitable? Or that I'm rude and that my raincoat needs dry cleaning?"

"I'm definitely recommending that she meet you," said the woman proudly. "Definitely. She'll take it from there."

"Gee," I said, "are you sure? Without even checking my references?"

"You're getting the wrong idea," said the woman. "I've really given you a terrible impression of her."

"Tell her I graduated from Radcliffe," I said angrily. "See how she likes that. And tell her I'm not a social worker by nature, either. Tell her I love my parents and I'm doing just fine."

"Radcliffe!" the woman repeated. "How wonderful."

"Cum laude," I added.

"She'll be tickled," said the woman. She held out her hand as if I'd just earned an introduction. "I'm Sonia Friedberg. I'm a dear, dear friend of your mother's." She lifted her sunglasses up to her forehead and said, "The resemblance is chilling, which is marvelous. It really makes things just that much . . . easier." She squinted at my hair and asked if I used something on it.

"What?"

"Your hair has an auburn cast to it. And a bit of a wave. You don't get that from her."

"My hair's just brown."

"Her natural color was brown, too," said Sonia. "And the eyes. You look like her especially through the eyes. That same deep brown; that same intensity."

I moved a step away.

"You have a sweeter face than she does. But still, it's marvelous. She'll be delighted."

"Who is she?" I asked angrily. "And what is so marvelous—that I look enough like her to close the case?"

"Oh," said Sonia, "that was never the question! She's always known you were the one. She's known your name for years and years, but it's only recently that she's been ready for you."

"But not ready enough to come herself instead of sending a spy?"

"She's an extremely busy woman," said Sonia. "She's used to delegating."

I fitted my key into the mailbox's lock and saw my hand trembling. "She sounds despicable," I said.

Sonia opened her mouth to register surprise. "Oh, no. She's not at all." She shook off the misguided image and laughed, as if picturing something indescribably delightful. "She's fabulous," she said. "Fab-u-lous."

FOUR

Bernice Graverman was my mother, all right, and I hated her within minutes. She was striking in a slim, dark way that recalled Bess Myerson in her Catalina swimsuit being crowned Miss America. "Gabrielle," she said theatrically as she saw me. "Gabrielle."

I walked down the diner's central aisle toward that voice. I know this woman, I said to myself. I know her on some level. Her voice . . . her face. I thought: it's mine. Uncanny, really. A prenatal memory.

"Bernice has her own TV show," Sonia was saying.

I didn't get it immediately. Then I heard her—static overtaking a weak signal. The introduction registered: this knowledge of Bernice was not imbedded in my DNA. It was not that of a child finding her long-lost mother. It was that of a casual viewer, a channel-spinner. Sonia nudged me and I sat down.

Bernice Graves, Boston morning television: "Bernice G!"—a show in upholstered wing chairs and coffee poured on air from a silver tea set.

"It's the reason I found you," Bernice said while I stared at her Buster Brown pageboy, tinted blue-black and stiff with shine. Her skin was tanned, except for wet-look white eye shadow. "I did a very *very* powerful show on the subject of adoption. Some birth mothers and some orphans. Just before the credits, I looked into the camera and said, 'I've never told anyone this before, but I gave up a child thirty-six years ago.' " Bernice closed her eyes and recalled the pain and glory of that cathartic moment. "I didn't feel it coming. Next thing I knew it was out. . . ." Bernice opened her eyes. "You didn't happen to see the show, did you?"

I said I had not. I taught school every day.

"It made the papers, too. Jack Thomas's column in the *Globe* and Norma Nathan's in the *Herald.*"

"I didn't hear about it," I said apologetically.

"It was the only time I ever let my audience see me cry."

"You were on live?" I asked.

Bernice stared. Had I asked if she was on *live?*

"What I meant was—"

"The show is taped," said Bernice. "The moment was real. In that sense, it was very live. I thought about cutting it. I also thought about running it by our general manager and then I thought, This is as gutsy as it gets. This is raw emotion. I'll take the consequences. I'll turn my life upside down. I cried when I saw myself on tape. I cry every time I see it."

"I can't believe you had the nerve to say it," said Sonia.

Bernice smiled bravely, gratefully.

"Would you have called her if you had seen it?" Sonia asked me.

I said I didn't know. Maybe.

"But you knew you were adopted, correct? That there was a real mother out there somewhere searching for you?"

I said I'd always known, but hadn't assumed anything about my real mother, had no reason to think she was either out there *or* searching.

"How could you not have called me after seeing something like that?" asked Bernice. "How could anyone not?" She turned to Sonia. "Is it me? Am I the crazy one? Look at us."

"She wasn't afraid to take the biggest risk of her life for you," said Sonia.

"In what way?" I asked. Bernice waited prettily for Sonia's explanation.

"Branding herself 'unwed mother.' Not knowing if the truth would cost her her job—"

"Painting a scarlet letter 'A' on my own chest, as it were," Bernice interrupted.

I asked what *did* happen after the broadcast.

"The phone calls ran four to one congratulating me for having the guts to do what I did," Bernice said. "Only two said, 'Get this slut off the air.' "

Sonia, staunch ally, harrumphed.

"It's the lunatics," said Bernice. "They're always threatening to go to the FCC and get you off the air. I had a married priest and nun on once—adorable—and I asked them a routine question about premarital sex. The switchboard blew up, literally."

Bernice and Sonia commiserated. I was the forgotten player in their reunion drama. It was probably my fault for missing my cues, failing to respond in a way that would lead to my sitting before a camera in a wing chair with one of my hands clutched in two of Bernice's.

"Would you like to see the clip sometime?" asked Bernice.

I said, "Maybe sometime. Thanks."

"She's very . . . detached. I expected something different," Bernice said to Sonia as if I weren't there to hear.

"She's in shock."

"No, I'm not."

"I know how I'd react if my real mother found me," said Bernice.

"Which doesn't make your set of reactions right, or hers wrong," said Sonia psychiatrically.

"Are you sure I'm her?" I asked.

Bernice looked to Sonia.

"Of course," said Bernice.

"Show her," said Sonia.

Bernice reached into an enormous red leather pocketbook. She removed a business-size envelope and took out a newspaper clipping. Its edges had darkened to a pale coffee color, but it didn't look too old or too used. It was me, April Epner, age three, crying on the swan boat, the 1955 picture I knew from my parents' foyer. I took it from her warily, spooked to see our private memento in someone else's hand.

"It's me with my parents on the swan boat," I said unsteadily.

"So you don't deny that?"

I asked where she had gotten it. She repeated her question.

"Why would I deny it? My name's on it."

Bernice took the clipping back as if she'd better not trust me with so fragile a piece of crucial evidence. "I cut it out of the *Globe* in nineteen fifty-five."

"I don't understand what this proves," I said.

"It shows how long I've known who my daughter is. It showed me where you'd be if I ever needed to get you. It says you lived in Providence and you were the daughter of Mr. and Mrs. Julius Epner."

"But how did you know this little girl—me—was your daughter?"

"I knew your name."

"How?" I asked.

"Against all odds," she said. "A very obliging woman at the adoption agency took pity on me and divulged what might have cost her her job." Bernice tossed her head. "Besides, look at them. You couldn't possibly have come from them. I knew first of all that you had to be adopted. Second, you were three and a half. My daughter was exactly three and a half that same month. And you looked exactly like me in *my* baby pictures. Exactly. I showed this to my mother without saying a word and she almost fainted."

"Your baby was born April first, nineteen fifty-two?" I asked.

"Yes."

"You should see the two of you in a mirror," cooed Sonia. "This would be the coincidence to end all coincidences if you weren't the daughter she gave up."

"How come you didn't do anything then?" I asked.

"I was twenty, twenty-one. I was still thinking I had done the right thing. And I was still expecting to marry someone and have children the right way. All this picture meant was that I knew where you were. Don't forget—this happened in the fifties, way before people started meeting in church basements to help each other find their illegitimate children and vice versa."

I asked if her timing was a coincidence. Had she known that my mother died recently? My father two years before?

"More or less," she murmured.

"How?"

"Something they call a clipping service," she said. "I've subscribed for a while, not that it gave me much of a return."

I thought of the man and the sons on the sidelines at TV reunions. I asked, "What does your family think of your search for your long-lost daughter?"

"Family?" She looked at Sonia.

"Husband? Other children?"

"Only you," she said.

"You've never married?"

"Why? Have you?"

I said no.

Bernice shook her arms so that her bracelets settled at her wrists. She smiled and said happily, "Another thing we have in common."

We drank our coffee and refused refills. Bernice collected the three bits of paper that were our checks. "Thank you for the coffee," I said.

She turned to Sonia. "Unbelievable. She's thanking me for a lousy cup of diner coffee, as if I don't even owe her that much. As if I have nothing to make up for."

"She doesn't want anything!" said Sonia. "She's here as an emotional and an intellectual investment, not because you're Bernice G. I told you she had integrity."

"What about dinner?" Bernice asked me. "Would you feel compromised by the occasional dinner?"

I said I thought that would be okay.

"We'll get acquainted."

"Okay," I said.

"How do you feel about this?" she asked.

How did I *feel?* A television question. Did other people in airport reunions and adoption-support groups cry at this point, or touch? I didn't feel like doing either. "I guess I have some more questions," I said.

From across the table Bernice put her fingertips to my lips to gently silence me. "Later," she whispered. I leaned away so she couldn't touch me again with any grace. She reached into the enormous red bag and took out a brown leather book. "Let's make a date!" she said. "This week? Thursday."

Thursday was too soon. I said I couldn't Thursday.

"Sunday night? Dinner? Imperial Teahouse?"

"Fine," I said.

"You like Chinese food?"

"Love it."

Bernice smiled maternally. She and Sonia looked pleased together. It made perfect sense, didn't it? Any daughter of hers would have to love dim sum.

"You want to know who your father is, of course," said Bernice.

Sonia did not speak up to silence her, but braced me by laying five creamy pink fingernails on my sleeve.

"Wait—" I said.

"A famous man, now dead," said Bernice as if she had been savoring the phrase for thirty-six years and nine months.

FIVE

"I want to know everything about you," Bernice said as we were being seated at Sally Ling's. "Start from your earliest memory. Or start with your life today and work backwards."

I shrugged out of my coat and draped it on the empty chair next to me. I told Bernice I had expected to talk about her first, at least the part about my father.

She pushed away her place setting and leaned forward, arms folded, elbows on the table. Without preamble or protest, she recited her story. "I met him when I was sixteen. I worked in Stockings on the street floor of Jordan Marsh, a buyer in training. It was a more personal department in those days with a great deal of customer contact. Stockings came in boxes, not on racks like greeting cards. I spent my days folding back tissue paper, carefully splaying my fingers inside nylons to demonstrate color and sheerness." She paused. "Am I going into too much detail for you at this juncture?"

"Go on," I said.

"I met Jack at my counter just before Mother's Day. I recognized him as an educated man and spoke accordingly—"

"Jack who?"

"I'm getting to that. 'Doesn't this Schiaparelli have a lovely diaphanous quality?' I asked. I saw the effect immediately. He started, then smiled his brilliant smile. For good measure, noticing his Harvard ring, I said, 'I can't wear my school ring because it snags the hosiery.'

" 'Where did you go to school?' he asked.

" 'Girls' Latin.' I lowered my voice so the other salesgirl wouldn't hear. 'I'm going to be a senior. They think I'm staying on here full-time.'

" 'And where do you live?'

" 'Brighton,' I told him. He grinned again and held out a tanned hand. 'I hope to be your next congressman.'

"I said something like 'You do?'

" 'I'm running in the Democratic primary. Maybe you could put in a good word for me with your neighbors.' That's *exactly* what he said.

" 'With pleasure,' I said.

"He patted his pockets and found a parking ticket to write on. I offered him my Jordan Marsh ballpoint. He wrote my name and address. . . . Nothing!" Bernice smiled triumphantly.

"Nothing?" I repeated.

"No flinch at the 'Graverman,' no reneging on what I sensed was sexual rapport between us out of anti-Semitism. Nothing! He asked if I'd like to help out in the campaign. 'Pretty girls are always needed,' I think is what he said. I blushed, of course. I was totally inexperienced and hadn't learned how to accept compliments graciously. 'If you think I can be of some help,' I said.

"He wrote a phone number on my sales pad. I said I'd call his headquarters that night. He was a beanpole then, and not terribly smooth, but I sensed his greatness. I should have kept that sales slip. It would be worth a lot of money today. And did I mention the stockings? A Mother's Day present for Rose."

Bernice ended her story with a quivering, pained smile.

I laughed. For the first time in her presence, I laughed.

"How dare you," she whispered.

"You're saying my father was Jack *Kennedy?*"

She stared for a long time, then said, "I know it's not what you were expecting to hear."

"Do you have proof?" I asked.

"He knew about you, if that's what you were wondering."

"John Kennedy got you pregnant?"

"We were deeply in love."

"Wasn't he married?"

"He hadn't even met her yet!"

"Why didn't he marry *you?*"

She patted her stiff bangs. "I loved him too much for that."

"His career, you mean? You were being altruistic?"

"Of course. It would have been political suicide for him to marry me. He'd have been crucified because I was pregnant and it would have been worse that I was a Jew. Jack would have come to resent me, too. Ironically."

"Why 'ironically'?"

"Because if he had chosen me—us—he'd never have been elected. He'd be alive today."

I asked if she was mentioned in any of the Kennedy biographies.

She stared at me again—it was my own schoolmarm's

stare, refusing to answer a question of such sass and ill will. "What sells books?" she asked finally. "You tell me: Bernice Graverman or Marilyn Monroe?"

I wanted to tell her that she was either cruel or crazy and in either case insulting my intelligence. I considered "You are a sick woman," or "You're lying." I settled on "I don't look like him at all."

"You don't," she agreed.

"Wasn't he tall?"

Bernice reached for the glass ashtray and placed it in front of her with a petulant clink.

"You're annoyed," I said.

She shrugged.

"Did you expect me to believe you?"

"When you're telling the truth, you don't worry about being taken for a liar."

"So you said to yourself, I'll tell April I'm her mother and President Kennedy was her father, and then she'll know. Period. That'll impress the hell out of her. Something like that?"

Bernice poked a long red fingernail into an almost flat pack of cigarettes and found one more. She lit it with a silver lighter and exhaled gracefully toward the ceiling. "I'm not an analytic person," she said. "I act first and live with the consequences."

"How old was he?"

"Twenty-nine," said Bernice, "but he looked twenty-two."

"I can't believe someone twenty-nine years old, running for public office, would seduce a sixteen-year-old campaign volunteer, practically on the spot."

"You're very naive. You don't understand the way it was. Politicians did whatever they felt like doing, especially bachelor politicians."

"Where did you go for your trysts?" I asked.

"Charlestown. An apartment of someone he trusted."

"Was he your first?"

"Of course!"

"How long did it last?"

"Weeks, months." Bernice looked away, then added: "For me, a lifetime."

I smiled, thinking that for all her drama she was a terrible actress. I asked if they had managed to be together often.

"Whenever we could. His schedule was impossible."

"Was he good?" I asked in a low voice.

Bernice smiled indulgently. "Terrible, by today's standards. All business. And his back always hurt."

"Was he right- or left-handed?"

"Right."

"Was he circumcised?" I asked.

"If you're trying to trip me up, you won't."

"Why weren't you angry? Didn't you want to ruin his career after he abandoned you?"

Bernice closed her eyes and shook her head, *rattled* her head vigorously. One toad-sized clip-on earring flew off her earlobe.

I thought: This person is my mother.

"There's so much I want to know about you," she said chummily, her revelation behind her. We were eating our meal, the entire list of eight appetizers. Bernice had ordered for us and told the waiter we must not be disturbed.

I asked what she wanted to know about me.

"Why, for example, would anyone want to teach a dead language in a public high school? Don't most Radcliffe graduates with your inclinations become college professors in the romance languages?"

I told her I loved Latin. That it was fun. Once you knew the rules, it was so logical.

She leaned closer across the table. "Am I hearing something *real* now, something"—she made a cluster of her fingertips and touched her head and then her chest—"something about April . . . that she likes rules and logic? Am I hearing something significant about her?"

I helped myself to one steamed dumpling and one panfried dumpling. After a moment I said, "I'm not good at that kind of question with someone I don't know."

She said quickly, "I understand perfectly. You have a hard time with intimacy. What should we talk about that won't take me in too close? Your job?"

"I don't mind—"

"Say something in Latin. I had four years of it at Girls' Latin and all I remember is *'Gallia est omnis divisa in partes tres.'* "

I said, with feeling, *"Semper ego auditor tantum?"*

"Much call for Latin teachers?" she asked, unmoved.

I told her, no matter. It was mandated in our curriculum. And I was tenured. *Tenere:* to hold.

"I hated it," said Bernice proudly. "Who wants to learn a dead language when there's Spanish and French and Russian and Japanese around? With a billion people on earth speaking Mandarin Chinese?"

"There'd be no French and Spanish without Latin," I answered. "And do you remember how beautiful Latin poetry is? Catullus? 'Let us live and love, nor give a damn what sour old men say. The sun that sets may rise again, but when our light has sunk into the earth it is gone forever.' You find that dead?"

Bernice sat back against her chair, blotted her mouth, and checked the napkin for signs of color. She was disappointed. I hadn't done enough.

"I know it's not a glamorous job," I offered, "but it's very satisfying to teach something no one cares about."

She looked at my clothes: a long-sleeved cotton jersey,

which I owned in black, purple, celery, and white, my blue drop-waist Indian cotton jumper. Tonight, for dress-up, I had added a Guatemalan shawl.

"Your look," she said. "What would you call it? Collegiate? Primitive?"

"Not to your taste?"

She smiled diplomatically. "We have all the time in the world," she said.

SIX

As far as I was concerned, my real parents were Trude and Julius Epner of Providence, Rhode Island, who had adopted me in 1952 and named me April. I was their only child for seven years until a baby brother temporarily diluted the power of my office. I forgave them for that act of disloyalty; I forgave them for everything because they died two years apart—my mother just last year—too young and before I was prepared. Widowhood at sixty-four made Trude a teller of pretty autobiographical tales, uncontradicted by Julius's dour editing. Her stories were eulogies to him: their meeting by chance, their wedding, their finding a little daughter more perfect than their own flesh and blood could have fashioned, considering. Trude started talking right after my father's funeral, the first night we sat *shiva*. The upstairs neighbors came the first night, and a contingent of my grown childhood friends arrived and left in a clump the second. Then the rabbi, the cantor, the cantor's wife, the widow of the old rabbi, one fellow retiree from the shoe store my father had managed, one temple elder none of us knew. Trude didn't comment on the poor attendance, but shortened our memorial week to three nights.

Afterward, we still went into the living room after the dishes were done, wore our mourning clothes, put out the leftover pastries. Trude talked, and my brother and I let her, circled by the empty folding chairs the funeral director didn't take away for four more days.

They had met on a train from Providence to Boston. Trude was headed to Filene's Basement and Julius to Fenway Park. Instead, they spent the afternoon together in the Public Garden, whispering in the German they hadn't spoken aloud for the months they'd been lodgers in the States. Neither asked the questions Americans loved so much—how mothers, fathers, brothers, and sisters had been killed and how they, miraculously, had survived; instead they exchanged the facts. She was twenty-five, Viennese; he, twenty-nine, from Munich. Their fathers had both been furriers. He had a brother in Palestine, and she had no one she knew of. Neither had been religious or married. Belsen and Auschwitz.

At dinnertime Trude called Providence and said she'd be late. They had supper at Woolworth's, speaking English at the counter, and toasted each other with glasses of bright green punch. It was for both the first meal away from their American sponsors, who heaped unsolicited second helpings of dull kosher food on to their refugee plates. Both ordered BLTs.

They took a late train back to Providence after cavorting to South Station like furloughed G.I.'s in a Hollywood musical. Slumping cozily against each other in the last car, Trude and Julius kissed.

Julius knew that night he'd marry Trude; he hoped he'd have the willpower to keep from proposing on the spot. When the train pulled into Providence, Trude gave him her phone number and took his for insurance. They embraced with the intensity and joy of lovers reunited.

Trude told the Solomons about Julius at breakfast. Adele wrinkled her brow with the effort of placing these people, the Wallachs. She had not tried to contact other families who had taken in displaced persons; Trude's Americanization, she had thought, would not be served by inducing friendships with hollow-eyed shells of men unsuited to her joie de vivre.

But Julius Epner sounded promising.

"Tell me," Adele prompted. Trude smiled sleepily and cupped both hands around her coffee cup.

"He's very lovely," she said. "Big, big blue eyes that stick out a little. Very kind eyes. High forehead with this . . . this hair!" Trude laughed and outlined a wiry bush above her own head.

Adele and Sy Solomon exchanged prayerful looks. "Will he be calling you?" Adele asked.

Trude answered yes as if any other possibility were too ridiculous to consider.

Trude said she might never be able to give him a baby. "In the camp I never menstruated. None of us did. I picture my insides shrunk away. Now sometimes I do and sometimes I don't." Julius instantly adopted Trude's dilemma as his own. If she couldn't have children—so be it. Perhaps it was not realistic, asking their bodies to reproduce and bring forth healthy children. It would be a miracle, actually, for Trude's thin little body and tender bones to bear his child. And it was selfish of him to want children at the expense of her health. They had each other to love, and wasn't that already more than he expected from such a life?

"The English doctors said you were all right?" he would ask from time to time. "They looked at you and said you were all right?"

This is a wonderful man, thought Trude. A mature man I can discuss menstruation with. I was a girl before the war; I dated boys. We talked about music and films and about our girlfriends and boyfriends.

"I was a silly girl," she often said to Julius. "I cared about two or three things: that I was taken out on dates by handsome boys, that I had pretty clothes to wear, and that I was at least as pretty as my sisters."

"You were a young girl. That's what young girls think about."

"I'm different now," she'd say.

"Meaning I'm not a handsome boy?"

She'd wag her head back and forth as if considering the question, then reassure him playfully about being so very handsome indeed. But to herself she'd think: Look what it took to make me no longer vain and spoiled.

She wanted to believe that if she were still in Vienna, if the war had never happened, she'd have grown up, stopped worrying about whether her many shoes matched her many outfits, and would have loved a slightly gawky man like Julius Epner.

Trude worked behind the counter at the Solomons' bakery on Prairie Avenue. They eased her into a full-time schedule as her stamina increased. Customers loved Trude, or the very idea of Trude, and her brave allusions to Viennese confections.

Old men and women pushed tips into her hand, pleading when she refused, "Please, for your relatives, then. Perhaps someone who needs it." "Such a salesgirl!" they'd say loud enough for the bosses to hear. "I bought out the store!" Adele Solomon, sales up, put an empty baking powder tin, labeled "Hebrew Immigrant Aid Society," next to the cash register to assuage those bent on charity. Trude felt the clang of every coin.

Sometimes a group of children would come in and buy a single cookie. Trude knew from the way they pushed up to the counter and stared that they had heard about the blue numbers and had come to see the refugee. And so many customers noticed the tiny peppercorn of a diamond Julius had given her when they became engaged that Trude saw how Americans needed her in an odd way; how they watched her, would always watch her, to analyze her nimble survivor's fingers for clues about her life.

At their wedding, guests seemed bewildered by the music and the dancing. The rabbi of the Providence synagogue spoke obliquely of their past and reverently about their children's children. Just before Julius, grinning, stomped on the symbolic wineglass, guests rose to say the prayer for the dead.

The bride and groom kissed exuberantly at the end of the ceremony. They giggled and held hands, the only two present who didn't adopt a mood of soulful celebration, which everyone including the bandleader seemed to think fit the occasion. It was as if the leading roles had been miscast: Julius Epner and Trude Weiss were supposed to be married in a manner befitting a solemn love born of tragedy, yet there they were, two kids in love, dancing as if they hoped the sighing guests would vaporize and a Murphy bed would drop from the function-room walls.

Friends gave them presents instead of cash as if to say, Our silver trays and appliances will remind you that we Jews in America can have possessions without fear of losing them to greedy neighbors when we flee our homes and are next sent to death camps. Trude wrote notes in her meticulous European hand thanking guests for their thoughtful selections. Then she and Julius returned as many as could be traced to area stores and opened a savings account that would pay for the birth of a baby.

Their apartment was a barely renovated attic with a clothesline bisecting the one long room. They ate on a maple drop-leaf table, slightly warped from years on the Wallachs' porch. Trude washed dishes in the small bathroom basin; Julius dried each plate and fork and cup and walked it to the unpainted shelves. They considered the worn room-size Persian rug ugly and old-fashioned, though years later Trude would wish they hadn't given it away. Their bed was large and new with an Old World eiderdown; the only wall it fit against was designated as kitchen so that the big bed, freestanding, appeared to be the centerpiece of newly married life. They didn't entertain or dance to Julius's bachelor radio because they didn't want to disturb their landlord downstairs. They drank strong coffee, washed dishes, took walks, alternated Friday suppers at the Solomons' and Wallachs'. Every month they waited for Trude's period to fail to arrive.

Just after their first anniversary, they saw a doctor, who said to relax. Trude asked scornfully how her eggs and Julius's seed knew whether she was relaxed when they had relations.

The doctor smiled indulgently at the quaint and simple thought.

"What else can we do?" asked Trude.

"Do you know when your fertile time of the month is?" asked the doctor.

"We're educated people," said Trude, finding her voice after the insult.

"Don't be offended," said the gynecologist. "A patient

once asked me why she hadn't gotten pregnant, since she and her husband slept together every night."

"Why hadn't they?" asked Trude.

"*Slept* together," he said, putting his palms together and to one side of his head, pantomiming sleep. "That's *all* they did."

"Is that a true story?" asked Trude sharply.

The doctor nodded. "Now you see why I don't take anything for granted."

"Be assured we know how to make babies," said Trude.

"Give it a year," said the doctor.

Trude asked if being in the camp had damaged her.

The doctor said, "Many of my patients who have led perfectly comfortable lives cannot conceive. Don't blame yourself."

"Who said I was blaming myself?" she asked.

After two years, Trude called an adoption agency in Boston, chosen from the phone book because it bore a Jewish woman's name. "My husband and I would like to inquire about adopting a baby," she told the person who answered the phone. She went right to the salient detail, the camps. The woman on the phone was a formidable gatekeeper, but she recognized the unusual and the compelling. Trude was put through to a caseworker. For a second time she asked whether the agency disqualified people if they had been in concentration camps. The caseworker sputtered and said, *"Disqualify!* Why, why, we . . . *glorify* people like you!" At her end of the line, Trude smiled knowingly. She made an appointment for herself and Julius and reported to him, "Social workers! Everything's black and white to them. They love their little heroes."

They took the train to Boston from Providence, then walked from South Station to Boylston Street. At their interview, they were served lemon drop cookies and tea in china cups with gilded twig handles. "We have to ask for certain documents," the caseworker apologized. "We have to observe our protocol. But of course you needn't worry about that. We know that your records have been . . . lost." More tea? she asked. Water? A piece of fruit? Trude explained that she was a coffee drinker; had the social worker realized she was Viennese? The interviewer said soothingly, "We are here to help you in any way you might need." Her expression—a look that Trude and Julius knew by heart—said, This is why I went to social work school and this is what I hoped to find in the adoption field. You will be my helpless wounded bird and I will be your eyedropper.

"One thing that we cannot make an exception about," the interviewer began once Julius's cup had been refilled, "is your income." Trude and Julius thought, This is it. Here's where they say, "We glorify you, as long as you own a home with at least two bedrooms." Trude cut in and named a figure that was almost twice as much as Julius earned. She didn't think they would ask for proof; she figured that Adele Solomon could write a letter saying Julius earned extra money working weekends at the bakery. What did she care about lying? What moral nicety was stronger than giving the answer that would result in a baby?

The social worker looked pleased as she recorded the figure. Refugees with qualifying incomes! Then she left the office and came back with another woman—Florence Cohn of the Florence Cohn Agency herself! She shook their hands and looked into their faces with a compassion reserved for the very rich and the very celebrated who knew the tragedy of infertility.

"We are honored that you came to us for help," she said.

"How long will it take to get a baby?" asked Julius.

"Do you have a preference for the sex?" They said they did not.

"Six months."

"Six months!" they said. "That's all? Six months!"

On their next visit, there was a manila folder before the caseworker. There had been a match. Some question about the religion of the baby's father. Was that acceptable to them?

Trude said, concealing her annoyance, "Of course."

"What of the mother?" they asked.

"Intelligent. Very. Seventeen years old. Healthy, attractive, good family. Has availed herself of prenatal care. Her involvement with the father was not . . . typical of her. She believed they were engaged."

"What's she like?" asked Julius.

The social worker, with a patient smile, repeated more slowly, "Jewish. Very smart. Very pretty. In good health."

"What I mean," said Julius, "is—will she make trouble when the baby's born?"

The social worker shook her head emphatically. "She is absolutely committed to giving this baby up for adoption. She has specified Jewish parents"—she read from a card—"with many books in their house and who will educate the child as far as his intellectual needs take him."

"She said that?" asked Trude.

"She'll be going to college herself as soon as this is behind her."

Trude and Julius nodded to each other.

"When is the baby due?" asked Julius.

"The baby's here," said the social worker. "She has an April birthday."

"April!" repeated my mother and father. They smiled. *April.*

* * *

Frederick was their natural child. I was seven when he was born, an age considered grown up enough to accompany them in a well-behaved manner wherever they were invited. Trude's pregnancy was a personal affront to me; besides not being their flesh and blood, I was left at home—me, their little lady, a mensch already—with tiny Freddie and the baby-sitter.

I asked all the time, "Is Freddie a beautiful baby?"

"Yes," they would answer.

"Was I a beautiful baby?"

"So beautiful."

"Who was more beautiful?"

"You were the most beautiful girl and Freddie is the most beautiful boy."

"But what if you didn't know who was what? If you saw both of us lying side by side in a crib, which one would you say was the most beautiful?"

What harm would it do, my parents probably said; Freddie wouldn't understand the question or the answer.

"You," Julius would mouth, and Trude would affirm with a poke of a forefinger into my belly. *You.*

In fact, Freddie was the beautiful one. He had reddish lights in his fluffy brown hair; he had Julius's blue eyes. His little body was irresistible in every posture. I never knew a baby could be so adorable, or that the sight of veins crisscrossing a chest under pale skin could be so moving. Worst of all, he was a miracle, Trude and Julius's *lang ersehntes Wunschkind*. Did they think I didn't understand?

Visitors came to see Freddie—more friends than I ever knew we had. Some engaged me in a few moments of big-sister talk before rushing to coo over the bassinet. Some brought presents for both of us. Books were popular, and barrettes; little-girl toilet water in bottles shaped like teddy bears. Who were they kidding with their one or two halfhearted questions and their coloring books? Keep April distracted, the presents seemed to say.

I was yesterday's news in my pink-framed eyeglasses and new, big permanent teeth. How nice for Trude and Julius that, just as April's homeliness—no fault of theirs—was surfacing, a baby like Frederick should come along.

Freddie and I said, "Will you remember all this to tell the grandchildren, or would you like it on tape, an oral history?"

"These little stories?" Trude said. "Absolutely not. My voice on tape sounds like an old lady's. I have an accent on tape. Why go to such troubles?"

We didn't push. Freddie said, "Okay. We don't need them on tape—April with her good memory and all. Besides, you'll be around to keep the details straight. You'll tell the grandchildren—what am I saying?—the *great*-grandchildren."

She went along with this false good cheer, even though she didn't feel well. Even though I was thirty-four, unmarried, unwooed. Even though Freddie was living at home at twenty-seven, happy to have Trude folding his underwear and cutting his meat while he sneaked out to boink the unaccountably large number of women who found his cockiness and his red-gold Vandyke beard cute. My childhood friends noted his grown-up charms when they paid their respects. He looks like Julius, they told my mother, but with a certain, well, American robustness. Little Freddie. Who would have thought? Even during the week we were officially in mourning women called him. He'd get off the phone and say, "Just someone I work with. Just a friend. Heard about Dad."

"You weren't on the phone for very long," my mother would say.

"I know I wasn't. It was a business call, basically."

In private Trude would worry. "I did something wrong. He thinks it's shameful to bring a girlfriend home. He's waiting until I die so he can marry anyone he wants."

I'd say, "Stop it. You're not going to die just because Daddy did."

"Don't let a shiksa have my engagement ring. I'm leaving it to him, but you see that it doesn't end up on the finger of some little shiksa. You keep it for yourself if you think I wouldn't approve."

"Where are you going to be?" I'd always answer, "Florida?"

"These are the things I think about," she'd say quietly.

She died in an ambulance twenty-three months later while two paramedics tried to save her. They managed to start her heart up again, which made her just conscious enough to fight them off and split the lower lip of one. "Let me go," she cried.

They said she had had chest pain while Freddie was at work—real chest pain, finally; months of angina disguised as stomach cramps and hot flashes had failed to pique the concern of her semiretired internist. "Intestinal angina," a cardiologist said afterward. "Must have been. Fools a lot of good people. I would have done an angiogram if she had been under my care."

"They see their loved ones," the bleeding ambulance attendant told Freddie in the emergency room, "just like you hear about on TV. It looks so beautiful to them that they don't want to come back. That's why she was saying 'Let me go' like that."

"You didn't listen to her, did you?" Freddie yelled. "You still kept trying, right?"

"She coded," he said. "We kept trying and then the E.R. docs took over."

"How come other people get brought back?" Freddie asked. "Why didn't it work with my mother?"

"She's happy now," the EMT said. "We see this a lot. Makes you think they're goin' on to someplace better."

"We're Jewish," Freddie said. "We don't believe in that." He excused himself and said he had to call his sister. She lived out of state. He had to tell her.

"She's lookin' down at you," said the EMT. "She's watchin' over you and that sister of yours. You can bet on that."

Freddie called me at school and spoke carefully. When I cried, he said he had held up so far with the doctors and those EMTs but that now he was scared.

"I'll come right now. I'll be there in an hour. Will you be all right?"

"Are you?" he asked.

"Are you?"

"This guy said she was asking to die, and now she's with Daddy, watching over us." His voice cracked and he stopped.

"That's what people say. They think it helps."

"It wasn't like that. This guy saw something. He was *there*—he knew what he was talking about."

"I'm leaving right now," I said. "I love you."

It had been two years since Bernice Graves had found any clipping about the Epners of Providence in her monthly statement from the service. She complained about not even having enough for a scrapbook—not that she would have done anything so patently tacky as create a shrine to her lost child, anyway. We had been the least newsworthy family in America, she said. No engagements, marriages, citations, elections, promotions; just an obituary now and then. This one was headlined, "Gertrude Epner, 66, Holocaust Survivor." It said she was from Vienna, had survived internment in Auschwitz, had met and married fellow displaced person Julius Epner in Providence in 1948. Two children: daughter April of Quincy, Mass., and son Frederick, at home. At least this clipping stated explicitly where I was; and at least it brought her up to date on my family situation: I was fatherless, motherless, childless, and husbandless. Probably lonely and, even if I didn't know it yet myself, ready.

SEVEN

So once a week at the restaurant of her choice Bernice treated me to dinner. She quizzed me on my life in the form of coy questions often asked of celebrities in magazine sidebars: my favorite color, shoe size, most unforgettable birthday party, last book read. It was only a warm-up, though, a stab at intimacy before asking what she really cared about: me and men. Me and sex.

I told her I had had boyfriends.

"In high school?" she asked. "College?"

"Not really. . . ."

"Who was the love of your life?" she asked easily.

"I feel kind of funny talking about this," I said.

She looked puzzled. *Funny* talking about men?

"I don't have a lot to tell," I said.

"I'm not going to judge you by what you've done or haven't done. I need to know certain things for my"—she searched the acoustic ceiling tiles for the word—"to satisfy a *craving* I've had all these years. A craving to know you."

"Well," I said, "there was this man—my supervisor when I was student teaching—"

"What was his name?"

"Willis."

"How old was he?"

I shrugged. "Forty?"

"And you were . . . ?"

"Twenty."

She listened to my accounting and said, "Why, this is fascinating!" And: "It makes perfect sense. You were looking for your father."

I shook my head as she explained her theory: *abandoned,* looking for male validation. One didn't have to be Sigmund Freud to see it.

"I never felt that way."

"Consciously," she snapped.

"Ever."

She signaled for the waiter, a handsome young man with the presence of a moonlighting graduate student. She asked him about desserts; what he, off the record, would tell two reckless women to share. He held up a tanned finger, smiled, and returned with a slice of something runny and chocolate.

"You're a genius," Bernice told him.

"Do you know him?" I asked.

She said no, why?

"You seemed to."

Bernice looked at me evenly. "I make my living talking to strangers. If I can do it with millions watching me, I can certainly handle a waiter." She picked up a fork, poised it over the cake, and said, "You were talking about being in love with your principal."

"My supervisor."

"Tell me everything," she said.

Not much to tell: supervisor confesses on his student teacher's last day that he has these feelings of a personal nature. Student teacher is surprised, mostly flattered. Feels tenderness for pudgy red-haired bachelor whose upper lip and brow perspire when she is in the same room. They date for the summer. She realizes by August that flattery only goes so far. She doesn't take the job offered at his school, and that's the end of it.

"I never saw him again. I took another year of Latin courses so I could teach secondary."

"Where?"

"Wellesley."

"Escaping from the hard, cruel world of men and romance!"

"Well, I wouldn't exactly—"

"Never to return?" Bernice asked with her eyebrows arched.

Later after coffee and small talk about the station she asked, "And that's it?"

"What?"

"I mean after Willis. Anyone else?"

Of course she had to ask. It was the way she measured the intimacy between us—by how much we told each other. I asked how comfortable she would have been if her mother had asked her these kinds of questions.

"Understand something, April. Sex to me is . . . glorious. And fun. Not something you hide from your mother. When I talk about it or ask you about it, I'm asking you in the same spirit I might ask how you enjoyed a meal or a movie you shared with a man. I wouldn't talk to my mother about these things because she would get upset. You're right. She's from the old school."

I asked her if she was saying her mother *would*—present tense—get upset? Her mother was still alive? I had a *grandmother?*

"I'm barely fifty," said Bernice stiffly. "It's hardly an earth-shattering piece of news that my mother's still living."

"It is if you've never had a grandmother, if you've never even seen a picture of one of your grandparents."

Bernice frowned. "I know what you're saying, but she's not what you're looking for, believe me. She didn't want anything to do with a grandchild conceived out of wedlock. And that's her big tragedy in life—not that she didn't keep you, but that her only child could make such an embarrassing mistake in the first place."

I hesitated a few moments, then asked her what had happened when she came home pregnant with me at seventeen. Bernice closed her eyes and inhaled deeply through her nose. "I thought of taking my own life to punish her," she said. She opened her eyes and looked at me. "Does that give you an idea of how she carried on? I had to be the one, at seventeen, to make all the decisions, to say, 'Ma, it's not the end of the world. I'll go away. I'll have the baby. We'll arrange for it to be adopted by a nice family and then I'll come home and you can forget it ever happened.'

"She fell apart. She went screaming to my father, who was a son of a bitch and needed to be handled. I always led up to things gradually with him, about dates or a bad grade—small potatoes in comparison, but he still needed handling. But, no. My mother had to drop the bomb and see it explode on my head. I hated her for that, for the whole way she added insult to injury. I wasn't just pregnant! I was destroyed! I had been tricked by the oldest trick in the book—and then he walks away and I'm left at my parents' door . . . at my parents' *mercy,* which of course is a joke. I laugh when I read these articles about parents who rallied around their daughter after getting over the initial shock; how it *strengthened* the family. Not the Gravermans! It ruined the Gravermans. We all hated each other after that." Bernice dropped her chin slightly to signal the end of her soliloquy.

"I'm sorry," I said.

"What for?"

"That you had to go through that with your parents."

"Thanks," said Bernice.

"I didn't know you had a mother, and I certainly didn't know you were feuding all these years."

"She'd have forgiven me a long time ago if I'd gotten married and had children. That would have wiped everything clean. I would have been a good daughter who made a little mistake. Now I'm a daughter who gave her no *naches,* if you know what that means—nothing to be proud about. It's ludicrous! As if seeing me in a nice house in Newton married to some schmuck of an accountant son-in-law is her goal. Of course the irony here is that her bubby friends beg me for tickets to my show. They get their housewife daughters to take them and it's the high-light of their year. I'm a celebrity to everyone but my own mother. She still worries about what people think; that they remember I dropped out of sight for five or six months in nineteen fifty-two and they're still gossiping behind her back. I know there are people who have a feeling for their flesh and blood and can't stand the thought of giving their own grandchild away. But that never oc-curred to my parents. They'd be the last people in the world to have said, 'Who cares what the neighbors think? We raise our own!' "

I asked if she considered keeping me.

"How could I have kept you?"

People do it, I said. Run away?

"I was seventeen. I'd never had any responsibility. I had no money." Bernice forced a cynical laugh. "You've seen too many soap operas where the pretty young waitress from out of town works two shifts to support her illegitimate baby—while the bighearted landlady back at the rooming house watches the baby. That wasn't the life I had planned for myself. Or you.

Or you. Added as an afterthought. She was telling me her story, but didn't have the grace to embroider a little feeling for the baby who turned out to be me.

"How do you think I feel when you tell me about this stuff?" I asked.

Bernice looked puzzled.

"About how I ruined your life, your family life; how all of you hate each other because of me; how I was as unwanted as I could possibly have been?"

"Should I lie to you?" asked Bernice. "I could do that, and tell you whatever you want to hear."

"I don't want to hear how you've never recovered from the tragedy of having me. How am I supposed to react? Should I say I'm sorry? 'Forgive me for getting conceived'?"

Bernice picked up her wineglass and receded farther into her chair. She stared directly into my eyes. When it began to feel like a contest, I looked away. "You hate me," she said quietly.

EIGHT

I went with her to Brighton on a Sunday afternoon to meet my widowed grandmother. Bernice and I had known each other for a month. "What have you told her?" I asked as she rang the buzzer.

"Not the whole story."

"She knows you found me?"

Bernice rummaged through her purse, but stopped to scowl at my question. "Let me do the talking," she said. She returned to her search and came up with a key attached to a rhinestone diaper pin.

"Shouldn't we knock first?" I asked when we reached the apartment door.

"She can't hear with the television on," said Bernice.

My new grandmother was sitting at the kitchen table giving herself a manicure. The room smelled of nail polish remover and cigarettes. She had champagne-blond hair that looked newly cut and teased to its full one-inch height. She was wearing a black sweat suit that spelled "Rodeo Drive" in chrome studs across her bosom. Of course this would be what Bernice's mother looked like; what Bernice would look like in twenty years; and, I realized, who I might be in forty years.

"Ma," Bernice said, "I brought someone for you to meet."

The old woman rose from the table, not taking her eyes off my face, and shook my hand. "You're her," she said. I looked to Bernice for permission to answer.

"Of course she is," said Bernice.

I readied myself for her embrace and her tears. Instead she shrugged and went back to the table. "I don't know what purpose this serves," she said to her daughter.

"You don't know what purpose this *serves?*" Bernice answered derisively. "Well, can you imagine any possible reason I might have for bringing you the daughter I gave away, my only child, your grandchild; that there's a *movement* in this country of lost mothers finding their lost children?"

"Don't get crazy," said the old woman, "and don't make me say things that will hurt this young lady's feelings." She turned to me with a newly pleasant smile. "What about your life? They gave you to a nice couple?"

"Yes."

"Jewish? They were supposed to try."

"Refugees," said Bernice.

Her mother squinted at her unhappily—a signal, apparently, that she hadn't heard properly.

"Refugees," Bernice repeated louder. "From Hitler."

Her mother looked at me and back at her daughter. "They gave her to refugees? From Europe?"

"What's wrong with that?" I asked.

Bernice rolled her eyes. "I'm talking about opportunities."

"They gave me opportunities."

Bernice faced me squarely and put her hands on my shoulders. Before she spoke she glanced at her mother as if making certain she had the floor. "With the stroke of a pen I had the power to make you the first Jewish president of the United States or a classical pianist or an Olympic ice skater," Bernice began. "It was a seller's market even back then, and I could say, 'I want her to go to a family with means, a family who values education and travel, who will give her piano lessons and surround her with music. I want a Jewish family—not too young, not too old. I want her to learn languages and to take ballet. Material things are less important to me than the . . . the intangibles.' " Bernice's voice turned snappish. "And that's what they retained, 'the intangibles.' I was probably the only sap who went on in that vein, about the things money couldn't buy being so important to me. I gave them carte blanche to give you to two war-torn refugees who were rich in *intangibles*."

"Your instincts were good," I said quietly.

Bernice looked at me wearily. "I know. Your marvelous-parents-and-happy-childhood speech. I've heard it."

"Would you be happier if I had had a lousy life? So you could rescue me?"

Bernice considered my question for longer than it should have taken.

"That has some appeal, doesn't it—the abused orphan rescued by her glamorous mother?" I asked.

Her face brightened. She dropped her hands and sat down in a kitchen chair. "Glamorous? Do you really think so?"

I could see her mentally taking her pocket mirror from its suede sheath and studying her face with new objectivity: My daughter thinks I'm glamorous. Am I really?

Bernice smiled and leaned back against the padded

plastic as if we were embarking on an expansive and cozy topic. "Tell me what you imagined I'd be like," she said.

I shook my head, not understanding.

"As a child—you know—when you knew you were adopted. Didn't you wonder about your real mother?"

She looked confident that I would say flattering things about her. She believed so thoroughly in her own excellence that she could not conceive of answers other than ones that would conclude with me saying, "And you are my dream mother, so beautiful, so celebrated, so well dressed, so hip."

"I really didn't think about it," I said. "My parents were who they were, and I didn't sit around thinking about it."

"You were so contented, then?"

"I was not the kind of kid who sat around daydreaming about things that weren't going to happen."

Bernice turned to her mother. "Doesn't every kid imagine she's the lost-long daughter of a movie star? Isn't that typical of some stage?"

Mrs. Graverman said, "Maybe she didn't have much imagination."

"Or maybe she's not telling us the whole story."

I wasn't going to say it here in Dora Graverman's kitchen: I hated having refugee parents. I was embarrassed by my parents, by their accents and their disdain for easy American lives. Friends would ask, "Where were you born?" meaning "Are you a foreigner, too?" and I would answer, "Here," ignoring the complications surrounding my birth. Their mothers had short hair, permed into waves and curlicues, and perfect eyebrows that were darkened with pencil into velvet arches. Trude had long hair pulled tightly away from her face into a bun, exposing the gray. I wanted a young American mother who wore pedal pushers and sleeveless blouses. I asked them to speak English at home when we had visitors. It was awful to have a friend ask what language they were speaking and for me to answer "German" and then to explain, when my friends' eyes popped out, that there was German and there was German, that my parents had been, well, prisoners during the war, *definitely* on the side of the Americans, in any case.

If I said Trude and Julius were a trial as parents, Bernice would make me her informer, brainwash me, turn me against them, plant her flag in my captured head.

Bernice took a cigarette from her mother's pack on the kitchen table. She lit it by leaning into a burner on the stove.

Her mother asked me, "Are you married?"

"No."

"You go to business?"

"I'm a teacher," I said.

"So they sent her to college," Dora said to Bernice.

"Everyone sends their kids to college," said Bernice.

"Maybe if she had an unhappy childhood or they weren't good people . . ." Bernice's mother shrugged.

"What are you shrugging?" Bernice demanded, mimicking and exaggerating the shrug. "What? That I should walk away from her and send her back where she came from?"

"She thinks the other one, the refugee, was her mother," said the old woman quietly.

"I'm not looking to mother her. I'm only seventeen years older than she is. I thought we could salvage some kind of relationship. But there's obviously too much hostility there. I am what I am, and she doesn't like it."

Dora Graverman said to me, "Look. She did what girls did in those days when they got into trouble. They went away and had their babies and came home when they were skinny again. It wasn't anything personal. Jewish girls didn't have babies at seventeen and keep them."

"I didn't say she should have."

"Ma! She's saying just the opposite—she's saying, 'Go fuck yourself, Bernice. I don't want you and I don't need you.' She's *glad* I wasn't her mother."

Dora turned to me for confirmation. "So what do you want with her?"

"I don't know," I said.

"You came here. You met me."

"She's got no grandparents," said Bernice. "They were all wiped out."

"Gotteniu," murmured Mrs. Graverman.

"She never knew them," Bernice said flatly.

"You seem to be a very nice young lady."

"Of course she is."

"And you seem intelligent."

"She went to Radcliffe," said Bernice. "And she teaches classical languages."

"A boyfriend?" asked my new grandmother.

I told her no.

NINE

Anne-Marie, the school secretary, was twenty-five and had a mouth. She wore leotardlike clothes year-round, and earrings that looked like Calder mobiles. Senior boys with high self-esteem asked her out.

She was the one who screened Bernice's phone calls to me, ruling that nine out of ten were not urgent medical or psychic emergencies. Bernice insisted it was ridiculous that I couldn't be pulled from my classroom on demand or, preferably, reached directly with a twentieth-century Centrex system, which the rest of the world had managed to install thirty years before. She also wanted to know, as I answered one of these calls in the main office, who this battle-ax was who screened my personal calls.

"Anne-Marie."

"What is she?" Bernice asked.

I hesitated, then said, "She's just doing her job."

"Which is what?"

"Secretary," I said.

Bernice thought over this affront. "Is this secretary a friend of yours?"

I said, "I can't really talk here."

"I get it. She's right there. What you're trying to say is, this woman is a problem, but she's been there for a hundred years and the union won't let you get rid of her."

I laughed and said, "Anne-Marie is the sex symbol of Quincy High School. Ask anyone."

I was standing by Anne-Marie's desk. She smirked and said, "Yuh, right."

"Sex symbol?" asked Bernice. "Is that code for 'she fucks the principal'?"

"Do you want me to ask?"

"No. Is she married?"

I asked Anne-Marie, "Have you married since the last time we talked?"

"Yuh, right. I married Dwight Willamee."

I laughed.

"Who?" Bernice asked.

"It was a joke," I said.

"Do I know this person?"

"Our librarian," I said. Anne-Marie poked the bridge of her nose, pushing up imaginary glasses. Repeatedly. A tic of Mr. Willamee's. I laughed again.

"It's rude to exclude a person from the conversation," Bernice complained. "Rude and annoying."

"Oh, we're rude, all right," I said.

"Who are you talking to?" asked Anne-Marie.

Bernice, I mouthed.

"Tell her to call you at home, please."

"Did you hear that?" I asked Bernice.

"Does she know who I am?"

"Do you know who this is?" I repeated to Anne-Marie.

"Bernice Graves. No one else calls you here."

I said to Bernice, "She's most contrite. She didn't know who she was talking to."

Unhappily, Bernice asked, "No one else calls you there? Ever?"

"I've gotta go. I've got fifteen minutes to eat."

"You're a slave," she said and hung up.

I gave the receiver back to Anne-Marie, who checked first to see if any students were in the office. It was empty. She gave the phone the finger.

I ended up eating my sandwich standing up in the office, telling Anne-Marie why Bernice was calling me every day.

"Did she tell you who the father was?"

I said evenly, "John Fitzgerald Kennedy."

Anne-Marie didn't consider it for more than a second; she whistled. "Seriously demented."

"That's her story."

"He's big with the crazies, you know—JFK, Christ, and the CIA. My aunt works at Bridgewater State, and those are the big three there."

"She doesn't believe it. It's an act she worked up to impress me."

"Does she think you bought it?"

I said no, she couldn't. She'd have to think I was a moron to believe that. I certainly didn't *act* like I believed her; at least I didn't think I acted like I believed her. . . .

"She thinks you bought it! She thinks you're looking at yourself in the mirror this minute and saying, *'That's* where I got such white teeth.' "

"Uh-uh," I said. "She knows I know."

Anne-Marie shrugged. She liked to use her dancer's shoulders. "Go look it up. Maybe it could be true."

"You can't look this kind of thing up. You think there's a footnote in a history book that says, 'Conceived illegitimate child, nineteen fifty-one. *See* Epner, April'?"

"How do I know?" said Anne-Marie. She stabbed at the bridge of her nose again, repeatedly, pantomime for "Go see the librarian."

I said okay.

I had seventh period free. There were no JFK biographies on the shelf—it seemed they were all displayed in a glass case outside the principal's office to commemorate Citizenship Day—so I waved to Mr. Willamee for help. He came out from behind the circulation desk, extremely tall and thin with long feet in tan suede bucks and a sad skeleton's face. Elbows that stayed close to his body when he walked left an unfortunately effeminate impression. Someone should do something about that, I thought; there wasn't a wise guy in school who could resist imitating Dwight Willamee when his back was turned.

He asked what I was researching about Kennedy, as if it were a delicate but necessary question.

"The dates he was a congressman—when he first ran, actually."

Mr. Willamee brought me the J–K volume of the *World Book* and said, "It's all here. Everything you need to know." I thanked him and sat down at a library table to study the photographs. Could the genes of Bernice Graverman and Jack Kennedy have produced a child who looked like me? Could I be half sister to Caroline and John Junior? Cousin to those Joes and Kathleens and Patricks?

Mr. Willamee approached the table with another book. "Would you be interested in *Profiles in Courage?*"

"I think I have what I need. Thanks."

Mr. Willamee looked disappointed to be of no further bibliotechnic help. The library was deserted. I wanted to say something reassuring—that I had obtained exactly, but *exactly,* the right information in no time at all. . . . Silly for me to ask for a biography when I should have known to go straight to the encyclopedia. Mr. Willamee said it was his job to know where to look things up; his first love was research, after all.

I felt uneasy accepting his help, using his time. I shouldn't have let Anne-Marie make fun of him in the middle of the office. He could have been outside the door on his way to collect his mail. I had encouraged her, and he might have heard me laughing—a colleague, a mature teacher of Latin, someone who always said hello and gave an impression of perfect respect. So I told him as he stood there awkwardly, poised to unlock the display of biographies if needed, overtending to his only patron—*confided* in him that a woman had come to me, the woman who had given birth to me and given me up for adoption; that in the course of our reunion she had told me that the man who was, who she *said* was, my biological father was . . . President Kennedy.

Mr. Willamee didn't laugh. He asked calmly, "And what year were you born?"

I told him—1952. April 1, 1952. He smiled faintly.

"What?" I prompted.

"April. Your name."

"Charming, isn't it?"

He looked at the biographical data, skimming the column with a bony middle finger.

"I know it *is* possible," I said before he pronounced the obvious—that technically, historically, medically, any which way, it certainly was possible.

Mr. Willamee listened. He stabbed at the bridge of his glasses and asked, "Is she a credible person?"

I said I didn't know yet.

"I mean—is she sane and rational? Not schizophrenic or . . . impaired?"

"It's Bernice Graves," I whispered. "From TV. She has a show called 'Bernice G!' A local talk show."

Mr. Willamee grinned slowly and shook his head in disbelief. He said, " 'My time with you is precious'—that one?"

"What?"

"That's her tag line. She closes the show that way. My mother watches."

Encouraged, I continued: "She told me Kennedy came into Jordan Marsh where she was working and they started talking. She found out he was running for the Democratic primary in her district, and one thing led to another—"

Mr. Willamee's eyes and fingers drifted back to the *World Book*. "Primary?" he repeated.

"Something like that."

He studied the page for confirmation. "He was in his second term in 'fifty-one." He pointed to the date.

"No kidding!"

"Of course, he did have a reputation with women," said Mr. Willamee, "and one that has since been documented." He waited politely for my response. Oh, God, I thought. Please don't let me laugh in his face. Mr. Willamee closed the book, his finger marking the page. "If you wouldn't mind, I could work on it. I'm not that busy."

"Okay," I said. "Sure."

I thought it was unnecessary, but his offer made me sad. I wanted to show the generous side of my character, the side that didn't make fun of homely people, especially those with no friends and nothing better to do. Mr. Willamee looked up as two students entered the library holding hands; he blushed as if he had been caught doing something flagrantly outside his job description.

Good. Let them see Mr. Willamee having a pleasant conversation with another teacher. Let them see there are people in this school who treat him with respect. "Thank you very much, Dwight," I said. I raised my voice. "So I'll check back with you on this . . . when?"

"Tomorrow," he said. "Or whenever it's convenient."

I turned at the door and called, "Nice talking with you, Dwight." I checked my audience, two stupid seniors all in black, and added, "As always."

I saw Mr. Willamee again that week, this time out of school. He was grocery shopping at a Quincy supermarket with a tall woman in surgical stockings, his mother, I presumed—she had the graying version of his Vaseline-colored hair. The appearance of two generations of Willamees made me realize he had an age, a birthday. His mother looked about Trude's age, maybe sixty. Was he forty, then? Younger?

He was pushing the cart, commenting agreeably on her choices, looking happy as if food shopping was a favored activity. I stayed back, pacing my own cart one aisle behind them. At one turn, before I retreated, I saw Mrs. Willamee offer him a four-pack of applesauce. He protested, laughing, and she put it back on the shelf with a shrug. I was relieved. Snack-packs of applesauce for his lunch box would have been sadder than I wanted to know about.

TEN

I wrote Bernice a letter and told her that after a superficial checking of facts, I had confirmed that President Kennedy was elected to the U.S. House of Representatives in 1946 at age twenty-nine; served 1947 to 1953.

She called me at work and got me: it was an emergency, Anne-Marie said. Urgent.

Without preamble Bernice said, "What does this letter refer to?"

"It refers to my not believing your story."

There was no answer at her end. "Bernice?" I asked.

"I can't talk here," she hissed.

"You called me. Do you have proof of some sort?"

"You must have misunderstood what I told you."

"You said he was running for Congress. When he introduced himself at Jordan's he said, 'I hope to be your next congressman.'"

"I distinctly said 'incumbent.' I never said he was running for the first time."

"Don't call me again if you're going to lie," I told her.

Sonia called me at home on Bernice's behalf. I said I would not see her or talk to her again, or—as much as I hated to be rude—to Sonia, either. I would speak to a lawyer about my privacy if it came to that.

"If she sends you a letter of apology, will you read it?" she asked.

"No, I will not," I said.

I passed the library on the way to the basement and remembered Mr. Willamee's independent project on my behalf. I hadn't checked back with him and it had been a week. The library door was closed. I could see through the fire glass that he was eating at a table with his back to the door. Ignoring the first knock, he rose immediately when he saw it was me—or at least when he saw I wasn't a student. I apologized for the interruption; I hoped he hadn't gone to any trouble with the research, because I had just severed my ties with the woman who lied about JFK.

"Can you come in?" he asked.

I stepped inside. He hesitated before closing the door. I walked over to the table and studied his lunch: peanut butter on whole wheat pita bread, Fig Newtons, carrot sticks, and an undisclosed beverage in a serious thermos. I hoped it wasn't soup. He took his seat and asked if I was on my way to lunch.

I didn't react right away, so he pointed to my brown bag.

"Isn't that your lunch?"

"My sandwich."

"Would you like to eat here?"

"I buy my milk and a bag of chips," I said. "Thanks anyway."

He unscrewed the stopper of his thermos and poured black coffee into its plastic cup. "All those kids in one teeming mass," he said, offering it to me.

I smiled, accepted it, and sat down tentatively. "What about you?" I asked.

"That's okay."

I told him the coffee was delicious, and it was—a French roast, strong and perfectly brewed. Dwight said it was his weakness: he ground his own beans and made a fresh pot just before leaving for school. He was a coffee snob— couldn't drink the stuff in the teachers' room; got mail-order beans from San Francisco.

Gay, I thought immediately. Of course he was gay.

"I haven't come up with anything substantial about Kennedy," he began.

I said it was just as well. I didn't want anything further to do with this woman.

"I'm checking the *New York Times Index* and *Globe* microfilm."

"For what?"

Dwight chewed politely and wiped his mouth before answering. I brought forth my own sandwich. "Trips. Vacations. Operations . . . something that placed him in Washington or out of the country or in the hospital for the whole time frame we're dealing with. Then at least you could refute her claim with some hard evidence."

"It isn't worth your time," I said. "I appreciate your trying, but it's not worth the effort. Really."

Dwight said solemnly, "It's no trouble, April."

I was startled to hear him call me by my first name. I thought I should use his, too, then remembered I already had—last visit, for the students' benefit; Dwight hadn't realized I was going after an effect. I wrapped up my uneaten sandwich, apologizing: now the library would smell like tuna fish.

"Not at all," he said. "It's nice to have the company."

What could I say that wasn't a lie? I told him his was the best coffee I'd ever had.

ELEVEN

Dear April,

I know you are angry with me, and you believe that I am not a teller of truths. Sometimes the people we love are not perfect, and we have to decide if perfection is the most important thing in life. I am your mother. At least you don't dispute that. I am used to being judged for my mistakes, and I've learned how to take care of myself. I have lived longer than you, and I know that you can't remove a person from your life the way a dermatologist can take a mole off your skin. I will always be a fact of your life, whether or not we have a life together. You have been a fact of my life for more than thirty-six of its years. I have much more to say to you and hope that this is not my last opportunity. Among those things we should discuss is your father, who was an intelligent, thin man of Irish extraction and, like myself, healthy with no congenital diseases or allergies that I knew of.

Bernice Graverman

I agreed to one more dinner. "A thin man of Irish extraction" sounded plausible.

"He was handsome and freckled, with a touch of red in his brown hair"—Bernice studied my hair critically—"and with a great deal of self-confidence. 'I find Jewish women extremely beautiful,' he said to me at Jordan Marsh. 'I think they are the most beautiful women of all.' I was vain then. I believed that kind of thing.

" 'You wouldn't consider having lunch with someone who was forward enough to ask you without a formal introduction, would you?' he asked. He was so good at appearing boyish—it's a midwestern thing they can do, this 'yes, ma'am' stuff, with their clean freckled faces. Women from the East aren't prepared for it. He said his name was Jack. He went to Harvard Medical School—"

"Last name?" I asked.

"Didn't I say that? Flynn. Jack Flynn."

"Okay," I said. "Go on."

" 'What time is your lunch hour?' he asked. I looked at my watch and could tell he was staring at my hands. I had the softest-looking hands. 'Fifteen minutes?'

" 'I'll be back,' he said with a charming grin.

"We ate cream cheese on date nut bread at Bailey's. I asked him about school. 'I'm at the hospital all day and I study all night,' he said. 'It's a very boring life.' It didn't occur to me to ask what he was doing at Jordan Marsh looking ruddy and refreshed at noon, midweek. Medical students took lunch hours like everyone else, I thought. He asked again about the propriety of a date with a virtual stranger. I smiled reassuringly and said that waiting on strangers all day had made me quite a good judge of character.

"He was waiting for me after work, and it was a beautiful late spring night. We walked and walked, across the Common, through the Garden, all the way up Commonwealth Avenue. He wanted to take me over to his lab to show me his cadaver. We got as far as the main door— some building at Harvard Med. 'I can't believe they locked it tonight,' he said. 'There's a big anatomy exam on Monday.' We walked back down Brookline Avenue and kissed at frequent intervals . . . in the twilight."

Bernice lit a cigarette and watched my reaction. She looked proud of her narrative and checked to see if I found her story as poetic as she intended.

"I was in love," she resumed dramatically. "I was drunk with love. It had been so simple—working at Jordan Marsh and finding love among my customers. And I truly believed, in the way that only a seventeen-year-old can believe, that it was fine to kiss this way, to give your . . . passion this way, when so fine a boy reciprocated your feelings.

"He had an apartment on Park Drive—L-shaped with an unmade bed at one end and a kitchenette at the other. There were two radios. We danced in one spot to whatever was playing, advertising jingles and all.

" 'I want to take our clothes off,' he said. Yes, it would be all right. He loved me; he was crazy with love. The naked body was a beautiful thing, et cetera. Had I seen a man in the state of love without his clothes on? He was not ashamed of his body.

"He went first. His back and shoulders were freckled. He held me against him—I was still completely dressed and waging this internal war over what I should do. I knew it was his penis down there, hard against my skirt; I knew men got that way when they were aroused. And then I decided: it wasn't fair of me to hide my body when he was showing me his. I was a modern girl in many ways, thinking of equal rights many years before it was fashionable.

" 'Just your sweater,' he said. It was a mint-green lamb's wool cardigan from R. H. Stearn's with mother-of-pearl buttons. I was wearing a white dickey, and worried how silly I'd look in just a collar and bra. He liked it fine.

" 'Please,' said Jack. 'Let me see you with just the collar. I know you have beautiful breasts.'

"I said no. He kissed me softly on my forehead, cheeks, nose and then unhooked my bra. I must have been saying no, but it was the kind of no, no, no you say when you've lost control. So there I was, my breasts peeking out from the starched dickey and Jack telling me I looked like Cleopatra. He was very skilled, if you haven't already picked that up, working his way through my skirt, my garter belt and stockings, my half-slip and panties.

" 'You'll be much happier when you're completely naked,' he told me. 'Something wonderful happens when you're naked, because our inhibitions are in our clothes.'

"I believed him. He never stopped talking to me, gasping at each new sight, telling me that I had the most beautiful body he'd ever imagined. 'I've never seen a woman naked in person,' he said, 'except in anatomy lab.'

" 'What about patients?' I asked. 'You must see them naked.'

" 'That's not until next year,' he said.''

Bernice picked up her fork, approached one of the scallops on her plate, put the fork down again. "There's an ironic tragedy here that I have to point out," she said. "I didn't know then that he was right, that I did have a fantastic body. I was too inexperienced to appreciate what he was saying." She leaned across the table to bring her face as close to mine as I would allow. "He was the only man ever to see me with that perfect body. First and last. Childbirth changes your skin tone. Places that used to be pink turn brownish."

She slumped back against the booth as if the observation had exhausted her.

I asked if that was it—my conception.

As if responding to a cue, she continued, "He walked me to his bed. He straightened out the bedclothes and got in. He held his hand out lovingly and said, 'Let's just hold each other for a while.' I followed him. He put his arm under my neck and nestled me in the crook of his arm. He sighed contentedly as if this was all he'd ever need. We kissed. He was a great kisser. He said I had great technique—a natural. He asked if he could lie on top of me. . . . Of course, before long he had talked his way in.

" 'I'll get pregnant,' I said. At least I knew that much.

" 'Not the way I do it,' he said. 'I'll withdraw before I ejaculate. It's easy to control.' I whimpered, my chin hooked over his shoulder. He pushed hard. 'You're a virgin,' he said.

" 'What did you think?'

"He said it was okay. He wouldn't hurt me. He was thrilled. Men love deflowering virgins. It's one of the big ones in their catalogue. He worked himself all the way in. 'There,' he said. 'The worst is over.' He moved his hips back and forth without a sound and pulled his body away abruptly. He jumped expertly out of bed onto his feet. He leaned over and kissed me on the lips. 'Congratulations,' he said. 'It's all behind you now.' I got up and went into the bathroom. I didn't ask him what exactly was dripping into my underpants."

"Did you ever see him again?" I asked Bernice.

She studied my face as if considering the pros and cons of possible responses, and said finally, "Yes. We had a relationship. Friday night dates and lots of lunches."

"And then you got pregnant?"

"My period was late. Jack hadn't come into the department for a whole week. He didn't have a phone, so I couldn't call him. It took me a couple of days, calling on my breaks, to confirm through the registrar that no Jack or John Flynn was enrolled at Harvard Medical School. 'Try the college,' a woman advised me with some compassion. 'Maybe he said pre-med at Harvard and you misunderstood.'

"Finally he dropped by the stocking department on Thursday to confirm our Friday night 'date,' and I asked, 'How is it that you can get away from classes on a weekday afternoon?'

" 'I just do it,' he said cheerfully.

" 'You don't get into trouble?'

"He smiled and leaned across the display case to pinch my nose—God, he was adorable—and said, 'Just with you, apparently.' I had never known a pathological liar before, so I really expected he would have an explanation for everything.

" 'There are some things I'd like to talk over. I've been trying to reach you all week,' I said.

" 'What are they?' he asked, no longer smiling.

" 'Not here,' I said.

"He took the ballpoint pen out of my hand and wrote on the serrated edge of a Jordan's bag, 'preg.???' I scribbled over his writing until it was a blue blob, then crumpled it up in my fist. 'Tell me if you are,' he said.

" 'Could I be?' I asked.

"He backed away as a customer approached. 'I'll call you,' he mouthed. It was the last time I ever saw him, leaving Jordan Marsh in his poplin suit and blue shirt, heading back to . . . what? An office job in an insurance agency or a cash register somewhere? I never found out."

I stirred my coffee with a demitasse spoon, around and around. Finally I said, "That's it, then?"

"I'm afraid so."

"Jack Flynn."

"Who the hell knows what his name really was."

After a moment I said, "What is this thing you have about Jordan Marsh?"

"I worked there! I don't have a *thing* about Jordan Marsh."

I took a sip, added a sugar cube, stirred some more. "So this is the real story? Jack Flynn is my father."

"Yes, he is," said Bernice. She winced—the pain of such poor judgment.

"And you never tried to find him?"

"Where? He didn't even live at that place he took me to, and he certainly didn't give me his real name."

"And you know that because you called every John Flynn in the Boston phone book and none was this Jack."

"Why would I do that?" she asked calmly. "He didn't want me. And he was a bum. A piece of shit."

"No clipping service?" I asked sarcastically.

"Sure—and I'd be buried by now under a truckload of newspaper clippings about the seven million John Flynns in America."

"That's convenient," I said.

"Convenient?" she repeated.

"Convenient: you were too young to know any better. You were an innocent, he was a cad—but a cad with a common name who posed as a medical student, which God knows explains the attraction. He seduced you, lied to you, abandoned you. And did it all under a false name and occupation. That's what's convenient."

She closed her eyes. "Unbelievable," she said. "Unbe-fuckinglievable."

"Me?"

"Yes, you! I'd like to know who did this to you?"

I shook my head, not understanding.

"Your paranoia! You're suspicious of everything. You mistrust everyone. Can you explain this—what made you this cynical and . . . unromantic? It certainly wasn't my genes."

"I consider myself extremely romantic," I said.

"This is not the outlook of a romantic person, believe me. You don't even know how negative you're being."

"I have good reason," I said.

She raised her eyebrows. Good reason? Something juicy and confessional at long last?

"I meant your JFK story."

She looked away, gathering patience and strength. "I apologized for that! Am I going to have to do penance for the rest of my life?"

No, I told her. Just tell the truth. I can tell the difference.

She stared for a few moments, then said, "I just hope you remember this smug little accusation. Memorize this moment so you'll feel like a goddamn fool when you get to know me better."

I said, "I'm sorry. I hope you're right."

She said slowly, "Call me naive and stupid for letting it happen. Call me promiscuous. Call me a lousy historian. But don't tell me who put his dick in me and got me pregnant. I'm the only one who knows that."

I said quietly, "And it was Jack Flynn? You stand by that story?"

Bernice opened her purse and extracted a cigarette. She shook it at me in warning. "Memorize this moment," she repeated.

TWELVE

Bernice enlisted Anne-Marie as her informer. Was there anyone at school for April? Perhaps a widower with children, someone a fussy woman might overlook on the first, second, or third inspection?

"Forget it," said Anne-Marie, taking it all down in shorthand for transmission later to me. "The ones who aren't already married you wouldn't want to know about." I was walking into the office as she said it. She handed me the receiver. I covered the mouthpiece and said, "You were having a nice chummy conversation."

Anne-Marie swatted away the remark. Go on, talk. You're tying up my line.

"Is this important?" I asked Bernice.

"Hello to you, too," she said.

"I'm not supposed to leave my class—"

"Blah, blah, blah. What are you doing tonight?"

I asked why.

"How does this sound: Double. Date."

I made a screwy face for Anne-Marie and said, "Sorry, I can't."

"Why not?"

"Work. Quizzes I promised I'd hand back yesterday."

"That's not a reason," said Bernice. "That's the excuse of someone who is avoiding a social life. Look, you bring someone and I bring someone and we have dinner together, the four of us."

"I think not," I said.

"Because you're truly too busy or because you don't want to?"

"Because I have work to do and a deadline."

"In other words, you don't have anyone to ask."

I said, "This is not an emergency phone call. I thought we agreed that only emergencies warranted phone calls to school."

"What about a fix-up?" Bernice asked. "I've had some marvelous fix-ups over the years. I'm sure if I thought about it I could come up with someone."

"No, thanks," I said.

"Why not?"

"I've never had a fix-up that wasn't a disaster."

"That's ridiculous. That's like saying, 'I'm going to shut myself off from a huge number of potential men out of a false sense of pride.' We'd all rather meet a man on our own in some natural, spontaneous way. But it doesn't always work out that way and we have to keep ourselves open-minded about the B-list."

Anne-Marie signaled that I should wrap it up. She needed the phone.

"I've got to go."

"Are you happy?" asked Bernice.

"This minute?"

"You know what I mean."

"Am I in love or anything like that?"

She didn't prompt me further, but just waited the answer out.

"No," I said. "I would have to say no."

"Listen," said Bernice, "I'm not happy either, but I do something about it. I'm not sitting passively by the telephone waiting for Mr. Right."

"I hate that expression," I said.

"Look, you come up with someone at your end, and I'll be going through my list of possibilities and Ted's," said Bernice. "I'll call you at home later to see if you've come up with anything."

"You can call, but I won't have." Ted? I thought. Who's Ted?

After a pause, Bernice said, newly tranquilized, "Fine, April. Then I won't bother you at home."

"What's the matter?" I asked.

"Nothing is the matter."

"You sound mad." Anne-Marie looked up, engaged, granting me an extension.

"I thought you had to get off," said Bernice.

"I do."

She said easily, "It bothers me that you don't want your friends to meet me."

"That's not true." I rolled my eyes.

"Have you told *anyone* about me?"

"Sure, I have." I shrugged at Anne-Marie. Haven't I? Don't you count?

"Have any of your friends said, 'Wow, I'd love to meet her'?"

"Well . . . sure. Implicitly."

"Who?" demanded Bernice. "Who have you told?"

"Oh," I said. "Anne-Marie, of course. She's very interested in our relationship. And"—I dragged it out, surveying a mental list for the most convincing white lie—"Rita and Sheryl—"

"Whoever they are."

"Teachers I eat lunch with, and . . ."

Anne-Marie mouthed a name. I squinted, and she mouthed it again.

"And, of course, Dwight Willamee," I said, nodding my thanks.

Bernice's tone brightened. "I've heard that name," she said.

Anne-Marie refused my invitation. She said it was a double date, no matter what I wanted to call it; it had to be a man. Let Bernice fix you up, she said. Or find someone yourself. Or ask Dwight Willamee, for God's sake; any warm body would do. She considered her own advice and decided it might not be such a bad idea; might shut Bernice up about the great supply of men around this convent.

I did ask Dwight to join us for dinner. I didn't want to embarrass him, and I didn't want to see him turn purple at the suggestion that my invitation was remotely social. It was not my business that he was gay; he should not have to confide what he so far had kept hidden. I went to the library carrying my brown bag and displaying my milk money.

"Don't feel you have to accept," I began, "but the bane of my existence is offended that I haven't told anyone at school she's found me, and I thought you might be interested in meeting her, since you've actually seen her show."

Mr. Willamee almost smiled. He said, "She's offended that you haven't told anyone about her, so you want me to meet her so she'll know you told someone?"

I nodded.

"Sure," he said.

"It would be for dinner, if that's not too weird."

"Not too," he said.

"She'll be very charming. And she'll probably pick some pretentious place."

"I thought you were breaking off communication with her," said Mr. Willamee.

"So did I. But she retracted her JFK story, and we reached an understanding about telling the truth. You know: nobody's perfect, life is short, the whole bit."

"Did she tell you who your real father is?"

"A Jack Flynn. Another Irish-American who picked her up at Jordan Marsh—that part I'm beginning to believe— who posed as a medical student, seduced her regularly, walked out when she was pregnant. I sat there politely and listened to every detail of what he said and what he did and what parts of her body he touched in which order."

"Doesn't sound half bad," he murmured.

I smiled uncertainly. Had Dwight Willamee said that? Would a gay man say that? Had I heard a clue to his sexual preference, or had I imagined the words and the emphasis?

He said, serious again in a way that erased his moment of wryness, "She's a talk-show hostess, and they're all exhibitionists of one sort or another."

"Yeah," I said, still off balance. Then: "I think she thinks I'm fascinated, though, and that she's giving me an education."

Dwight blushed. He used both hands to rearrange the lunch in front of him: two sandwiches, one banana, one large, lumpy homemade cookie; his thermos.

"Please go ahead and eat," I said.

He swiveled to look at the wall clock behind him, and said he might have to begin.

I reiterated: *So.* Just a dinner. He and I could talk about school. Bernice loved to hear about school. He must not feel he has to create any kind of false impression that I talk positively about Bernice. And he mustn't feel he has to pretend that we had worked more closely than we actually—

I understand, said Mr. Willamee.

"You're being a good sport," I said.

"It's fine."

"I don't know why she makes me so crazy."

Mr. Willamee said, blinking for effect, "Your birth mother appears out of the blue and tells you your father is John F. Kennedy and you wonder why she makes you crazy?"

I smiled and said, "Thanks. Good point."

"What time tonight?"

"I'll call you," I said. "Are you going to be home after school?"

He patted his breast pocket for a pen. I pulled one out of my purse and offered him my lunch bag. He wrote the numbers carefully and handed me back both. "Don't throw it out with your crusts," he said, smiling.

"I eat my crusts."

"And don't ask for Mr. Willamee or you'll get my father."

"Okay. Dwight."

"Good," he said.

THIRTEEN

She asked me to meet her at the piano bar at the Ritz. There would be a man with her. My Indian imports, she said, were nice, entirely suitable for the classroom, but would I dress up tonight? Did I have something chic?

"I'm bringing Dwight Willamee," I said.

She paused. "Why do I know that name?"

"He works with me. I mentioned him on the phone."

"*Seee,*" she sassed. "Look and ye shall find."

"It's not a date."

"Dwight? Isn't that a man's name?"

"He's a colleague."

"Married?"

"Married?" I repeated.

"You're such a prude," said Bernice. "Was he ever? Is he now?"

"No."

"Good. Sort of."

I didn't pursue it. I didn't want to hear her version of why not being married was good, sort of.

"What does he look like?"

"Tall—six feet five or so. Gangly."

"What's his mouth like?" she asked.

Dwight's mouth? "A regular mouth. Teeth. A big face; bony."

"What color eyes?"

"Why?" I asked.

"What color?"

"Bluish, I think. Or hazel. And glasses."

"Good-looking?"

"God, no. Just the opposite."

Bernice paused in her questioning. After a few moments she said, "So what you're saying is, he's not conventionally good-looking, but he has his attractive qualities."

"Not at all," I said. "He's the librarian—the one Anne-Marie joked about when I asked if she'd run off and married anyone."

"Not good-looking, then?"

"He's just a friend. And when you see him in person—"

"I've never been attracted to conventionally handsome men, either. I've always been drawn to personalities first. Their looks are secondary."

She was lying, of course, but she believed it. If I had challenged her, she would have argued her thesis until I was sold. At that moment, Bernice was rewriting her sexual history, inventing attractions to homely men of character.

"Is he outright ugly?" she asked.

"Some people might find him ugly."

"Some people are jerks," she said. "It's what's inside that counts."

Thank you, Mother, I wanted to say; thank you for that kindergarten lesson in social relations.

"What do the other women at school think of this Dwight?"

"I've never discussed him with anyone at school. There hasn't been any reason to discuss him with anyone. But I think, in general, he's seen as geekish."

"Why?" she asked indignantly. "Are they all married to male models?"

"No."

"Would they be jealous if you became involved with him?"

I laughed. "I can safely say no one would be jealous."

"Will I like him?" she asked.

I thought, Actually, no; politically, having given lip service to a beauty's-only-skin-deep policy, she'd pretend to. I said, "He's a fine person."

"Of course he is," she said warmly. "I can't wait."

I arrived before Dwight. Bernice wore all black, her pageboy covered by a turban of black jersey. People glanced at her, said something to their companions, and glanced back discreetly. Her escort was gray-haired, pink-faced, strongly perfumed. He was introduced as Ted Dichter, the man in her life. "Where's yours?" she asked.

"Dwight's meeting us." I asked how Ted and Bernice knew each other.

"Through real estate," said Ted.

"Buying or selling?" I asked. He laughed appreciatively as if I had exhibited a precociousness for real-estate jargon.

"Both," said Bernice.

"I was a guest on the show," said Ted.

"It hasn't aired yet. You have to see it: Boston's most eligible bachelors over fifty-five. We had a lawyer, a gynecologist, a politician, a developer." She prompted him, "Who else was there?"

"A professor, the colored guy."

"That's right. Is that five? Isn't that a great premise?"

"Great," I said.

Ted Dichter looked at Bernice with a coy smile. "And when it was over, she touched my hand and said, 'Whoever the woman in your life is, she's very lucky.' As it turned out, there wasn't a woman in my life, so I took the liberty of asking your mother to have dinner with me."

"Why, just like Marlo and Phil!" I said to Bernice.

Bernice touched his arm to signal time out. Would he check on our reservation in the dining room? As soon as he walked away she said, "I think I'm going to marry him. He keeps asking me."

"How long have you known him?"

"Almost a month."

"Isn't that a little soon?"

"He's sixty-one, and at that age no one wants a long courtship." She looked up. Her features were being assembled into a joyless smile of salutation. "Dwight?" she said.

He was there suddenly, in a gray banker's suit and yellow bow tie, expressionless and still, as if reporting for duty. I stood up. "Bernice," I said, "this is Dwight Willamee."

She let her hand move up slowly from her thigh to shake his. "I'm so pleased," she said.

"I never miss your show," said Dwight with the faintest of smiles.

"You're lying," said Bernice. "You have to be. I know you're at work at nine. You're just flattering me, but I love it."

"Mr. Willamee never lies," I said. Bernice looked at me

knowingly as if I had slipped and called him by a private pet name.

"Hi, April," said Dwight.

"You look nice," I said.

"There's Ted!" said Bernice. We looked up. He was motioning for us from the doorway.

As soon as we were seated and I had introduced the men, Ted said, "Did your mother tell you I'm trying to get her to say yes to marrying me?"

Bernice smiled prettily and studied the menu.

"Just this minute," I said.

"How does that sit with you?"

"Well, I've only known you—"

"In theory, I mean. Any objections to her getting married?"

"Not at *all*," I said.

"What about you, son?" asked Ted.

Dwight looked at me, all innocence, and said, "None whatsoever."

Ted took Bernice's hand in one of his and mine in the other. "I know it's been just the two of you for such a long time, it might be hard for you to share her."

I looked at her. No lies ever bothered her. With deliberateness I said, "Bernice and I have only known each other since September."

Ted continued to smile as if he hadn't heard me.

"I have no say in her decisions," I said, taking my hand back.

"Your mother seems to think you do."

"Yes," I said.

"You're a pretty girl."

"Thank you."

"You're even prettier when you smile." He heh-heh'd in Dwight's direction. Dwight heh-heh'd back, deadpan.

"I told him you were a sourpuss," Bernice explained.

"You're the image of her," said Ted.

"Around the eyes, maybe," I said.

"So what do you think? Could you stand having a stepfather around the house?"

I looked quickly at Bernice, who returned a maternal stare that said, Speak when spoken to, April.

"You know I have my own apartment in Quincy?"

Ted smiled determinedly at Bernice: I'm doing my best; let me try again.

"Bernice told you the whole story, right?"

Ted said very solemnly, "Yes, she did, April."

"So you know that her getting married wouldn't change much, for me?"

"I know that's how you see it."

I looked at her quizzically: I'm trying to humor him, but you're making this difficult. Help me out. I don't want to say the wrong thing.

"She can be maddening," Bernice said to Ted.

"I'm a little confused," I said.

"I did tell him about our history," said Bernice.

"I'd like to know what she told you," I said.

Ted put down the roll he was breaking, and dusted his fingers on his napkin. I waited. "Bernice said, 'April is angry over certain things in her childhood. She's rebelling against me.' She said you weren't acknowledging her as your mother." He glanced at Bernice, who looked as pleased as ever.

I saw the problem. Bernice had prepared him with a nicely ambiguous psychological profile of me, leaving out the salient details about my birth and adoption. Ted had assumed—and why not?—that my rebelliousness took the form of claiming some dead couple, imaginary or idealized, as my real parents. And now Ted, who had probably read a book on stepparenting in preparation for tonight, was trying to make things right. I sighed as if caught in the act of abusing my long-suffering mother. O-kay. You've got me. She's right. I'm a terrible person. I smiled a weak smile, which Ted took for an apology.

"Let's change the subject!" Bernice said brightly.

Dwight coughed into his fist and raised his eyebrows at me.

"Let's have champagne!" said Ted. He telegraphed his order to a waiter without actually speaking and without asking the price. He was happy now; he wanted to hear about me, about school, about his future stepdaughter.

"I teach Latin in Quincy. I've been there fourteen years."

"Your mother's very proud of that fact. I used to think it was only Catholic priests who knew Latin."

I said, no, there were a few of us everywhere.

"Well, I think it's just great to have a specialty that's not a dime a dozen," said Ted. He smiled broadly. We all did.

"What about you, Dwight?" Bernice said.

Dwight pushed his glasses up with his index finger. "I'm the librarian at April's school," he said.

"That's fascinating," she said.

Dwight laughed.

"It's not?"

"Most people don't have that reaction. Most don't know what to say after I've said, 'I'm a librarian.' "

"Most people are jerks," said Bernice. "I've always greatly admired librarians. I think they're unsung heroes, and I've never met one who wasn't keenly intelligent."

"Thank you," said Dwight.

"Maybe you could do a show on librarians," I said. "They could talk about their jobs, and about their filing systems, and since they're all keenly intelligent, it should be fascinating."

Bernice smiled sourly. She touched Dwight's hand to signal they should ignore me, back up their conversation to the point before I interrupted.

"What do your parents do?" she asked.

"They're retired."

"And before that?" she asked lightly.

"My father worked for the city of Newton in the Department of Public Works and my mother worked in the library."

"The library! So this is a family legacy?"

"She wasn't a librarian. She just worked at the circulation desk."

"But she passed on to you a love of books?"

Dwight looked at me; I could see he wanted to smile.

"And a keen intelligence," I added.

"Where'd you go to college?" she asked.

"Harvard?" he said, and checked with me. I knew that inflection. It was the way I said, "Radcliffe?"—quietly. A small liberal arts college in Cambridge you might have heard of . . . ?

"You *did?*" I asked.

"April went to Radcliffe," Bernice confided across the table to Ted.

"What year?" I asked.

"Seventy-one."

"Seventy-four," I said.

"You're just finding this out?" asked Bernice.

"Which house?" I asked him.

"Adams."

"Lowell."

"How come you're just finding this out now?" Bernice asked. "Hasn't it come up in conversation before at school?"

"We talk about other things," I said.

"I guess you do," Bernice said unhappily.

"So how'd a Harvard man end up as a librarian?" asked Ted.

"Low lottery number."

Ted squinted. "I don't get it."

"I would have been drafted without a deferment, so I went to graduate school to get my M.L.S."

"But you must like it if you're still a librarian," said Bernice.

He shook his head. "Death by tenure."

Bernice, nodding energetically, said, "But it's hard to leave a place when you've been there a long time and you've made a lot of good friends?"

"No," said Dwight. "I don't have any friends there."

She looked back and forth between us, waiting for one of us to crack the code. "Is that true?" she asked.

"I don't mind," said Dwight.

"Except April. Is what you're saying?"

Dwight looked at me kindly, granting me license to paint more friendship onto the canvas than actually existed. Bernice would have her easy answer and we could move on. "Of course, except for me," I said.

Bernice beamed. How nice it was to have a daughter with the right values, a daughter who befriended someone the other kids wouldn't play with. I let her think that, and I let her boyfriend preen like the lucky family man he felt he was becoming tonight. I wanted to pass the test, if only because I wanted him to say later, "She may seem difficult to you, hon, but I find her delightful."

I ate enthusiastically, the way a well-adjusted stepdaughter would; I shared a rack of lamb with Bernice and a Caesar salad with Ted. Dwight ordered a modest breast of chicken, as if making no assumptions about being anybody's paid guest.

After dessert, after the flaming crepe for two, over

coffee, Ted sent a folded five-dollar bill to the pianist. Instantly, the music changed to "Blue Moon." Across from each other, Bernice and Ted exchanged long looks. They clasped hands through the flowers, their arms drawing a line across the table, Dwight on one side, me on the other, wondering where to put our large free hands.

FOURTEEN

The phone woke me just after six the next morning. Something's happened to Freddie, I thought, the only one I have left.

It was Bernice. What had I thought of Ted and did I like his looks?

Still disoriented I said, "Yes. I did. Yes. I think so."

"Are you all right? You sound like you're out of it."

"I got nervous when I heard the phone ring at this hour."

"Sorry. I needed to ask if you thought I should marry him."

Even half asleep, I didn't hesitate. Ted approved of Bernice, of her drama and her affectations—her *mishegas,* my parents would have said—even of her show. He actually loved her; I could see that over dinner. I thought Ted was someone with whom I could enter into a satisfying conspiracy: take her and I'll be nice forever. I'll be her long-lost daughter and her maid of honor. Move to another city; *develop* another city—I'll write faithfully. Get her angry and I'll take your side. I will be so happy for you and so helpful that you will keep a picture of me in the family constellation on your desk and say proudly, "My stepdaughter, April."

"Of course you should marry him," I said.

"He sure was crazy about you."

"I tried. Did you give him an answer last night?"

"No!"

"Because he's rushing things?" I asked.

"He wants to get engaged so he can fuck me," said Bernice.

A warning flag flickered in the corner of my internal vision. "What do you mean?" I asked pleasantly.

"He's from the old school. There are women you sleep with and women you marry, and never the twain shall meet. Except if you're officially engaged. It's very quaint."

I said she must be mistaken. Besides, did she tell him it was okay with her to sleep with him before they were engaged? Maybe he was being chivalrous and thought she needed a commitment.

"It's a health thing," said Bernice. "Did you notice how meticulous he is? I think he's got an AIDS phobia—like you could catch it from casual sex but not from your fiancée."

I said slowly, "I think you should get engaged. Get tested for AIDS. Show him he won't catch anything. Find out how he is in bed." I said this with effort, with a Cosmo girl's casualness forced for effect.

"I know how he is in bed," Bernice said impatiently, as if we had been discussing an entirely different man.

"Oh," I said.

"I meant he wanted to get engaged so he can fuck me on a regular basis and spend the night. Of course we've slept together. He's a normal man, for God's sake."

I had no advice left. She asked me if I could see him as a father.

"Absolutely."

Bernice was quiet for a few moments. "He's loaded, you know."

"I didn't know, exactly."

"Which doesn't matter to me one iota."

"I know," I lied.

"Don't humor me, April. I know you think I'm interested in appearances, but you don't know me very well if you think I'd consider marrying someone just for his assets."

"I know that."

"Good. Because I meet rich men every day and I'm not impressed. I wouldn't even wear a diamond if Ted wanted to get me an engagement ring. I'd wear a simple thin gold band, very understated."

"That proves it," I said. "True love."

"Aren't you going to ask me what I thought of Dwight?"

"No."

I heard her take a drag on her cigarette, then exhale slowly. "You can do better than him," she said.

I sat up straighter in bed, switched the phone to my right ear, looked at the clock. "That's a nasty remark," I said.

"Why? I thought he was just your friend."

"You don't think a friend would take offense at that remark?"

"I meant as a boyfriend you could do better."

"You're not listening."

"He has no charm," said Bernice. "I can get by without a lot of things, but I insist on a man being charming."

"How deep of you," I said.

"Do you find him charming?"

"Who cares? It's not high on my list, especially for my librarians."

"I see. And that's the story you're sticking with?"

"Yes," I said.

"Would you tell me if you *were* involved with him?"

"Yes."

"You wouldn't be embarrassed?"

"You're ridiculous," I said.

"Because I care who you go out with? All mothers care about that. At least I don't object for boring reasons like he doesn't make any money or he's not Jewish."

"We're just friends," I said again.

"What would your adoptive mother have said in this situation?"

"She wouldn't have passed judgment," I said.

"I can't help it. I value your opinions and I assumed you valued mine."

"Why do you care if a friend of mine is handsome and charming or not?"

She laughed. "It's the producer in me: How will he play? How will he look on camera?"

I reset my alarm so it rang. I said I had to go, had to jump in the shower.

"What time is it?" she asked. I told her almost six-thirty. I also told her—not that I was redefining anything, not that it had any relevance to anything at all, but speaking objectively, as a platonic friend—I thought Dwight had been a little charming the night before.

Bernice groaned, said she had to get up, had to wake Ted, too, who wanted to be out the door by seven.

FIFTEEN

Kimberly Fusco dropped a stapled note on my desk at the beginning of second period and said smartly, "It's from Mr. Willamee." The oohs started in the back of the room and rolled toward me.

"That's enough," I said.

"Aren't you going to read it?" asked Kimberly, who had sauntered to her desk but was still standing.

"You guys are nerds," I said. "We used to do this to my teachers when *I* was in high school. It's very passé."

"Read it!" someone yelled.

I opened the note and said loudly, "Miss Epner, your library book is overdue. Please return it at your earliest possible convenience." I reached behind me for my book bag and threw the note in. "Some of you might check your lockers for overdue books, too," I said. "Kimberly, how would you say the nominative plural of 'books from the library'?"

Charles Lopes, a chronic wise guy whom I actually found quite funny, hitched his shoulders up to his earlobes and lisped, "Please return it at your earlieth possible convenience, Mith Epnah."

"What did you say?" I asked.

Charles's buddies laughed.

"What did you say?"

Charles stopped smiling. "Sorry," he said.

"How would you like it if you heard that a classroom full of people laughed when your name was mentioned—not at one of your hilarious jokes, but at you. Something about *you*. Would you like that?"

"No, Miss Epner," I heard, and at the same moment, "Faggot." From another corner, from an unidentifiable male voice—faggot.

I looked to the approximate source. "Who said that?"

"I didn't," said Charles.

I made a face: Of course you didn't, jerk. I was looking right at you. "I want to know who said that," I repeated.

"What are you gonna do if you find out?" asked Kimberly.

"Kill 'em," said someone.

"Make 'em suck Willamee," said another ventriloquist.

I pretended not to hear. I went to the blackboard, picked up a piece of chalk to write, turned around, and said, "If anyone says one word, this entire class will get detention." I turned back and wrote *"libri ē bibliothecā"* on the blackboard. There were murmurs, but no discernible epithets. The girls in front shushed the potential troublemakers and we continued.

At the warning buzzer I said, "I want you to be decent young men and women, even if it's just for these forty minutes a day." I thought about saying, "And furthermore, not that I should even dignify your name-calling, but Mr. Willamee is almost certainly not a homosexual."

93

Of course, I didn't. I waited for the bell to ring and the classroom to empty. I took Dwight's note from my book bag and read what it really said: "A rare opportunity. Thanks. Dwight."

I wrote back on yellow math paper, "A rare *ordeal* is more like it. I owe you one. April." I walked mine to the office and put it in Dwight's mailbox. He would realize by example that this was the only safe way for innocent parties to pass notes. I would tell him in a nice way that confident and popular students could not be trusted, that the Kimberly Fuscos of the world didn't understand the finer points of friendship.

I went to the cafeteria for lunch and found the usual fourth-period crowd in the faculty room. I sat down between Kiki Broustas, adviser to the cheerleading squad, and Frank Scanlon, a fussy English teacher with a bad chestnut brown toupee. Frank asked me without greeting if I remembered Kyle Bui, class of eighty-five, maybe eighty-six; a Vietnamese boy? He'd just sent Frank a letter from Notre Dame—the damned nicest letter—saying Honors English had been a good foundation and he was majoring in English.

I said I'd had him for three years, was disappointed he chose Notre Dame over Columbia, but I was glad he sounded happy.

"Kyle Bui?" Kiki asked, frowning. "Did he play any sports?"

"I doubt it," I said.

"Notre Dame's a big jock school," Kiki informed us.

Frank looked distressed that Kiki was of his school, his profession, his species. "Kyle was a reader," he said, again to me.

I reminded him that Kyle had won the Latin prize his senior year. Frank smiled. He knew I was the only judge, and grade-point average was the only criterion. He had come to the right place. There was a lull in conversation that made me look up. Dwight Willamee was in the doorway with his industrial thermos and his lunch, staring at the nearly full table.

"Dwight!" I said, his only greeter. He hesitated before walking slowly to the one empty seat. Before he reached it Kiki said, "Lou sits there every day. He'll be down in a sec."

"Sorry," said Dwight.

I stood up and moved my chair to one side. "Here," I said. "Pull one over and squeeze in." My colleagues picked up their chairs by the seat and put them down again one inch farther away. "More," I said. "Norman, Chuck, you, too, please." No one stood to say, Never mind, I'm just about to leave. You can have my seat. Or How ya doing, Dwight? I motioned again for him to bring a chair from the other table and sit with us. Look—all the room in the world.

Dwight hesitated. I could tell from his pained expression that he was about to back out of the lunchroom murmuring, No. Please. I'm disrupting you. I'll go back to the library. I'm obviously not wanted.

"I was going to find you for a postmortem on last night," I said loudly.

"You were?" said Dwight.

"Are you going to sit?"

He hoisted a chair up in the air, landed it in the negotiated space, and sat down. He took a sandwich out of his bag and removed the plastic wrap. People were listening, waiting to hear what Mr. Willamee could possibly have to say to me about the evening before. He shook his head very slightly and smiled, just shook his head and smiled as if he needed more time and fewer interested parties.

I said to the table, "Dwight got dragged to a family

dinner last night, which turned out to be excruciating."

"Whose family?" asked Kiki.

"Mine."

"What was the occasion?" she asked.

"No occasion," I said.

Kiki looked around to see who was catching this. She squinted at me—C'mon, April. Are you serious or what? "Are you two on a committee together?" she asked.

"Sort of," said Dwight.

"Dwight's been helping me research something about my family."

"That's nice," said Kiki. She stood up, cocked her finger at two phys ed teachers in windbreakers. "See you guys." She walked away, tray in hand, the green soles of her aerobic shoes flashing against their white uppers. I pushed her chair away from the table and claimed the space.

Frank Scanlon spoke around me to Dwight. "What kind of research is Miss Epnah doing on her family?"

Dwight reached for his thermos and unscrewed the stopper. "Miss Epnah can probably tell you herself," he said.

"Genealogical," I said.

"A new hobby?" asked Frank.

"Coffee?" Dwight asked. I nodded.

"What are you?" asked Frank.

"Jewish," I said.

"I mean your nationality."

"American."

"And before that?"

"Nothing," I said.

Frank said, "We all came from somewhere, even the Indians."

"Except me," I said. "I didn't."

Dwight leaned forward and said, "April's a little discouraged with our research."

"Everyone comes from somewhere," Frank repeated. "Even the Jews of Eastern Europe who made their living as peddlers and owned no land."

"That's a relief," I said. I took a sip of coffee from the cup Dwight offered and asked if I could get a Styrofoam one for him. He shook his head.

Frank squeaked his chair back noisily as he rose to leave. "Nice to hear an update on Kyle Bui," I said.

"Don't be discouraged about your roots," Frank counseled.

At the other end of the table, the phys ed teachers were discussing a cretin football player who was being heavily recruited by midwestern universities. Closer, a white-haired teacher of shorthand was discussing early retirement incentives with a bald man I didn't know.

"Sorry," I said to Dwight.

"About what?"

"Your first trip down here in fifteen years and there's no seat."

He reached in his bag and brought forth a second sandwich. "A bit territorial when you're not in with the in crowd."

"I'm not in with the in crowd," I whispered. "I don't even like anyone at this table."

"It's all right if you do. Frank's a decent guy."

"He was done eating. He didn't have to sit around for another ten minutes and fiddle with his tea bag while you rearranged the furniture."

"It's okay. I'm a big boy."

"They're jerks," I said.

He smiled at something but didn't explain.

"What?"

He shook his head no, but spoke after a few moments. "I'm fascinating and they're jerks?" Bernice's words; her emphasis.

I opened my mouth to protest, but Dwight said, "You're not like her. It was just that one word. You spit it out with the same . . . distaste."

I allowed myself a few bites of my sandwich, finished my potato chips. "What did you think of Bernice's boyfriend?" I asked finally.

Dwight's mouth was full. I waited. "Ted. A man possessed."

"They've only known each other a month," I said.

"Which means what?"

"That he's rushing things. Putting pressure on her, proposing every day."

"A month's not that short a time to know someone," said Dwight. "Besides, something tells me Bernice can handle it."

I laughed. "Did you find her completely full of shit?"

"In an endearing sort of way."

"You're kidding!"

"She certainly went out of her way to be charming to me."

I laughed. "That's true." And thought: *charming*.

He picked up the second sandwich and stared at it. After a few moments he asked lightly, "Has she met other friends of yours?"

"No. Why?"

Dwight automatically reached for the black plastic cup, then remembered it was my coffee.

"Go ahead." I pushed it toward him. He took a sip, handed it back, said carefully, "Was Bernice expecting you to bring a boyfriend or something?"

"Why?"

He shrugged. "Ted's demeanor. The place, the music, the champagne . . ."

"Because he knew he'd be proposing every five minutes. He's the type that goes for the grand gesture."

"I sensed they were expecting it to be a foursome." And more softly: "I guess we all felt awkward."

Well, I said. Well, that's their problem. I told Bernice a hundred times I was bringing a friend. Apparently that concept is foreign to her. Males are not friends in her book. Males are dates, period.

Dwight fingered the cup but didn't pick it up. "So she did see me as a date?"

"Well," I said, "you were, more or less."

"You know what I mean."

"Dwight—" I began.

"And she wasn't too thrilled."

"Bernice is completely self-absorbed. All she talks about is should she marry Ted or shouldn't she. She woke me up at six this morning to tell me he's only proposing so he can sleep with her and then it turns out he's in bed next to her. If she had any thoughts about my taste in friends, she didn't share them with me." I folded my empty potato chip bag into halves, then quarters, as if something important rested on the sharpness of my creases.

He stood up slowly, threw his balled-up lunch bag neatly across the room into the open barrel. The grace of his set shot surprised me. He smiled down at me and said, "Liar." I watched him collect the rest of his trash and reassemble the thermos; he took my coffee cup and swallowed the rest like a belt of scotch. The huge Adam's apple dipped; below it, his blue pinstripe shirt was unbuttoned at the neck. A few chest hairs poked through a small hole in his T-shirt. I felt a sudden pull in my gut for no reason—a poignancy I might feel over another kind of man with a tiny rent in his T-shirt and the first glimpse of chest hair. But Dwight's shirt? Dwight Willamee's chest hair? It made no sense at all.

"I'll see you," he said.

"Coming back tomorrow?" I asked.

He rolled his eyes. "Not until someone dies and gives up a seat."

It registered as funny, but I didn't laugh. The Girl Scout cheer and the charitable smile I had for weeks bestowed on Dwight no longer fit.

SIXTEEN

Bernice said no to Ted, and he broke it off completely. I fretted about how she had ruined everything; how she'd never grown up. I had argued myself into believing that Ted was some kind of answer.

She began to tell me things: his proposing on their first date; his jealousies; his accusing her of being interested in whatever male guests appeared on the show.

"Why didn't you tell me this before?" I asked.

"It was sweet at first! Harmless little questions about what I did. 'Tell me what you did today,' he'd say. Harmless. Then he started with the 'Is he attractive?' and 'Do you like him?' I went along with that crap! I even started to feel guilty. I had to reassure him that whoever it was wasn't attractive, no, I didn't like him—about perfectly nice, attractive men who I could have liked. He would get belligerent—you wouldn't believe the crap he'd throw at me. 'Does he have a big prick?' he asked me after

I had Bobby Orr on the show. You know what I said? I said, 'I don't know. I can't tell by feeling the outside of his pants.' "

I laughed. Bernice said, "Funny, right? Well, he has no sense of humor. He sulked for the rest of the night."

"Why didn't you tell me this part before? This is serious crazy stuff. No wonder he's sixty and proposing on the first date."

Bernice shrugged. "You hope it's not permanent, or you attribute it to his being so madly in love he can't think straight. Because one thing I've learned is, Don't spit in the water. You may have to drink it."

It was Saturday. We were at Saint Botolph's in the South End for lunch. Bernice was wearing a huge white shirt over black jersey calf-length pants. We sat quietly, smiled politely as the waitress brought menus. After ordering, I asked softly, "Why is it, do you suppose, that you haven't met someone you like enough to marry?"

Bernice looked surprised. "I wasn't selfish enough to put you aside and work on my life," she said.

I said I didn't quite understand. She knew where I was, even if she hadn't made her move yet. Under the circumstances, I hardly took up any of her time.

"After a certain age, I told every man about you. I spilled my guts on first dates to every schmuck I went out with. It scared plenty away. They knew I was a serious person with a cause. I'll tell you—it separated the men from the boys. Once in a while a guy would act as if he understood my pain. Most of them, nineteen out of twenty, would say, 'I don't get it, Bern. You were seventeen years old. You got pregnant, you gave the baby up for adoption instead of ruining your life and probably the kid's. He probably went to a rich family who's giving him everything he ever wanted.'

" 'She,' I'd say. 'It was a girl.'

" 'Oh,' they'd say. 'What kind of music do you like?' as if you were just a thing I brought up to make conversation."

"Why *did* you bring me up?" I asked.

"Because you were my theme song. You were the way I announced myself, identified myself. It's as if I were saying, 'Here's what I am all about. If you don't like it, leave.' And that's what made me a success on television, that same attitude: I'm going to talk about what I want to talk about, and if you don't like it, change the channel."

After a few moments I said, "I find that hard to believe."

"What do you find hard to believe?" she asked, crimping her voice to imitate me sounding prissy.

"That you let me get in the way."

"Then you don't know me at all."

"Would you have married Jack Flynn if he hadn't abandoned you?"

I could see the mild surprise in her eyes, as if Jack Flynn's name didn't sound familiar. She said she had been too young then, definitely too young to have been married at seventeen. And now she was too old.

"It's time people knew about me," she said over dessert.

"They do," I said. "You're semi-famous."

"Not that part of me. I meant, it's time people know you found your mother. Your brother, for instance. What have you told him?"

"Nothing yet. I don't want him getting nervous."

Bernice withdrew, shrinking back. I knew these withdrawals; had seen her do them driving, smoking, talking. Now conversation stopped; she set her face to the task of eating. Her table manners became exaggerated in their precision. If conversation was to resume, it had to be through my efforts.

"I didn't mean you weren't important news," I tried.

She chewed a tiny bite daintily, long past what was necessary.

"What I meant by nervous was that Freddie took my mother's death badly. He was there, and he had lived at home. He's very protective of them. And he might see you as a threat to his own security—the biological mother taking back the child. I'm his only family."

"You're thirty-six years old! People worry about biological mothers coming back to get their babies, not grown children!"

"He's very protective of them," I repeated.

"They're dead, for God's sake."

I put my dessert fork down and leaned closer across the table. "They lost everyone they loved in the war. Freddie would still see it as a loss for them. He thinks they're watching over us."

Bernice smiled a tight, knowing smile. "Well, here it is, finally. The war. I was wondering how long it would take for you to open that can of worms. The precious war. That's what I'm up against, aren't I?"

It was my turn to eat and ignore her—difficult because we were sharing one dessert. After a few bites, I lost my resolve. I needed to reprimand her. "That was an unbelievably insensitive thing to say about my parents."

Bernice shrugged. "At least I riled you up. You're so goddamn . . . judicious. Every time I talk to you, I can see how you think before you speak, measuring if it's going to bring you one step closer to acknowledging me or if it's going to keep you evermore the Epner—uncommitted, nice and safe."

I shook my head impatiently throughout her speech. "I'm talking about what you said, not me. Not the way I act or don't act. What *you* said about 'the precious war.' That's really the way you think, isn't it? Some foolish war in Europe now gives my dead parents an unfair advantage in your tug-of-war over a mutual daughter?"

Bernice said, "I have the utmost compassion for your parents' ordeal."

"No, you don't."

"I most certainly do. I feel as if I were related to them. I think of them as I would some European cousins I never met. I felt terrible when I heard they were gone. And I certainly feel the bond of having shared a daughter with them. Of course, all that extends to Freddie, too. I view him as a kind of long-lost son."

"Is this new?" I asked.

"It occurred to me as we were discussing your parents, actually. He's your brother. You're my daughter. Of course my heart would go out to him."

"Have you contacted him?" I asked.

"No."

"Please don't try to talk to him before I prepare him."

"I won't."

"I want your word that you won't call him or write him or make an on-air appeal to him. I mean it."

Bernice tapped the end of a new cigarette smartly on the table and looked pleased with herself. "And if there's a medical emergency? If you were lying in a gutter somewhere, unconscious—"

"And I suppose you'd be notified first? Yours is the first name on my Medic Alert bracelet?"

"Can't you have a hypothetical discussion? You can be so damned literal."

I leaned closer and enunciated carefully. "Don't call Freddie. I'll tell him soon."

"Life is unpredictable," said Bernice. "I could find myself seated next to him at Legal Sea Foods and he could walk over and ask for my autograph."

"Don't test me on this one, Bernice. You'll lose whatever ground you think you've gained."

"Now she's threatening me! The little *pisher* is threatening to . . . what? Stop giving me a weekly audience? Stop letting me feed her at fashionable restaurants? I beg your forgiveness, Your Highness."

"Don't turn this around so that you're the insulted one. I'm asking you nicely for a simple favor: leave Freddie out of this for now. I'll eat with you. I'll be your long-lost daughter. But it's between you and me."

We didn't speak while the waitress removed the dessert plate and refilled our coffee cups. When she was gone, Bernice sat back, toasted me with her coffee cup, toasted our contest, and said, "I'm not worried."

SEVENTEEN

 y phone rang the next night during "Masterpiece Theatre." I was watching "The Flame Trees of Thika" for the second time, thinking how I was definitely growing old if Hayley Mills was playing Elspeth's mother.

It was a man's voice saying, "You don't know me, but I was given your name by Bernice Graves at Channel Four. I'm Bob."

"Yes?" I said.

"It's my account. I'm the rep for Digital. She gave me your name."

I waited for him to state his business.

"Do you hate this as much as I do?" asked Bob.

"I'm not sure what you're talking about," I said.

"Calling someone up out of the blue and making small talk. I'm not very good at it."

Instead of being helpful and saying, "Not at all. You're doing fine," I said, "You were calling me about . . . ?"

"Going out some time!"

"I think there's been some mistake," I said.

"Are you April?"

"Yes, but Bernice didn't discuss this with me first. I wouldn't have agreed to it."

"She said you were tough," said Bob, pleased with a confirmation of sorts.

"I don't do blind dates. Bernice took this upon herself without asking me first."

"She said you'd put up a fight. She told me to be persistent. Anyway, what've you got to lose?"

"Look," I said, "it's nothing personal, but I'm seeing someone."

"Oh, that's it," said Bob.

"That's it," I said. "Too bad Bernice didn't ask me first. It would have saved you the trouble."

"She doesn't know about it?"

"No."

"She told me she's your mother."

"She is."

Bob laughed. "But who tells their mother everything, right?"

"We're not very close," I said.

"Not to hear her talk."

"I was going to tell her one of these days. But you want a relationship to jell before you bring your parents in, you know what I mean?"

"Yeah," said Bob.

"She's quite opinionated."

"And she might not like this guy?"

"Why do you say that?" I asked.

He laughed nervously. "She's a tough cookie. And

you're it, her one and only. Kind of puts the pressure on."

"She doesn't run my life," I said.

"Well . . ." said Bob. "What can I say? Good for you. I hope it works out. With your mother, with the guy. Invite me to your wedding."

"You're a good sport," I told him. "Considering."

"It's a crapshoot," said Bob. "You can't take it too personally when a girl turns you down if she's never even laid eyes on you. At least you were nice about it."

"Thank you," I said.

"Want me to break the news to your mother?"

"Which news?"

"About the guy. She'd love hearing there's someone. I get the feeling she'd be relieved." He laughed. "She must've felt a little desperate to tap me for the job."

"Au contraire," I said politely.

"Well, April—nice name—if things don't work out with this guy, you know where to find me."

"Thank you," I said. "I will."

"What'll I say if Bernice asks me what happened? I know she will."

"Tell her I refused. You don't have to put yourself in the middle of anything."

"I told her I'd work at it, though."

"Some people hate blind dates. She'll assume I'm like that."

"Are you?" asked Bob. "Actually?"

"Yes," I said.

"How'd you meet this guy you're seeing?"

"I can't really talk," I said. "I should call Bernice up and straighten this out."

"Okay," said Bob. "I don't want to be obnoxious. So . . . lots of luck. Have a nice life. Call me if I can ever do anything for you."

I said, Thanks, I would.

"And don't come down too hard on your mother. She saw me around and thought, Someone ought to snatch this guy up! Might as well keep him in the family." He laughed unconvincingly.

"I'm sure she did," I said. "But I've got to go now."

"Take care," said Bob. "And good luck."

"You, too," I said.

There was a message in my box by the end of first period Monday. "Call your mother at the station." I waited until lunch and called from Anne-Marie's phone.

"Don't you have something to tell me?" Bernice coaxed.

"Do I?"

"A man in your life? Someone serious enough to make you reject the overtures of other interested men? I'm all ears."

I rubbed my eyelids with my thumb and forefinger. Anne-Marie perked up. I said, "Didn't you figure out I was making that up?"

"You can't talk now," she said. "Is that it?"

"Yes, I can. There's nothing to tell."

"You made up some romance to get Bob off the scent?"

"Right."

"Shit," said Bernice. "Shit, fuck, piss."

"Don't you ever tell a white lie to get off the hook? Or do you accept dates with every strange man who calls you up?"

"That's different."

"Why?"

"I have all sorts of crackpots calling me. I'm a television

personality. You're a Latin teacher. This particular guy was hand selected by me."

"Look—it's not worth getting agitated over this. You don't see me mooning over a lost date, and I'm the one who's allegedly missing out."

"You missed the point, April—I could give a crap about Bob Turits. But when he told me that you were in love with another man, I got excited. I didn't know you were capable of thinking on your feet that fast—in social situations, that is. I assumed you had to be telling the truth."

I laughed and said I thought there was a compliment buried in there somewhere.

"You'll notice I'm not laughing," she said dourly.

"Forget it. It wouldn't have worked out anyway."

"You know that for a fact? A sixty-second phone conversation and you *know* it wouldn't have worked out? This is what depresses me more than anything."

"It's not your problem, though, is it?"

"I'll concentrate on the up-side of this," she said. "There *is* an up-side to this setback, you know."

"I'm glad," I said, careful not to ask what that was.

"A little voice inside me was saying, 'It's that librarian. He's the reason April's turning away blind dates with good-looking guys. He's the mystery man.' So in that regard, I'm relieved."

I didn't say anything. Bernice said, "Did you hear what I said?"

I turned my back so Anne-Marie wouldn't hear, wrapping myself in the cord.

"April?"

I told her I had to get off. Really. I'd gotten memos about phone abuse.

"Do they understand 'important' there? Can't they distinguish between truant parents and real life?"

"Sometimes," I said.

"That's it for today, then? The bad news and the good? I've got everything in perspective and we can both go back to the drawing board?"

I handed the phone to Anne-Marie and said, my hand over the mouthpiece, "I can't get her off. You try."

My choices for lunch were: return to the faculty room and talk about my roots with Frank Scanlon and the rest of the private club, or keep Dwight company in the library.

I crossed the overpass between buildings, passed Helen Langevin and Harold Drouin on their way to the lunchroom. They both telegraphed friendly, quizzical looks— No lunch today? Aren't you going in the wrong direction? "I have a meeting," I said, passing one, then the other. "A meeting."

The library door was closed, Dwight's lunchtime convention. Through the glass panel I saw him at his customary table, holding a disk of pita bread in his left hand and a pen in his right. He was writing, stopping, thinking, writing on yellow math paper. He finished, folded the page, wrote something on the outside. He tipped his chair back and reached behind—the window didn't give me the peripheral vision to see where—and came back with a stapler. He stapled the note closed, three times on every side. Another reach with his long arm to set the note a safe, clean distance from the food and the coffee; a return to lunch—a bite of pita bread after its dip into something saladlike. I didn't knock or go in; I couldn't interrupt him, even now, even with the task finished and stapled, ready to be posted. I went back to my empty classroom to eat at my desk. It was one thing to find the yellow note in my mailbox and carry it away for a private reading, another to collect it in person and confess I had spied on its creation.

The note appeared in my mailbox after fifth period. It said only, "Dear April, Don't you have an overdue library book—or something? Yours, D.W."

EIGHTEEN

Anne-Marie was cutting out an article from *USA Today* when I walked into the main office. "Checks are in," she said. I emptied my mailbox. One yellow note, one pink telephone message. "Here," she said, handing me the clipping. "Might come in handy."

It was advice distilled from a how-to book on keeping office romances discreet. The author had eight important don'ts: Don't close the door if you're in an office alone together. Don't pick lint, threads, or dandruff off your lover's shoulder in public unless you do this for everyone. Don't kiss or touch each other at the office. Don't sit together at staff meetings. Don't travel together; stagger your travel schedules even if you're rendezvousing later. Don't send love notes through in-house mail. Don't use your secretaries as go-betweens. Don't commute to work together or leave work together in the evening.

"Why did you give this to me?" I asked Anne-Marie.

"I think you know," she said.

I dropped it on her desk and walked toward the door.

"I've got eyes," she said. "And I've got ears."

I walked back to her desk, checking for eavesdroppers. "And what do you think you're seeing and hearing?"

She poked the bridge of her nose, once, twice.

"Cut that out," I said.

She smiled smartly. The proof she needed. "I've got eyes," she said.

"You need glasses."

Anne-Marie pointed an unbending finger at the mailboxes. Today's long-sleeved leotard was a deep burgundy. "What's with the notes, then? Two today, one yesterday, one Friday."

"Do you read my mail?"

"I don't have to read it! And I heard about dinner."

"Did Bernice say anything to you?"

"Of course. She tells me everything. I don't ask for it, but she unloads on me. She's all hot and bothered over this."

"And what do you say?" I asked after a few moments.

"I say, 'It's none of my business who April likes.' "

I picked up the clipping and waved it in her face.

Anne-Marie batted away the piece of paper. "What are you afraid of?" she whispered, her eyes darting in an automatic office check. "This is the twentieth century. You won't get fired for dating another teacher."

"Dating? We're light-years away from anything resembling a date."

"Why? Because you're both retarded? Go ask him. *Jesus.* You think he's going to turn you down? He'll die of happiness, that's all."

The bell rang and the corridor stampede began. "It might be all in my head," I said.

"It's not," she said firmly. "What's your other excuse?"

I cocked my head toward the masses in the corridor. "They're brutal."

"So what? You're entitled to a life."

"They're hard enough on him," I said softly.

"Cut the shit, April," said Anne-Marie.

I returned Bernice's call from a phone booth so the operator could cut me off after three minutes.

"Did I do the right thing in turning down Ted's proposal?" she asked.

"I think you did."

"I taped a show this morning with a jealousy expert. He said marriage sometimes tames the impulse because the person feels more secure."

"Ted's nuts, though. You're probably only remembering the good parts in retrospect."

"You're right," she said. "I really know that in my heart of hearts."

I hesitated, then said, "Are you a little down?"

"Of course I'm down. I'm fifty-three years old with no social or sexual prospects."

"You have more prospects than anyone I've ever known. You always meet people."

"I'm going to stop looking. Seriously. I don't need a man to validate my existence. I've got a career that's totally fulfilling; a daughter . . . in fact, a daughter I can use as a role model, who is independent, who doesn't look at her life and see it as half empty. You've taught me that."

"I have?"

"By example. You have your life, your work. You don't bitch and moan about Saturday nights and about your biological clock. I'd like to think that some of that came from me—maybe from some latent part of me I haven't used yet."

"I think about men," I said.

"Of course you do. But you're not obsessed with them. It's a marvelous way to be."

"I think about them a lot. I just don't talk about it all the time."

"Which isn't healthy, either, you know. But that I blame on your Germanic upbringing."

I paused and said, "That may be."

"Really?" said Bernice. "You're acknowledging that?"

"They discouraged a lot of things. Some men, some opportunities . . ."

"I want you to come to dinner tonight," said Bernice.

I stayed in the phone booth and opened my note from Dwight: "April—New bean today, Zimbabwe. Yours, D.W." I wrote back below it, unsigned, my handwriting cramped to its tiniest script, "Are you doing anything Sat. nite?"

I went there after school, to the library. Dwight stood behind the circulation desk talking to a student. He looked up, smiled, and said, "Miss Epner."

I signaled, Go ahead. I'll wait.

I watched him. I saw that a V-necked sweater over a flannel shirt filled out his upper body. I saw that he had a fine nose. Eyes. I just stood there pretending to wait my turn with Mr. Willamee. And I thought: If he looks up again, he'll know.

The student was saying, "She goes, 'Not *Catcher in the Rye* and not *A Separate Peace*. Everybody picks them.' "

Dwight took a sheet of white paper from the student and read it, frowning. He slapped it with the back of his hand and said, "Here you go—*Call It Sleep*. Great novel."

The student turned the paper around and studied it. "Do you know how long it is?" he asked.

Dwight looked up at me and said, *"The* single most important criterion when choosing a book for a book report."

"It's due Friday," said the boy.

Dwight laughed and pointed to the card catalogue. "Under title or author. Go."

"Thanks," said the student.

Dwight waited a few seconds and said quietly, "Next."

"Hi," I said.

He reached inside his V-neck to his shirt pocket, flashed our note, and returned it to its hiding place. "Is this from you?" he asked.

I nodded.

"Disguised your handwriting."

Didn't mean to, I said.

He patted his breast pocket. "Were you serious?"

I nodded.

"I accept," he said. He looked at me then the way I imagined we'd look at each other away from school, weeks from now.

"This Saturday?"

"I'm free," he said.

"Good."

"Where are you taking me?" he asked.

"What do you like to do, besides drink coffee?"

"Go to movies. Eat pizza. Same things you young folks like to do."

I smiled.

"What?" he asked.

"You're funny. No one gives you credit for that around here. But you can be quite . . . I don't know."

"Droll?"

"You don't let everyone see that side."

"Just you," he said lightly.

I checked to see who was watching. "Why do you suppose that is?"

He pushed his glasses up, pretended to be reading a notice taped to the circulation desk, and quietly intoned, "Let me count the ways."

Another student, a girl wearing several gold wires through each earlobe, approached with a note. Dwight read it and said, "Fine." She thanked him and left, smirking at me as if I'd understand.

I muttered, "Not a conflict for Saturday night, I hope?"

He laughed. "Just my type."

"Because I asked first."

He touched his breast pocket again. "I wasn't sure you had. I thought it might have been a trick . . . Anne-Marie intercepting my note and toying with me."

No trick, I said. Absolutely not.

"Good."

"Besides, you should have recognized a behavior pattern here. It wasn't the first time I asked you out."

He shook his head.

"No?"

"That was different. That was an accident. That was when you were a Kennedy."

"That was before," I said.

"Before what?"

I smiled. He stared at my hair for a few seconds and then lowered his gaze to smile back. I said, "I'd better let you get back to work."

"Why?"

"You know."

I moved a half-step backward, but returned. "Come for dinner?"

"I'd like that."

We said bye, just mouthing the word. See you tomorrow.

Maybe I'll give you a call tonight, he said.

Dinner at Bernice's tonight. But tomorrow night? I'll give you directions, I said. We'll set a time.

We'll talk, he said.

NINETEEN

 Bernice peered critically into my face across her dining room table and said, "You look different."

I said my hair had been trimmed a good half-inch. She shook that answer off impatiently and said, "That's not what I'm seeing."

I shrugged.

Bernice pushed her empty dinner plate toward me to make room for her elbows and assume a position of greater intimacy. "How's Dwight?" she asked smartly.

Fine, I said.

"It's him. That was a lie detector test and the needles went haywire."

I asked what it was she thought I was not telling her.

Bernice touched her cigarette briefly to her lip and peered again through a squint. "You've slept with him. That's what's coming across."

I said, "I know this is your favorite topic of conversation, but it's not mine."

"How do you know? We've hardly touched on the subject. You might enjoy it."

I said no. I wouldn't. And just for the record, Dwight and I had never even had a date, let alone sex.

"I have a very good reason for asking you if you've consummated your relationship. It has nothing to do with prurient interest."

"What's the reason?"

"Don't jump down my throat."

I said I wouldn't.

She straightened up for the announcement. "I think Dwight's gay."

I didn't answer immediately. Then I said, "I used to think that before I knew him."

"Something's missing—a male-female connection. You know what I'm talking about? It isn't there."

"Where?" I asked.

Bernice held out her hands and interlocked her fingers. I was supposed to know what that symbolized. "The connection," she repeated. "A look that men send out. An attitude. Something in the way their pupils dilate."

"Dwight's not at ease around women, if that's what you're picking up. I think you're used to ladies' men."

"Ladies' men! That's such a dated term. In my experience—and I see a lot of men in a lot of different contexts—they look at you and you know. Not that they're coming on to you, but that they would if they could. I'm not talking action, either. Cardinal Law was on the show once and I felt, even there, a certain *presence*. A muted sexuality."

I asked if she was saying this so I would testify to Dwight's heterosexual activities. Because, actually, I had only recently—long after that dinner at the Ritz—acknowledged that I have feelings for him. We were going out Saturday night. For the first time.

"I'm only telling you what concerns me. Men can make friends with women for appearance's sake. Let's say they have a high-visibility job and want to have the trappings of a heterosexual life. Men marry women for appearance's sake. And have children."

"And you think you're the litmus test? No man can resist you and if he doesn't drool when he talks to you he must be gay?"

Bernice clucked in annoyance. "Why do you think I brought this up?" she demanded.

Because. This is how you think, and view the world, and this is how you carry on conversations. I said, "I have no idea. Tell me."

"Because I don't want you used and I don't want you getting hurt."

"You don't think it hurts me when you characterize Dwight as a closet gay? Or worse—as a conniving closet gay. Or at best, a sexless heterosexual?"

Bernice got up and went into the kitchen. I could tell she wasn't mad, but that for her things were just getting interesting. She was doing something about dessert and coffee so she could return to the conversation undistracted. I followed her into her Pullman kitchen, all black in startling ways: black porcelain sink, black granite counters, black marble tiles on the walls.

"I've got some Girl Scout cookies in the freezer, unopened," she offered.

I said, "No thanks, just coffee."

"One of the cameramen nailed me for his kid. I said, 'Sure, one of each.' I couldn't believe they get two-fifty a box. I figure it's a write-off, though."

As I listened I experimented with speeches: *I know you don't find him attractive—I didn't either at first—but I feel this*

. . . this tenderness when I see him. Part of it has to do with the way he looks. Those bones sticking out. It turns my heart inside out when I look at him now. Same face, same long arms, everything I used to find homely . . . I said, "I feel as if you've spoiled something. That it's your own vanity and it has nothing to do with Dwight."

She turned around, surprise making her expression friendly and inquisitive. Then: "What makes you so insecure? You certainly don't get it from me."

"Criticizing you makes me insecure?"

"You need one hundred percent approval. You want me to like everything you do and love everyone you love: your brother, your dead parents, Dwight, *Latin*. A really secure person doesn't need positive reinforcement for everything."

"I'm not looking for your approval. I just want to have a conversation with you that makes me feel as if we're moving forward and not circling each other like wrestlers on the mat. It's incredibly frustrating because you never just listen and say, 'That's nice, April.' You always have to make a big deal out of everything. Sometimes I don't care, but this one really offends me."

Bernice looked excited, even happy. "Just tell me I'm wrong, then. Say: 'Dwight is incredibly sexy and you don't know what you're talking about!' "

"I will."

"Good." She handed me a molded plastic tray, black, with cups, saucers, and packets of Equal. I followed her obediently into her living room, which was dominated by an immense curving sectional sofa unholstered in fawn-colored suede. Bernice sat down and faced me, still looking happy and expectant. We sipped coffee. I asked her what bean it was.

"Bean?" she repeated. "How do I know?"

"It's very smooth," I said.

"Doesn't all coffee come from Colombia?"

I said, God, no. Africa, Jamaica, Sumatra, Hawaii, Costa Rica . . . Didn't she go into coffee specialty shops?

"Since when did you become a coffee maven?" she asked.

"Dwight got me interested. He mail-orders his beans."

Bernice was not impressed. What did one expect an effeminate librarian to get through the mail if not coffee beans?

I said, setting my cup down first on the coffee table, "Ever think about where Jack Flynn might be?"

I thought I saw a flash of confusion in her eyes, as if the name Jack Flynn didn't match any signal in her brain. She said quickly, "Ah, the handsome Jack Flynn."

"Do you have any ideas?"

"In jail, probably, for statutory rape."

I confessed I sometimes looked in the phone book under John Flynn, just to see how many there were. Maybe to see if one might jump out at me.

"You wouldn't be interested in him."

I shrugged—for my medical history. Maybe I had some half sisters or brothers.

"You certainly haven't demonstrated any great interest in your birth *mother*," she said. "Are you hoping something will click with him?"

"You don't think I'm interested in you?"

Bernice released a forced "ha," then clamped her hand over her mouth as if such rudeness had escaped against her will.

"You think I'm cold?" I asked.

"You're pretty goddamn Germanic."

"Trude and Julius's fault, of course."

"Let's just say you're not the cuddly type."

I said I knew. I had always been sarcastic. Dwight made me laugh, though, and I was laughing more these days. Had she noticed Dwight had a very dry sense of humor, even a zany streak?

I couldn't bring myself to stop. She seemed to sink farther into the cushions of the couch. Usually a silence meant she was pouting, but this seemed different. I asked if something was wrong.

"I'm exhausted," she said. "And I've got vegetarian cookbook authors coming on tomorrow."

"You look more sad than tired," I said. Then I saw tears in her eyes. She looked away.

"What is it?" I asked.

She rubbed the nap on the suede seat beside her, forcing it one way, then the other. "I get sad at night," she said. She abandoned her design and sipped from her mug.

I said, "I know. I used to get sad at night, too."

"But not anymore!" she sang with a false brightness. "Now you've got a date Saturday night. And your marvelous family memories. Everything's peachy keen."

I knew what would cheer her up. I paused a few moments and volunteered: "My parents would have been upset about my dating Dwight."

Everything about her brightened: her eyes, her posture. Her grip on her cup changed as she tried to subdue her excitement. "Why?" she cried.

"Not Jewish. German-American."

"He's *German*?" she breathed.

"Way back."

"But they were German- and Austrian-Americans, too!"

"Big difference," I said.

She put her cup down on the smoky glass coffee table and lit a cigarette. "Do you know this for a fact, that they'd disapprove?" she asked.

I nodded gravely.

The fingers holding the cigarette formed a V in front of her nose; her thumbnail was caught between her teeth. "What haven't you told me?" she finally asked.

I slipped off my shoes and pulled my legs up under me on the couch. I held my mug with both hands. When I was twenty-nine, almost thirty, I told her, when they were both still alive, when Freddie was in his early twenties, living at home, I had this boyfriend, Peter.

"Not Jewish," said Bernice.

"Polish," I said. "Pieciak." I went home for dinner on a Friday night by myself to tell them I was seeing him. I worked it into the conversation—my friend Peter this, my friend Peter that. They didn't react. Finally I said, "He's a brother of someone I knew in graduate school. We're dating."

My father asked what his name was and I told him. They consulted their plates, pushed some brisket onto the backs of their forks. Not a Jewish name, their food seemed to tell them. Not a Jewish boy. Not right for April. Or us. I said something like "Sorry to have to bring you such sad news."

"Sad news?" they repeated. Not sad news. "Did we say something wrong?"

"I thought you might think it was good news I was dating someone."

"But we don't even know him," they said.

I said, "I'm thirty years old. I'm getting old for finding boyfriends."

"Oh, that," they said. "That's what Americans think, that women are over the hill at thirty."

I said, "I almost brought him along tonight. I wonder how you would have treated him."

"We're always cordial to guests in our home," they said.

"I think I'm in love with this person," I said. "It's what I came home to tell you. And more important, he's in love with me."

Then it was time for their speech on my loyalty, my industriousness, my superior intelligence; their catalogue of April's wonderful qualities that made her the best of everything. They believed it, too; they thought men fell in love with industriousness and neatness and tenure and safe driving. How could they worry about my staying single, about such a treasure lying unclaimed?

"It's never made me popular," I told them.

"Popular!" they spat. "Of what importance is *popular?*"

"You never get over being unpopular," I said. "It forms the way you look at things. At yourself. At men."

"But who's right now, sweetheart? Didn't you just tell us that a young man is in love with you. What does your *popular* mean in this case?"

One by one we resumed eating. Trude asked what he did. A graduate student, I said. Still? they asked. At what age?

Twenty-eight, I said.

Twenty-eight? they repeated. "Young. Younger than you, April."

"It doesn't bother me," I said.

"When did this come about?" my mother asked.

Since the summer, I said.

A signal passed between my parents then, one that said, Well, of course—it's only been months and she's calling it love. That's what this is.

I said, "You and Daddy were engaged a few weeks after you met."

"That was different," said my father.

"He'd like to meet you sometime," I said.

They nodded pleasantly.

"You could drive up and meet us for dinner."

"What is he?" my father asked.

I knew what he was asking. "Catholic," I said.

"Does he go to church?"

"I don't know," I said. My father made a noise, a grunt that meant, You know nothing.

"What's the matter?" I asked angrily.

"What did you think we would say? You thought we'd be pleased you're in love with a Catholic boy who's a Pole?"

And Freddie said, "You knew they wouldn't be happy, April."

"They were worse than the Nazis," said Trude. "They loved killing Jews. They'd point to Jews who passed as Gentiles to save their lives and say, 'There's one. Get her.' When the war was over the Poles still had pogroms!"

Julius said, "Should I say I'm pleased when I'm not? That it makes me sick to my stomach that when my daughter finally falls in love it's not only with a *shagitz,* not your regular Gentile, but a Pole. Is he blond and blue-eyed, too, for good measure?"

"He wasn't there," I said. "It wasn't him. It's not all Poles. And it's my life anyway. Not yours, mine."

Julius was on his feet suddenly, crouched, his hand raised and open flat. I burst into tears. He sat down and said, "I'm sorry, I shouldn't have done that."

"What did I do that was so terrible?" I said.

"You should have known," my mother said.

"What'd you expect, April?" said Freddie. "A *Pole.*"

"Nothing happened," said my father. "I apologize."

Bernice's hand was over her mouth. She slid it off slowly and said, "Wow. A primal scene. What happened with this guy, Peter?"

"Nothing."

"Because of them?"

"Because of me."

She narrowed her eyes. "How often did he hit you?"

"Never," I said.

"Just this one time? Is that what you're saying?"

"It touched something off—"

"I don't care what it touched off! You don't slap your adult children around unless you're a sickie. And you shouldn't be apologizing for him!"

"He didn't *hit* me."

"And what did your mother do—what did your brother do—while this little drama was being performed? Applaud? Or did they apologize for him, too?"

"We all knew why," I said. "The war."

Bernice stubbed out her cigarette after a final, angry puff. "When are you allowed to say, 'They were difficult people. My life was harder than it might have been if someone else had adopted me'?"

"You don't know that."

"I know you can't do anything about their being in the camps. You can't erase that, no matter how good a daughter you are; no matter how Jewish your boyfriends might be."

I fought the quivering that had started in my chin. I managed to say, "What if I am making excuses for them? I know what they went through. It doesn't hurt anyone."

"It's not fair to you," she said. "And it's not fair to Dwight."

Dwight? I said.

"This is what this is all about: falling in love with someone who'd make them turn over in their graves. *And* breaking the news to little Freddie who has a hot line to heaven, apparently."

"I can handle Freddie," I said.

"You'd better! Tell him there's a man in your life—an upstanding, fine German-American man. That he's highly intelligent and devoted to you; that you're compatible, emotionally, intellectually, and temperamentally."

I smiled. So much for gay Dwight.

"You have to confront these prejudices head on. Take a stand. Don't let him play Daddy. Who's he going to choose—his dead parents or you? Force his hand."

"That's not the way I do things," I said.

Ordinarily she would have said, "That's right! And look how far that's gotten you!" But tonight she could feel my adoption unraveling and her stock rising. All she had to do was be nice, be the sympathetic one and wait. The key was being in Dwight's camp. With great restraint she said, "You're right. The important thing is to work on your relationship with Dwight and not let ancient history erode what you two have together." She smiled the smile of a wise and loving confidante, a marvelously judicious one.

I said yes, that was pretty much the way I had decided to handle it.

"I'll have you all to dinner!" Bernice cried. "You, Dwight, Freddie. It would be on neutral ground. We could all relax and get to know each other."

Maybe sometime, I said. I was going to take it one step at a time. Dwight and I hadn't even had one date.

"Your brother wouldn't have to know who I was. I could just be a friend who was having a dinner party. We could have a girl here for him. A gorgeous shiksa."

"Let me think about it," I said.

Bernice put one index finger to her chin and held it there primly. After a few moments she said, "I'm coming on too strong. I'm asking you to do something for my own selfish reasons. I want your happiness so badly that I'm trying to direct everything."

"That's okay," I said. "You meant well."

"I do. I really do," Bernice said earnestly.

"You'll meet Freddie one of these days. And you'll like him in spite of his being a prick. He's very charming."

"Good. I want to meet him. And I want to see more of Dwight. I think he and I have a lot in common. We both—" She stopped, changed her mind; said instead, "Where is he taking you Saturday night?"

TWENTY

We took his car because mine was unreliable and the drive was six hours, round trip. I read to Dwight from the guidebook in my lap: "There are no living Shakers at Hancock Shaker Village, but visitors sometimes get confused." It was Saturday morning. We were driving west on the Massachusetts Turnpike in his white Honda Civic.

"Why is that?" he asked.

I read further. "The re-creation of this nineteenth-century Shaker village is so authentic that the staff purposely does not wear the full Shaker dress in an attempt to keep the confusion to a minimum."

"Don't you get carsick doing that?" he said.

I put my finger in the book to mark my page, lowered the seat back a few inches, and closed my eyes.

"Are you okay?"

I smiled, didn't answer.

"You're not having second thoughts about this trip?"

"I seem to recall it was my idea."

He smiled. "You mean you don't catch sight of me out of the corner of your eye and say to yourself, Ye gods! What am I doing in a car driving across the state with Dwight Willamee?"

I looked over, noticed how his complexion was healthier in sunlight than it appeared under the fluorescent lights of the library. His skin looked pink, softened by a careful shave and a hot washcloth. In a moment, eyes back on the road, I said, "I know exactly what I'm doing here."

Dwight had called me the night before to get directions to my apartment. We had talked about Bernice; he told me he had taped her show and watched it.

I had asked him what he thought.

"Painful," he said.

"Which one was it?"

"Pet owners."

"Oh, God."

"Who comes up with her show ideas?" he had asked.

"She takes credit for the good ones."

"What's her idea of a good one?"

"Eligible men. That's how she meets them all. Of course there's some other pretense for their being on— they cook or they've sailed solo around the world."

"Sort of her own dating service."

"Exactly. And everybody at the station knows it."

"You have to laugh about this, you know. If you see her through the eyes of a television critic, you'll be annoyed all the time."

"I *am* annoyed! You wouldn't believe the stuff she thinks of. She carries around a notebook to scribble ideas in, then hands her notes to her production assistant when she gets a bunch saved up. She'll write something ridiculous down like 'Shetland ponies,' but then some nice woman approaches her at a restaurant and says she has a book coming out on Shakers or Quakers that sounds really interesting, and she writes it down on a napkin and crumples it as soon as the woman walks away."

"It was probably on Shakers," Dwight had said.

"The ones who don't have sex. They just recruit members for the community and adopt orphans."

"Shakers."

"They're extinct, except one woman in Maine."

He had asked if I remembered the author's name. I hadn't; a woman, though, the scholarly type. Bernice would have booked her if she had been male, surely. Dwight had said, no matter. In a few months he'd check *Books in Print*.

"Do you have a thing for Shakers?" I had asked.

"I guess I do, sort of an inverse voyeurism one could have only for people who don't believe in sex."

Dwight liked sex, he was saying. He was a sexual being. He couldn't imagine a life devoted to no sex; it was so peculiar to him that he was going to go out and buy a book and try to fathom how people lived that way.

"Have you ever been to the Shaker Village in the Berkshires?" I had asked carefully.

In the car, I studied his profile when I thought he wouldn't notice. Without taking his eyes off the road he said, "Now you're really making me nervous."

I waited awhile, turning to appreciate the October foliage bordering the farms on my right. Finally I said, "You're not nervous. You're good at this—better than you let on. I think you know what you're doing."

"Is that bad?" he asked slowly.

"No."

"I didn't deliberately hide anything or mean to suggest that I'd never talked to a woman or never sat in a car with a woman." He smiled. "Tell me I wasn't *that* pathetic."

"I see you differently, that's all. It's hard to remember old impressions. Now I see . . . other things."

He grinned, didn't answer right away. Finally he said, "And your favorite fairy tales all had frog princes in them."

I laughed and said his self-image needed work; for example, how long would it have taken him to ask me out if I hadn't asked first?

"It depends. I'd like to think I'm not totally devoid of social grace. On the other hand—"

"We could have kept on passing notes for years."

"You could be right, pal," Dwight said. He took one hand off the steering wheel to pat my knee. I caught the hand as he withdrew it. We looked at each other, the first eye contact acknowledging these were our hands and our nerve endings. A few hundred yards later, his hands back on the wheel, he said, "Maybe we can still do dinner tonight. If you're not too tired."

"I won't be," I said.

"Herbs were very, very important to the Shakers," said our guide. "Dandelion extract was used as a diuretic and to purify the liver." Dwight and I began making faces. We were only on the third stop of the tour. The Poultry House, the Brick Dwelling House, the famed Round Stone Barn, the Sisters' House and the Brethren's Shop, the Ministry Wash House and the Meeting House, were still ahead. The Good Room *in* the Meeting House for souvenirs; the demonstration of Shaker music and dance.

"Whaddya say?" I asked. We were straggling behind the group, uncommitted.

Dwight consulted his visitors' map, then his watch.

"We could slip away"—he read: "to the attractive lunch-room, furnished with reproduction Shaker chairs and tables, offering sandwiches, soups, beverages, and Shaker rosewater ice cream."

"Or we could leave."

"That bad?"

"Do you like it?"

"A bit attenuated," he said. "I like the House of the Seven Gables–type tour, up the back stairs and down the front. Buy a postcard and leave."

"Shorter might have helped," I said.

He put his arm around my shoulder to confide, "Full frontal nudity wouldn't help this place."

The tour group turned a corner. We held back, retraced our footsteps, admired the famed Round Stone Barn from a distance, and drove to Pittsfield for lunch.

It was four o'clock and we were in Northampton, only one hour closer to Boston than we had been. We drank cappuccino at a sidewalk café next to a bookstore on Main Street. Up the hill, if you leaned far enough toward traffic, you could see the gates of Smith College.

Dwight said, "Total anonymity. Not one person who knows us."

I lowered my voice. "Except that the ghost of every Quincy High School student who went to Smith over the last fourteen years is dancing before my eyes."

He moved his chair closer. "I know it sounds crazy, but I've heard there are people out there, adults like us, who don't whisper in public and don't travel two hours out of town for dates."

"Obviously not high school teachers."

"Or not paranoid high school teachers." He shook his head: what a life.

Why do you do it? I asked. You're obviously unhappy.

Why don't you get out now? Quit before you're burned out.

Dwight rolled his eyes as if to say, too late for that.

"You could get a job at a real library. Or a *college* library. What about Widener? Or do something else entirely."

"I look periodically. I get the *Chronicle of Higher Ed.;* I get a listing from Columbia every two months. I sneak out for interviews when things come up, but the good ones are mostly outside the area." He cocked his head toward the brown awning two doors down. "Bookshop" was painted discreetly on the scalloped edges. "That's what I'd really like to do—a bookstore with readings and signings. Maybe classes."

Why not? I asked. Why not do it?

"Money."

I hesitated, taking a sip of coffee, then said, "You help your parents?"

He nodded.

"What about your sisters?"

"They visit, but they have their own lives."

"And you don't?"

"You know what I mean—kids, husbands, in-laws, dogs."

I did know what he meant: lives without spouses or children didn't count; didn't register on the meter of meaningfulness.

"Do they encourage your . . . getting out socially?"

He laughed. "They know."

"You told them about me?"

He nodded.

"That's flattering."

He mimicked my words.

"It's not?"

"They'd heard your name in passing before."

Before? I thought. When before?

Dwight said, "You'll meet them. My mother will do her cream of mushroom soup over pork chops for you." His arms were folded on the table. He smiled, slid his elbows closer to me.

"What?"

"Think they'd mind if we went up to my room after dessert and made out?" he asked as if it were a reasonable and commonly debated point of etiquette.

I rubbed his sleeve above his wrist, just a touch with my fingertips. It was a great bump of a hairy wristbone with enormous appeal.

He drove me home to Quincy, even though I said the Green Line and then the Red Line took me practically to my door. "Nonsense," he said.

We were parked in a visitor's space. "Should I invite you in?"

"Uh-oh," said Dwight. "Here it is. The awkward moment."

"Are your parents expecting you?"

"I'm thirty-nine years old," said Dwight. "A backward thirty-nine-year-old, true. But I assume you have a telephone."

"It's after eleven. Maybe we should just say good night."

"Fine," he said quickly. "I understand."

"What do you understand?" I reached for his hand and held it firmly.

He smiled and said, "Nothing. I forget."

"Good."

"Maybe we can do this again sometime."

I laughed and said, "Is that right?"

"Next Saturday?"

"That long?"

"When?"

"Do you go out on weekdays?"

"Sure."

"Thursday, for dinner? Here."

"That's right—you owe me a dinner."

"Okay," I said.

His face came closer and we kissed. We checked with each other and smiled. He kissed me again, the definitive one. Soft and expert; effortless. Everything in the right place. A talent.

TWENTY-ONE

Bernice did not call to interrogate me about my date. My phone was not ringing when I came in Saturday; no tries on Sunday, no messages on Monday.

Anne-Marie, on the other hand, was waiting.

"I've already seen him this morning," she announced smartly, "so you don't have to keep avoiding me." She summoned me by flexing her index finger. I walked to her desk. "You won't believe this but he was standing by his mailbox, leaning one shoulder against the wall reading something and I looked over and I swear to God for a second I thought he looked cute."

"C'mon."

"I swear to God. Of course I didn't say anything. He doesn't know I know anything."

I walked over to the mailboxes, pictured Dwight leaning into the wall, glanced tenderly at his name.

"You got it bad," said Anne-Marie.

* * *

Dwight came to my homeroom just as the bell was ringing to signal the beginning of first period. He stood just inside the door as the students filed out. A few of the confident boys patted him in that patronizing way they egged on the nerds with girlfriends. Kevin Caruso, not usually ill-behaved, called out, "Miss Epner, your boyfriend's here."

"Mr. Willamee," I said pleasantly.

He nodded his professional nod to the students still straggling by. "Move along," Dwight said two or three times until the room was clear.

"Hi," I said.

He winked. "Come for lunch?"

"Sure."

"I've got some ideas," he said.

"About what?"

"Jack Flynn."

I made a face.

"Not good?" asked Dwight.

"What kind of ideas?"

"Phone books."

"Where?" I asked.

"Boston. South Shore. West suburban. North. Lots of John Flynns listed. Those are the logical places to start."

I put an imaginary receiver to my ear. "Hello, you don't know me but did you inadvertently impregnate Bernice Graverman in nineteen fifty-one?"

"Nah. We're smoother than that."

"I'm not doing it," I said. "I don't even care about Jack Flynn."

Dwight smiled and said, "I know. Just like you don't care about Bernice."

"I didn't go looking for her."

I looked up at the clock above the door. The minute hand clicked another notch and a buzzer sounded. "I've got a class," I said.

"We won't do anything drastic at lunch. We'll just discuss it. I can't turn back now that I'm in my Sherlock Holmes mode."

"Maybe," I said.

The kids in Latin II had heard. There was a cued tittering as I strode in and over to the desk. "How's Mr. Willamee?" said Jennifer Platt smartly.

"Why?"

When she didn't answer I asked, "Just trying to make a federal case out of one teacher passing another in the hall?" That's all I said. That's all we teachers ever said about our personal life and the most we ever said when teased.

I couldn't concentrate very well during class. I felt a nagging annoyance with Dwight for coming to my homeroom and exposing us. People didn't do that. Students sniffed out faculty romances with fewer clues than Dwight was supplying. I settled down at some point. One of my C students was struggling with a translation, stumped by a gerund; the others were getting restless with his pace. Then the loudspeaker went on: Anne-Marie asking blandly enough if Mr. Willamee could come to the main office—a routine announcement any day but today. My class erupted, oohing in one crescendo as if they'd rehearsed.

I smiled cynically, the way you do in these situations. I said wearily, when I heard the refrain of "Goin' to the Chapel" being sung from the back of the room, "That's enough."

They still made noises. I said, "Do you think this is very civilized?" The A students stopped as I made eye contact with each one. The creeps got louder. Alison Chin said, "Shut up, you guys." They directed some jeers at her, and faded out.

I didn't look up, but leafed ahead with a mission in Caesar's *Commentaries on the Gallic War*. I announced that they had just earned themselves double the homework assignment, which I would be collecting at the beginning of class the next day. I picked up my books and left the room seconds before the bell rang.

Dwight thought I took the teasing too seriously.

"Did you have to come to my homeroom?" I asked.

"I assumed I'd be welcome in your homeroom, April."

"I'll never hear the end of it."

"Good. It's character-building. Besides, they like you. They're doing it affectionately." He smiled. "They probably like the fact that you're being swept off your feet."

"I'm too crotchety to be swept off my feet."

"That hasn't been my experience."

"I'll never hear the end of it. Neither will you."

He grinned. "I can take it."

"You don't have classrooms full of them."

"You just want a boyfriend everyone likes that you don't have to apologize for."

"That's not true," I said.

"You don't like the students knowing because Mr. Willamee is a dork and you don't want to be known as a dorkette. You don't want anyone to know."

"Look," I said. "Give me your tie clip. I'll wear it. Do people still do that? I'll do it."

"Only a dork would wear a tie clip," said Dwight. "And only a dorkette would think it was cool to parade it around school."

We were sitting at a table in the library. I squeezed his thigh under the table, a reckless gesture for school. He tried to pry me off after a polite few seconds, but I caught him by the bony fingers and held on. I smiled and said, "Do you take it back?"

"Yes. Uncle."

"Good." I let go. Then, "We're still on for Thursday?"

He prodded his glasses up and said, "Are you kidding?" He stared the way people stare just before they are moved to declarations; I stared back, a convert at the altar of bony sockets and hollows.

One of us—me, probably—brought up Jack Flynn to break the hold we had stared ourselves into. Dwight said he'd looked the name up in the Boston directory first and in the others he had in the library. He said he could make the calls for me. It was research, after all, and he had enough distance on the subject to handle it with professional objectivity. He would say he was a researcher looking for the Jack Flynn who lived and worked in Boston in 1951, perhaps much longer, and would be approximately fifty-five to sixty-five years old now.

I said it wouldn't work. If he was the least bit suspicious or had ever been in trouble, he'd deny it. Dwight said no; one makes it clear from the first that it is family business and confidential.

Imagine, I said: fifty-five or sixty years old. The Jack Flynn who picked Bernice up at Jordan Marsh, the one who was young and dashing with a freckled back. . . .

He might still be dashing with a freckled back, Dwight pointed out.

No, I said. You'll never find him. He was a slippery character then and he still will be. He's not going to be found unless he wants to be. And from what Bernice says, he could have seduced young women all over Boston. He may have been hunted down a dozen times by his illegitimate children.

"Do I have your permission to try?" asked Dwight.

I thought of Julius. Dwight would never meet Julius. All of this would be unthinkable if he were alive. "It would be one thing if I were curious, or if I had any feelings toward this man," I began.

"How can you not?" Dwight asked.

"He's nothing to me."

Dwight shook his head.

"*You're* curious, not me. You said it yourself—it's a puzzle for you and you like puzzles. It's a way to extend the Bernice puzzle. You've met her, so that's no longer shrouded in mystery. So on to the next clue."

Dwight listened carefully and said, "There's probably a good deal of truth in what you say—"

"You're bored. This gives you a nice research project."

"What do you think Bernice would say about my making some preliminary inquiries?" he asked.

"She claims to hate him," I said.

"But she's so vain. She'd want him to see that she turned out to have her own TV show, that she made good and is svelte and everything else she tries to project over the airways."

That was true. Bernice believed people enjoyed looking at her and listening to her. Jack Flynn could be a guest on her show! "I haven't seen this man in thirty-six years and three months," she might say quietly as her introduction. First she'd rerun the clip from her illegitimate-daughter confession. Then a dissolve to Jack Flynn, age sixty, watching Bernice's taped declaration. Bernice would touch his arm or take his hand in her on-air-empathetic way. A tight shot of her face as she repeated, "I have not seen this man in thirty-six years and three months. Can you guess who he is?"

A housewife in the first row would say, unamplified, "The father of your child?"

Bernice would nod to her audience, her best friends for this half-hour, with disbelief and reverence. Do you believe what is whirling around me? Do you believe what you're seeing? This, this man; this reunion; this bone-deep personal moment?

Bernice would turn to Jack. "Why?" she would ask. "What are you feeling right now?"

He would smile nervously, search the audience for empathetic male eyes. Hey, guys! Help me out here! I got laid and she got pregnant. Now I'm supposed to feel something?

I sketched the fantasy for Dwight, but added that it was not what I wanted. A photo was enough, perhaps a photo of him as he was then, the young Jack Flynn who looked like a young JFK and who had seduced Bernice. I told Dwight that if he had to pursue this Jack Flynn thing to some kind of conclusion he should, in the interest of research, start with Bernice. She might tell him whatever she was hiding from me.

I called her Wednesday.

I expected her at least to pretend she was delighted that things were going well and that I had thought to report in. But she was quiet and distant, and I was sorry I had called. I asked if something was wrong. She said she was busy. Work was getting to her today.

"I thought you'd like to know," I said.

"I do."

I should have said, "Okay, catch you another time." But I kept trying to engage her. Dwight was coming for dinner tomorrow night. . . . I thought I'd make that shrimp over linguini she had made for me . . . a salad.

No reaction, just a disembodied silence.

"And something chocolate for dessert," I added.

She murmured something affirmative, still distant.

Usually I peeled myself away, begged to get off the phone and back to class. This time I was the one who pressed, "Talk to you soon?"

TWENTY-TWO

Dwight arrived promptly at six-thirty. He had gotten a haircut since I'd seen him at school; when he kissed me hello, I smelled the clove scent of barber's talcum. "Delicious," I said, resting against him, our first stand-up embrace.

He had tapes of two movies and a chilled bottle of white wine—a Sancerre, he said.

I told him I still had my collegiate corkscrew, the bamboo kind from Varsity Liquors on Mass. Ave.

"I had one of those."

"I keep meaning to get a decent one."

"I'm sure it's fine."

I stood in one spot while he helped himself to a hanger in the coat closet. He stopped what he was doing. "Is something bothering you?"

I gestured around my apartment. "I don't grind my own beans. My dishes have pink and gray sprays of flowers on them. My albums are a catalogue of Coop markdowns, nineteen seventy to seventy-four.''

Dwight hung up his raincoat and closed the closet door with deliberation. He walked into the living room and assembled himself easily in my rocker. "I love your apartment. It looks like Harvard Square meets turn-of-the-century Vienna."

"It's my parents' piano, and the teacups were my mother's anniversary collection. Freddie doesn't want his girlfriends to think he collects knickknacks, so I took them. They're not exactly my taste either."

He smiled and rocked.

"What?"

"Are you going to apologize all night?"

"No," I said.

"Don't be a nervous hostess," Dwight said.

"I am."

"Maybe we should have gone out to dinner. I invited myself over without giving you an out."

"I wanted you to come."

"It's just that I'm your most cool and urbane dinner guest, so you're a little flustered?"

I laughed.

"Good. Enjoy yourself. I know you're thrilled to have me."

"I am," I said, and I stopped smiling. I stared into his face. He studied mine to see if something was wrong, if my silence was an unhappy one. I walked up to his chair, so close that he had to stop rocking.

He loved my dinner, or at least praised every ingredient. Capers in scampi was a stroke of brilliance; black-pepper fettucini!

So easy, I said. Cut back on the garlic, add some lemon juice. Don't overcook the shrimp.

We drank his entire bottle of Sancerre and left the kitchen, happy to stagger on to the living room couch like sitcom lovers under the influence of unaccustomed wine.

"Let's make out," said Dwight.

And just as it happens with sitcom lovers, after we had just started kissing, after his lovely hands had slipped to the back of my neck, the doorbell rang. We jumped. I waited for the interval it would take for a caller to ring a second time, assuming it had been a mispressed button, a false alarm. But the bell sounded again. Dwight gave me a boost up to my feet and I spoke into the intercom.

"It's me—Bernice," said the voice. "Can I come up?"

I turned to Dwight before buzzing her in. "Bernice," I mouthed. He shrugged as if interested, as if letting Bernice in wasn't the worst catastrophe to befall a second date. "I can't believe it. She's never dropped over here," I said.

"Better buzz her in," said Dwight.

I said no. I was going down to the lobby to explain to her that I had company and that it was an inconvenient time. The buzzer rang again.

"Be right down," I called into it.

"Oh, let her up," said Dwight. "She won't stay when she sees me."

"I wanted to be alone with you."

Dwight pulled me by the hand until I let myself fall back onto his lap. He tipped me back for a Hollywood kiss as if to say, "Just wait."

I got up from the couch and buzzed Bernice in. Seconds later, she was knocking at my door.

"Of all people to take it out on," she said, embracing me and releasing me quickly.

"What?"

"The show!" She was several steps into the apartment and had just received some innate cue to pretend to be surprised by Dwight's presence. "Oh, no," she said, pressing my arm to stop both of us. "You have company!"

Dwight stood up, looking enormous. Not enthusiastically I said, "You remember Dwight."

Bernice swept toward him, murmuring apologies to him and back over her shoulder to me.

"I mentioned on the phone when I called you that Dwight was coming for dinner," I said pointedly.

Bernice stopped her march and said simply, "You did, didn't you?"

"I said I was making shrimp."

"Mea culpa," said Bernice. "It totally flew out of my mind until now. That's the state I'm in."

"What's going on?" I asked.

"We're stopping production and going into reruns for the summer," she said. "Do you believe it!"

"Is that bad?" asked Dwight.

"A talk show?" she asked.

"Not good?" said Dwight.

"I have a time line," she explained. "I get newsmakers and headliners—topical ones. Not six months late. I get the ones who are in the middle of their fifteen minutes of fame—you're familiar with the Warhol quote?"

Dwight smiled.

"I'm effectively off the air."

"That's too bad," said Dwight.

"It's not the first time they've pulled this one, believe me."

"And you never went off the air any of those other times?" I said.

"But this is different." Bernice sat down heavily on the couch. I sat down next to her, and Dwight took the rocker again. She looked around the room, remembering it was her first view of my apartment. "Cute," she said.

"Thanks."

"I know this is a breach of etiquette, bursting in on your little date. I should excuse myself and exit gracefully. But this whole mess goes beyond social convention. I had to see April; I instinctively reached out for her."

Dwight smiled politely. "I'm sure April is happy to help."

"Of course she is. She is a compassionate person."

Cued, I asked a compassionate question. "Tell us why this time is worse than the other crises."

"One word," said Bernice. "One fucking word: 'Donahue.' "

Dwight, doing Dracula in sunlight, recoiled, protecting his face with crossed hands. I giggled.

"They're putting 'Donahue' in the nine-to-ten slot."

"Why is that fatal?" I asked.

"Followed by 'Hour Magazine'? Where do you suppose they'll find room for a lowly local show?"

"How long have you been on?" asked Dwight.

"Eleven years."

"And the show is popular?"

Bernice set her lips primly. "It's carved its niche in Boston television," she said.

"They wouldn't just fire you," I said.

"No, you're right. They'd merely insult me by offering me a half-hour on Sunday morning."

"Just Sunday?" asked Dwight.

"Eight A.M. As I said, 'effectively off the air.' "

"What does your contract say?" he asked.

"My contract," she repeated. "Who the hell knows? No protection, I assure you."

"You should probably have a lawyer look at it. Even if they have the right to cancel the show, maybe there's some due process you're not getting."

Bernice ignored his comment and said, "A Sunday

morning show has a certain religious ambience to it. Do you think they're going to let me have call girls and male strippers on Sunday morning?"

"You don't know that for sure," I said.

"Boston television on the Sabbath. That's the unspoken guideline."

"You don't have to do anything you don't want to," said Dwight.

Bernice looked at him with discovery and amazement. She smiled brilliantly. "Jesus Christ—this man is *right*. I don't have to do a goddamn thing I don't want to do! I can say, Fuck you. No, thanks. I don't need your eight A.M. Sunday charity slot."

I looked at Dwight to see if he was flattered by her revelation. He sneaked a look at me, moving just his eyes, signaling that her performance was being noted.

"The word will get out," she continued. "I'll see that the word gets out that 'Bernice G!' is looking for a new home."

"There's always cable," I said.

"I don't know why this came as such a shock to me. I'm old for television, for a woman on television. They love their men *distinguished*—Donahue was nobody before he went gray—but they like their women to look like models in *Seventeen*."

"Do you think that's the issue this time?" I said.

"It is and it isn't," said Bernice. She signaled interest in a new topic by looking squarely at the remnants of cheese and crackers on an end table. "What kind of cheese was that?" she asked.

"Smoked Gouda and Brie," I said.

"With peppercorns," said Dwight.

She smiled coyly at me.

"Are you hungry?" I asked.

"Starved!" she shrieked happily.

I went into the kitchen and returned with a box of cream crackers.

"You're a doll," she said.

"We finished the wine," I said.

"Anything—soda, Perrier," she said between bites.

"Diet Coke?"

"Fabulous. I'll chug it down and get outta here, pronto."

Dwight stood up and said he'd get it.

"How tall are you?" she asked.

"Six-five."

"Ever play sports?" she asked.

Dwight said no, not seriously. He disappeared into the kitchen. Bernice didn't look at me, didn't try to catch my eye or signal her approval of him. When he returned with the can, half-emptied into a glass, she accepted both with excessive gratitude.

"Would you like anything?" he asked me. I shook my head no and smiled fondly.

Bernice caught the smile. It didn't seem to please her. "Were you named after Eisenhower?" she asked.

"My parents say I wasn't. They just liked the name."

"April was going to be named Gabrielle," said Bernice. "Her father's mother's name was Gabrielle."

"It was?" I said.

She turned to Dwight. "I assume you inferred from our last meeting that I'm April's real mother?"

Dwight said yes. He'd known from the beginning.

"I'd love to know what she's told you," Bernice said.

Dwight smiled a polite circulation-desk smile and said, "April hasn't told me too much about her real father or even who he is." It was a researcher talking, one who asked potentially embarrassing questions with equanimity.

Bernice didn't give the easy answer. I almost said for

her, "His name was Jack Flynn," but sensed that Dwight was conducting his own test. When she did say "Jack Flynn," it sounded deliberate, as if two adults were talking about the tooth fairy with a child present.

"She didn't tell you?" asked Bernice.

"It was confusing," he said.

Bernice, settling in, opened her handbag and withdrew her cigarettes and lighter. "Confusing?" she repeated archly. "You can imagine what it was like to live through it."

"Bad?" asked Dwight.

"The worst."

I went in to the kitchen to get a saucer for her to use as an ashtray. I put it on her lap and said, "Things have turned out pretty well for you, all in all."

"She hates me," Bernice said blandly.

"No, I don't."

"Every time I talk about what I went through, you get defensive and take it personally. All I'm saying is, you don't know what it was like."

We were supposed to respond by asking for the missing details. We said nothing. Her time was up; we wanted to be alone. Bernice posed, smoking artfully, and waited. I took her dirty glass and the drying cheese into the kitchen. I heard Dwight say after an awkward silence, "I'm going to ask April if she'd like help with the dishes."

He came into the kitchen as if exiting a stage and escaping with relief into the wings. I whispered, "She'll take the hint." In a few minutes, we heard Bernice gather her things and walk down my hallway. I left the kitchen in time to see her jerk open the door and bid me a quiet, wounded good-bye.

I waited for the sound of her heels clicking on the hall linoleum, and the elevator's chime. "Mother dearest is gone," I called to Dwight, as I returned to the kitchen. He was coaxing coffee from my dented electric percolator and supermarket grind. He seemed to graze the ceiling and fill the space with his long arms.

Later, watching the first of the two movies he had brought, Dwight asked, "Do you think she thinks we're sleeping together?"

I said no. She thinks I'm backward and undersexed.

After a few minutes he asked, "How would you feel about it?"

Good, I said, watching Woody Allen pretend to do things under the covers to Shelley Duvall. Good.

"Any other thoughts on the matter?"

I smiled. Stared straight ahead and said, "All the time."

Dwight slouched lower on the couch so our faces were level. "Let me get this straight . . ." he began and waited.

I looked at him. "What?"

"Am I slow? Have you been thinking, 'Is this guy retarded or what?' "

"This is our second date. We couldn't very well do it in the library."

He laughed. "You don't know how many times we did it in the library."

I said that was intriguing. How long had that been going on?

"You'll get a big head if I tell you. Or you'll think I'm completely depraved."

"Since before I asked you out?"

"No comment."

"Before dinner at the Ritz?"

Dwight grimaced, closed both eyes, opened one, and said, "Since the informational picketing at the School Committee meeting. . . ."

I had a vague memory of it—signs that said, "If you think education's expensive, try ignorance." Years before, maybe three years before. Christmas lights strung around evergreens on the City Hall lawn, Mr. Willamee in an enormous parka and earmuffs.

"When was that?" I asked.

"A few contracts ago," said Dwight.

"C'mon. Not that long."

That long, he said.

"Why didn't you say something?"

He sat up straighter. "I did."

"What?"

"School stuff. Latin. How are your classes going? Who's getting the Latin prize? Are you going to the meeting tomorrow?"

I squinted. "Vaguely."

"I can see I made a huge impression."

I touched his face. "I'm sorry."

Dwight shrugged unconvincingly. "A little crush. I was pretty used to having my crushes unreciprocated."

I put my other hand on his face. Rubbed the cheekbones with my thumbs. "Not this time," I said and kissed him on selected spots. We settled against each other to watch the rest of *Annie Hall*. As the credits were rolling he asked rather formally, "Do you want to watch the second one?"

I shook my head no.

"Kind of late?"

"Not for me."

"It's *The Big Easy*," said Dwight.

"It's supposed to be good."

"We don't have to watch it. It was two-for-one night."

"I'd like to see it sometime."

"Are you tired?"

"No. Are you?"

I said no, just drunk. I also said, "I'm sorry about not reciprocating back then. I should have noticed. If I hadn't gone to look something up about Kennedy—"

"Now you know why I have a soft spot for Bernice," he said.

Dwight patted my thigh just above my knee, a coach's two quick taps—*c'mon, kid*. He stood up, offered to pull me to my feet. Said, "Let's get it over with, Ape."

TWENTY-THREE

I called Bernice from home after school, even though I had resolved not to position myself as the apologizer. She answered the phone with a "Yes?" in the same martyred voice as her good-bye of the evening before.

"I know you're mad at me," I said.

She didn't answer. I tried again. "I could tell by the way you left."

Wearily Bernice said, "What am I supposed to say, April? 'Yes, I'm mad; I was just beginning to feel better after a foul day when you decided you had had enough of your mother for one night'?"

"You should have called first."

"You've made that eminently clear."

"You knew he'd be there," I said.

"So what?" she said angrily. "So fucking what? I was extremely upset and went to my daughter for solace without thinking it through to every last ramification. I'm a terrible person. I should be prosecuted for what I did!"

"You could've scared him off," I said quietly. "He's a shy person."

"Please. I can read a situation as well as anyone. There was no danger of him leaving. If I had thought I was going to drive him away, I'd have withdrawn quickly and with due discretion. Give me some credit."

I murmured something noncommittal.

"Did he leave?" Bernice demanded.

"No."

"Did I ruin the evening?"

"No," I said.

"You two seemed pretty thick, hiding out in the kitchen."

"We were just cleaning up," I said.

"I threw you two together, didn't I? Unwittingly, I admit. But something was going on there . . . something was being forged in the kitchen while I cooled my heels in the living room."

"Dwight was trying to help."

"He's not without charm. And I thought I did a fair job of drawing him out, by the way."

I grunted.

"Are you attracted to him sexually? He's obscenely tall."

"Six-five."

"I've never made love to a man that tall," she said. "I'm wondering if they're built proportionately."

I didn't say anything.

"I take it you know the answer?"

"Did Dwight and I go to bed after you left? No."

Bernice said, "I think that's probably wise."

Because you didn't like him, I thought. Because *you* wouldn't want to sleep with Dwight.

"He certainly adores you," she said.

"He does?"

"He never took his eyes off you. He *dotes* on you."

I smiled. Bernice meant Dwight didn't pay adequate attention to her.

"When are you going to let the poor man bed you?"

I laughed and said, "I'm sure you'll be the first to know."

She said, quietly but for effect, "I wish that were true." She asked when we were going out again. If Dwight was a decent kisser. What he had to say about her.

"Nothing," I said reflexively.

"You're the worst liar."

"I'm not lying. We talked about school . . . and some other stuff."

Bernice hesitated and said after a few moments, "Can I give you some advice?"

Okay, I said. Depending on—

"Don't get in the habit of defining your relationship by what I've said or done that day. Don't turn Dwight into your psychiatrist. Find things to talk about besides me."

I said, "We have lots to talk about."

"So I didn't ruin your romance?"

"That isn't the issue."

Bernice said gaily, "You're looking for an apology for my naughty behavior? All right. I'm sorry. I shouldn't have come without calling first. Okay? Are we back on speaking terms?"

"We never weren't on speaking terms," I said.

"You know what I mean. I want us to be close again. I want us to have dinner soon. Dwight can come."

"We haven't made our plans yet. I could speak to him and get back to you."

"Can I say one more thing?"

"What's that?"

"Don't you have something slinkier to wear when you're entertaining at home? If not, I'd get something. Jumpers in lumberjack flannel are nice for teaching—"

"There's my door," I lied.

"Does he know you're Jewish?"

I laughed.

"What's so funny?"

"That's the stupidest question I've ever heard."

"I hope he realizes your parents wouldn't approve the way I do. That they wouldn't be endorsing this or taking the two of you out for a lovely dinner."

One more thing, she said: You can tell me anything. I know you're falling in love. They wouldn't have known that. You wouldn't have been able to tell them. I'm good at this, though. This is the side of life I excel at. They had their strong points—I know that—but I'm better than they would have been about a daughter falling in love with a less-than-obvious choice. A hell of a lot better. Aren't I?

TWENTY-FOUR

 My brother called me at work to remind me that the next day was my father's Yortseit, the anniversary of his death. Three years.

I said I had remembered and already bought a candle; I had even expected him to call and remind me—the bright spot in all of this. "I miss you," I said. "When can I see you?"

"I'll drive up to Quincy," he said after a pause. "I like that restaurant we went to for your birthday."

"When?"

"Tonight!"

"What time can you get here?" I asked.

"Six-fifteen? Six-thirty."

"Meet me at home, and we'll drive over in one car."

He said okay. It had been so long he needed directions.

* * *

He arrived early and was starved. We drove to the Greek restaurant and were seated before Freddie asked, "What'd you want to talk to me about?"

"A couple of things. Important things."

"You need money?" he asked.

"No. Other things. Two things—"

"A guy?"

"Yeah," I said. "Finally. And stranger than that . . . I hadn't been looking for my real mother, my birth mother, but it happened. She found me. I know who the woman is who had me and gave me up."

"No kidding?" said Freddie. What about sharing a plate of mixed appetizers?

I said okay—the one with stuffed grape leaves and spinach pie, though. Not the one with the fried chicken livers.

"Do you want to hear about her?"

Yeah, he said. How old?

"Fifty-three. She's a TV star," I said.

"No shit! Who?"

"Bernice Graves," I said.

Freddie squinted. He repeated the strange syllables to see if they added up to a name he recognized. "Who's that?" he asked, still hopeful.

" 'Bernice G!' The morning talk show on Channel Four?"

"Never heard of it."

"She's on at nine A.M."

"Did Mom and Dad know?" he asked.

"Not that she'd found me. That was after. Maybe they only knew her real name, Graverman, and didn't connect it with the show. Maybe they *did* know. I don't think so, though."

"Why'd she give you away?"

"She was seventeen, not married."

"What about the father?" he asked.

"A guy she was in love with, thought she was going to marry. The usual story. His name was Jack Flynn," I said.

"Flynn?" he repeated, the way my parents had pronounced surnames to roll the ethnicity around on their tongues.

"Have you met him, too?"

I said I hadn't. Didn't know if I ever would, if I even wanted to.

"Does she have other kids?"

"Nope."

"Is she rich?" asked Freddie.

I tried not to snap at him. "Well off, I think."

"How much does she make a year?"

"I have no idea."

"You never asked?"

"No, I didn't. You don't do that."

"What kind of car does she drive?"

"A Mercedes, I think. Or a BMW. I've only been in it once."

Freddie huffed as if he couldn't believe my slipshod recall of pertinent details.

"She takes me to expensive restaurants every week," I offered.

Freddie was not satisfied. He knew cars, not Boston restaurants.

"How much money she makes isn't really the issue," I said.

"It is if you're her only child and heir," said Freddie.

I told him that was a cold-blooded way of looking at it. There was so much more to it—imagine at thirty-six meeting the woman who gave birth to you!

Freddie did not imagine anything, because the appetizer platter arrived. He did not ask if I was happy about finding my birth mother, or sad or mixed up. I did what Trude would have done at this point: served him one stuffed grape leaf, one triangle of spinach pie, one meatball, one portion of moussaka, a hunk of feta cheese and three calamata olives, then took a junior version of his plate for myself.

On the drive back to my apartment I asked, "How's your love life?" I always asked. Freddie always told me. "Anyone new?"

He shrugged.

"Anyone special?"

He shrugged again.

"Playing the field?" I asked.

"That's a nice way of putting it."

"So I don't have to worry about your being alone and lonely?"

Are you kidding? he said—no one waiting up for him? A house to bring his dates home to. An empty house all to himself . . .

"Just don't get any diseases," I said.

"Speaking of which," said Freddie. "Who's the guy?"

I turned into my building's parking lot. Dwight's car was there, which meant Dwight was upstairs waiting. I said, "Do you want to meet him?"

"No," said Freddie.

"Aren't you curious?"

I knew he wasn't. He had the passivity of someone whose food had been cooked and arranged on plates for too many years. All he had to do was eat what was in front of him. "You're a lump, Freddie," I said.

"I don't like meeting new people. I never know what to say."

"What do you say to all these women you end up fucking? You must have a few good openers."

He almost smiled. He moved his mouth in a circular motion and thought it over. "That's different. A lot of them come on to me. They smile. I smile back. I ask them what they do. I ask them to dance. With guys, you get introduced and they say, 'Nice to meet you,' and you say, 'I've heard so much about you,' and then you stand there like two fools. It's harder for me with guys."

"Then say something else! Say, 'So! Any friend of April's is a friend of mine.' Wink at him. Slap him on the back. Do the stuff Dad would never do. Play the old man."

Freddie smiled. He liked our new conspiracy.

"Give us the Epner blessing," I said.

Freddie opened the door and got out. He put his hands on his hips and squinted up to the imagined window where Dwight might be watching us. "Okay," he said. "Let's see this guy."

"You don't have to stay a long time. I'll tell him you have a drive ahead of you."

Freddie put his arm around my shoulder and squeezed briefly. He never did things like that; he had never been moved to affection by any words between us. I could almost imagine him with his arm around a woman, walking across her parking lot after winning her over at some bar with his receding auburn curls.

Inside the lobby, the elevator doors opened as if cued to meet us. Freddie's lips moved in rehearsal. "Introduce me as Fred" was the only thing I actually heard.

Bernice's laugh bounced off my head as I entered my foyer. Then there was audience noise. It was "Bernice G!" on tape—this morning's show being played back. I called Dwight's name and walked into the living room.

It was not a smooth introduction. Dwight bounded up from the couch to hit the VCR as if he had been caught watching something disgraceful. The TV crackled unbearably. One of us hit the power button and then there was silence. "Dwight Willamee—my brother, Fred Epner." The two shook hands manfully.

"Heard a lot about you," Freddie mumbled.

"Same here," said Dwight.

I took my coat off and remembered to kiss Dwight hello. He complied, looking miserable. "Were you watching Bernice?" I asked.

"I rewound it for you," he said quietly.

"Bernice?" repeated Freddie. "The gal you told me about?"

"My mother."

"The very gal," said Dwight.

"Wanna see?" I asked.

Freddie said sure. Dwight cued up the tape, and we sat down on the couch with me in the middle. "What's today's show?" I asked.

"Hair," Dwight said. "Hers."

Her guests were Avi, Tate, and Lawrence of D'Image, Topper's, and Kinks, respectively. It was one of Bernice's cute openings: pretending to be pouting into a hand mirror as she was introduced.

"You watch her every night?" Freddie asked.

"April's addicted," said Dwight.

Bernice was saying, "I'm proud of my gray. I can't believe people want to hide theirs." She put down the mirror and picked up her index cards. This would be another show approached in the pseudoscientific manner she used for such nontopics and nonspecialists. "What *is* gray hair?" she asked the panel. The guests nodded at one another and arrived at a quick consensus: hair that has lost its pigment and come in white. Gray is an optical illusion: white and black *equals* gray.

"Thank you, gentlemen," said Dwight.

"She doesn't have any gray hair," said Freddie.

"I want the God's honest truth," Bernice was saying. "Forget that millions of people are watching. Tell me what you'd do with me if I gave you carte blanche. I'm in your hands."

Tate announced she had marvelous bones while Avi squeezed and released clumps of her loose hair. Lawrence did nothing, only sat and looked superior.

Bernice faked a protest to her guests' considered opinion that her pageboy was sophisticated, versatile, feminine, and suitable to her hair, face, and life-style. "Come on, guys," she cajoled. "You mean you can't improve on this old tired bob. Nothing? Not even a new"—she twisted a lock into an improvised tendril—"anything?"

"Uh-uh," they murmured in unison.

They had little choice; Tate was the hairdresser who designed her hairstyle and groomed it three times a week. Bernice tried hard to make the evaluation look objective.

"Is this what they're all like?" Freddie asked.

Dwight nodded strenuously.

"You're not interested in hairdressing. A lot of people are," I said.

"She specializes in guests with shit for brains," Dwight said.

We paid attention to the next exchange: Avi announcing that a diluted vinegar rinse would bring out the sheen in black hair by restoring the acid mantle to the scalp—for pennies. *Pennies!* Yes, for her, too! The black in her salt-and-pepper was still . . . brilliant!

Dwight fast-forwarded during a commercial. We caught

Bernice reacting to her guests' next tip as if it were startling and important. "Let me get this straight: *nothing* repairs split ends? These products we hear about, the ones that claim to repair split ends, are gimmicks?"

Tate and Lawrence and Avi nodded with varying degrees of conviction. "You cut them. You get trims raygoolarly and you don't tease," said the one sitting next to Bernice. Bernice looked into the camera triumphantly. "Even those advertisements where they show the split end magnified, getting rejoined?"

The same one—Avi, an Israeli?—held up two fingers in a scientific demonstration. He splayed them, then united them, only to separate them again: split ends *do not fuse*.

"Mr. Wizard," said Freddie. Dwight laughed.

"Back in the late sixties I used to iron my hair to make it straight," Bernice told the panel.

"I hope you gave that barbaric practice up," said one.

Because . . . ? Bernice prompted.

"Because you can burn the hair and you can burn yourself. One of my clients came in with a red welt on her cheek like this"—he outlined an inverted V on his own face—"the point of her iron."

"My hair became coarse when I had my daughter," she said suddenly. "Does that happen often?"

We exchanged glances. Freddie was interested, finally. His eyes widened as if he couldn't believe the bull's-eye: the daughter, me, being mentioned the first time he tuned in.

On the screen all three men nodded sadly: the childbirth culprit. Changes in texture, in thickness, in color. No two women's hair reacted quite the same way, said Lawrence. The bangs of a client from his last salon grew in titian after twins!

I was spooked by her invoking me. I didn't want to see

her look into a camera and say, "Yes, April, *you*—you to whom I gave my sheen, my body, my youth."

I shut off the tape before, I imagined, the three haughty beauticians addressed the topic of ungrateful daughters. Nobody protested. Dwight supplied the missing tag line: "My time with you is precious!"

Freddie stood up, smiling, all but rubbing his hands together. "When do I meet her?" he asked.

TWENTY-FIVE

Freddie fiddled with the piano keys while I called
Bernice; Dwight stretched out on my couch and flipped
through an old *Harvard Magazine*. "Guess what I was just
doing?" I said to Bernice in greeting.

"Will I like the answer?"

"Yes."

"Is Dwight there?"

"Yes. And Fred."

"Fred?" she asked. "Who the hell is Fred?"

"My brother."

"I get it," said Bernice. "His grown-up name. They all
do that."

"We just watched this morning's show."

"Oh, God!" she shrieked. "I hated it—those pricks.
They don't get along and nobody told me until it was too
late. They're all ex-lovers or ex-rivals or something."

I smiled at Dwight. "Fred would like to meet the woman who gave birth to me," I announced grandly. Bernice loved it when I talked like that.

"You're kidding, right?"

"Would you like to come over?"

She asked what time it was.

"Almost nine," I said.

"It depends what you're looking for. I'm too tired to do Mother of the Year."

"Be yourself," I said. "Come as you are." Dwight distorted his features as if recoiling from such a prospect.

"How's this: meet me at the Ritz bar in a half-hour," she said.

"We're not dressed for the Ritz."

"What are you dressed for?"

I said I didn't know. Maybe a place where she wouldn't be recognized.

"You hate that," she said agreeably.

"I don't like to be constantly interrupted."

"Unless they raise their hands first?"

"You're so clever," I said.

"Okay. The White Glove. Down from Government Center. It's a Mass. General hangout. On Cambridge Street."

I covered the mouthpiece and asked if we wanted to meet Bernice in town for a drink. Dwight pantomimed, Me? You? *He's* the one who wants to meet her.

Freddie said, "Sure."

I uncovered the receiver. "Fine. Half an hour, or however long it takes to get there. We'll leave now."

I hung up and said, "I'll drive."

Freddie put his hand inches from his mouth and exhaled to test his breath. He asked if he could use my bathroom to wash up.

* * *

The White Glove was almost empty. Bernice, of course, was not there. She always swept in after me, even if that meant smoking in her parked car for ten minutes.

We took a booth and ordered a pitcher of draft beer. Two women in white nylon pants suits—nurses? physical therapists?—watched Freddie discreetly from a neighboring table.

"Those women over there think I'm highly desirable," said Dwight. "They're hoping I'm the unattached one."

Freddie looked over and acknowledged them with a nod.

"Did you see that?" Dwight said. "When no one else was looking the blond one licked her lips and whispered, 'Baby, baby, baby.' "

I laughed and landed a kiss somewhere near Dwight's mouth.

"Thanks a *lot,* April. Why don't you just hang a sign around my neck that says, 'Hands off. He's taken'?"

"I think they're looking my way," Freddie said as if adjudicating a serious discussion. "They're kind of young."

"Oh, darn," said Dwight.

I prodded Freddie's forearm across the table and said, "He's kidding."

"Does this happen often?" Dwight asked.

"Only when I'm out in public," said Freddie.

The door opened and Bernice rushed in. She was wearing a short, straight leather skirt in a hideous loden green and an oversize brown sweater that reached to mid-thigh.

Freddie rose and smiled lazily. "You don't have to tell me who *this* is," he said.

Bernice leaned over the table and kissed my brother's cheek. "Not Freddie?" she asked, taking his right hand in a slow handshake.

"Fred," he corrected.

"April never told me you were a hunk." She slapped her cheek with her free hand. "Why do I say these things? I'm incorrigible."

"Yes, you are," I agreed.

"Hello, darling! And Dwight. Good to see you." She nudged Freddie over in the booth and sat down.

"Beer?" she said, raising her eyebrows at me. "How reckless on a school night." She shifted toward Freddie, all ears. "I've wanted to meet you for the longest time. Now I see why your sister was holding out on me."

Freddie smiled agreeably.

"Tell me everything about you I need to know. Are you just like April, or are you fun?"

"I do programming," said Freddie.

"Let me guess—another brain: M.I.T."

"U.R.I."

Bernice splayed her fingers against her chest. "Thank God! I couldn't stand another one."

Freddie smiled, uninjured. "They're your genes. If she's a brain, you should thank yourself."

Bernice opened her mouth and clamped it shut as if Freddie's genetic insight had rendered her speechless.

"All you have to do is watch 'Bernice G!' once to pick up on the cerebral resemblance," said Dwight.

Bernice preened. I watched Freddie watch Bernice. He might have had a balloon floating next to his head reading: Attractive, yes. Should I go for it? Yes. Will she? Yes . . .

"What brought you up here in the middle of the week?" she asked Freddie.

"April and I had dinner together."

"At the Athenian Gardens," I added.

Bernice raised her arms above her head and snapped her fingers—Greek dancing from the waist up. Dwight and I exchanged our Bernice-being-Bernice look. "I had the most marvelous show with Greek-Americans during the primaries," she said. "Greek pride and all that. Half of them were restaurateurs who gave a fortune to Dukakis."

I said, "There's a thousand dollar limit on individual contributions."

Bernice gave Freddie an indulgent, bonding smile, one that said, Is this the kind of technical, unemotional conversations you've endured with her your whole life?

Freddie said, "I think I saw that show. It was really interesting."

"You didn't really," said Bernice.

"I must've been home sick. It rings a bell."

"Was it all men on the show?" I asked.

Bernice looked at me squarely. "April thinks I'm boy crazy. But what she fails to understand is that I'm unattached, that I feel as *young*"—she leaned into the word to press every drop of sexual essence out of it—"as I ever did . . . and none of that is a crime. Yes! I like men. *Mea culpa!*" She smiled, happy to employ Latin in an argument against me.

Dwight said, "We wouldn't want it any other way, Bernice. It enriches our lives immeasurably."

Bernice smiled uncertainly. Was Dwight making fun of her or defending her?

"You're a hot ticket," Freddie said.

"The hottest," I said.

"You must meet a lot of men who want to go out with a TV star," said Freddie.

Bernice raised her face to the ceiling, exhaled a mouthful of cigarette smoke, and said, "Ha!"

"*No?*"

"You'd think so, wouldn't you?"

"Yeah," said Freddie.

"People don't think I'm approachable. They're intimidated by me. Men don't ask for my phone number like they would an ordinary person. They think I'm not going to give them the time of day, that I'm only interested in power or fame or money—"

"It's lonely at the top," I said.

"There you go again," she said.

"You ask for it when you feed me such perfect straight lines."

"It's simple," she said, ignoring me. "I'm like everyone else. Looking for . . . love, if I dare use the word."

Freddie perked up. He had the answer to "looking for love" in his lap and he was happy to employ it. He said to me, the first time he had addressed me since Bernice's arrival, "It's really hard to find people out there. I don't think you and Dwight know what it's like in the real world. You found each other at school. You didn't have to scrape and claw your way through the bar scene. I know what Bernice is saying."

Bernice stared at Freddie for a few seconds. She turned to me and said, "Where have you been hiding this brother of yours?"

"I just met him for the first time myself," said Dwight.

Bernice smiled painfully. She could have cared less about Dwight's ideas. You couldn't flirt with Dwight successfully; you couldn't *perform* for Dwight and get any satisfaction. None of her tricks worked with him.

Freddie twisted around in the booth to see the bar. "Any food?" he said, searching for clues. Bernice studied him. She looked at his profile, measured his shoulders, hoping to be caught, I thought. On his way back around, he smiled at her.

This is remarkable, I thought. This ease. This purposefulness. He doesn't have to do anything besides look handsome and emit endorphins.

"You can't be hungry?" I said to him. Freddie hunched his shoulders and smiled winningly. Boys will be boys. Burgers and fries and shakes all day long.

"I could have a bite," Bernice offered.

"Good!" he said.

"There's no real food here. What about going to Chinatown? A movable feast!"

I said I was still full—I hadn't even needed the baklava I'd eaten two hours earlier. Dwight said it was getting late for him. An early day tomorrow.

Bernice consulted with Freddie through the unspoken language of the sexually engaged: Shall we abandon these two to their curfews?

"Freddie drove in with us," I said.

"That's not a problem," said Bernice.

"I could go for a pu-pu platter," said Freddie.

"Does your sister let you stay out past ten?" Bernice asked.

"Sure," said Freddie.

"Certainly with my mother," I said pointedly.

Bernice stood up, snatching the check before sliding out of the booth. She tried to look innocent—how nice that Fred's appetite gives us the opportunity to get to know each other over egg rolls.

Freddie followed, first shaking Dwight's hand and ignoring my look. "It's been great meeting you," he said.

"Thanks, Fred," said Dwight.

Bernice kissed her fingertips and fluttered them in my direction. "Ciao, baby," she called.

I let her see my thoughts: I know what you're up to. *Don't*.

Dwight and I stayed and ordered coffee. He said he had enjoyed every minute, every nuance of her performance; this was the way of the world and I shouldn't get my back up.

And wasn't there, really, if I was honest with myself, a fearful symmetry to the coupling of Freddie and Bernice?

* * *

179

Bernice had me paged at school the next morning. Anne-Marie had long been challenging the imperiousness of Bernice's calls and downgrading the "urgents" to pink message slips. The page meant Bernice had somehow prevailed.

I left my Latin I class with exercises to do at the end of the day's chapter; Anne-Marie handed me the receiver with a comic grimace.

"Yes?" I said.

"Nothing happened," said Bernice.

I asked what she meant.

"You know what I mean."

"My brother?"

"If looks could kill, you murdered me at the White Glove last night."

"It's hard for me to talk now," I said.

"That's not what I called about. I have something I want to run by you. But don't answer until you've given it adequate thought—"

"*Okay.*"

"A show . . . on the children of Holocaust victims."

"Starring Mr. Frederick Epner?" I asked.

"Not necessarily. I thought you'd be my centerpiece."

"I'm in the middle of class, Bernice."

"And I'm in the middle of a production meeting with my entire staff."

"I'm not going on television." Anne-Marie pricked up her ears. I shook my head at her signaling, Don't get excited; this is Bernice's idea, not mine.

"Fred wasn't opposed to the idea."

"I'm not surprised."

"Oh? Because you know him so well?"

I paused and measured how far I could open this particular Pandora's box in the main office. I said, "I just think he'd like to please you."

"What about the basic premise—the generation after and their scars?"

I paused, then said, "Did Freddie show you his scars?"

She ignored my baiting her. "We talked a great deal about your home life," she said.

"Any new insights?"

"Let's say, some history."

"Like what?"

"Like you weren't allowed to watch television during the week. That meant something to me."

"It meant they wanted us to do our homework."

"You really believe that?" she asked.

I rolled my eyes at Anne-Marie, who had given up all pretense of doing something else.

"Your brother and I hashed this over: your parents knew from the agency, the adoption agency, that I was a television personality. They were trying to avoid your turning on the set and coming face to face with your double."

I laughed.

"Of course you'd laugh. That's why I keep these things to myself. And that's why discussing these highly pertinent theories with a much less judgmental audience is a godsend."

"How could they have known?" I asked.

"The agency! You don't think they knew who I was?"

"But you weren't in television when they arranged the whole thing."

"Updates! They watch television. They knew my name. That much didn't change."

I knew it was foolish and time-consuming to argue with her. Okay. My parents forbade TV because of my famous mother, the talk-show hostess. And Freddie agrees. Good. I said, "I really can't stay on. I'll talk to you later."

"You don't have to humor me. There are people who consider my opinions worth listening to."

"Hundreds of thousands," I said.

"Millions," she snapped.

I said I had to get off.

Bernice released me with a clipped good-bye and hung up first. I blinked for effect at the mouthpiece and said before handing the phone back to Anne-Marie, "Wait, you didn't tell me how my brother was in bed last night."

"You're shitting me," hissed Anne-Marie. "Your *brother?*"

I snapped my fingers. "Like *that.*"

"Isn't he young?"

"Twenty-nine."

"How old is she?"

"Fifty-three."

"Good bod?"

"She thinks so."

Anne-Marie shook her head. "What a nerve, though, huh?"

"Him or her?"

"Both. Screwing his sister's mother. Seducing your daughter's baby brother. Some people don't give a shit."

"Sometimes I wonder how many men she's slept with and where she'd draw the line."

"Probably nowhere, if she likes what she sees."

I looked around. "She doesn't think much of Dwight as a sex object."

Anne-Marie asked what my brother looked like.

"Handsome. Reddish hair; big. Women like him."

Did I have a picture of him?

At home, I said.

"I wish she were on at night. I'd like a good long look at this dame."

I told her I taped the show every morning; it gave me something to talk about with Bernice when she wasn't quizzing me about my love life. I could lend her a few shows if she had a VCR.

"Don't let her give you any shit about Dwight. He's worth fifty of her one-night stands, no offense to your brother."

I was touched by her loyalty to Dwight and by the force of her conviction. "No offense taken," I said.

TWENTY-SIX

"**I**f it were anyone else, I'd be home in bed with him right now," Bernice told me at a fund-raiser for the Institute of Contemporary Art. She had asked me to go as her date; promised to introduce me by name only and not by filial association. Her sleeveless black wool dress fastened up the back with turquoise buttons the size of Ritz crackers. "I did it for you," she said. "I took a moral stand."

I doubt that, I thought. Something must have gone wrong in the seduction, and Bernice had decided to turn it into an ethics lesson. "What was the moral stand?" I asked.

"You. My daughter. I didn't want to antagonize you."

"Thanks," I said.

"I have a different social code that works for me, but I said, 'This is not a private act between consenting adults. This is a family affair.' So I asked him to leave."

"Did Freddie accept your decision?"

"Fred. He didn't have a vote."

"Did he want to sleep with you?"

Bernice looked at me. Had I seriously asked if a male—a robust young male with sexual proclivities—*wanted* to sleep with her?

I explained: I needed to examine the ground under her feet in this moral stand. When did she decide she couldn't? How heroic was her sending him away?

Bernice said, "Fair question."

"Because if you really did this for me, and not for some other reason that conveniently makes you look principled—"

"Like what?"

"Like Freddie didn't want to, or couldn't, or his underwear was dirty . . ."

"You have a hell of a nerve, you know," she said quietly. An anchorwoman from the station was approaching us. "Tracy Corcoran," Bernice warned me without disturbing her smile. She and Bernice kissed and wiped lipstick off each other's cheeks with practiced thumbs.

"I love your dress," said the young woman.

"It's a waste on-air. The buttons never show."

"Black is one of the colors they let me wear on the new set," said Tracy.

"They tell you what colors to wear?" I asked.

"The new set's gray. I can wear red, maroon, pink, black, charcoal, and a certain shade of orange."

"That's unbelievable," I said.

"What's unbelievable is that I don't get a clothing allowance."

"This is April Epner," said Bernice. "She's not in the business."

"What do you do?" asked Tracy.

"I'm a high school Latin teacher," I said.

"You're kidding!" said Tracy.

"Say something for her," Bernice ordered.

"*Tempus fugit,*" I said.

"Do you teach at Boston Latin?"

"Quincy High School."

"I went to Girls' Latin!" Bernice cried. "It was filled with girls like April."

"Dull and drab?" I asked.

"No! Serious. Conscientious. Bright."

I rolled my eyes: half "thanks, Mom," and half "you're full of shit."

"Are you two related?" Tracy asked, looking back and forth between us.

Bernice cupped both hands over her mouth and nose. "Oh, my God," I heard from behind her fingers.

"Did I say something wrong?" Tracy asked.

I waited for Bernice's explanation.

"Do I have your permission?"

"Go ahead," I said.

Bernice rearranged her features and said with a regal serenity, "April is my daughter."

Tracy clearly did not see what the fuss was about. "Oh," she said. "I didn't know you had a daughter. It's nice to meet you."

"Thank you," I said.

"Do you have more kids?"

Bernice said no, just this one daughter.

"Look," said Tracy. "There's Alan Dershowitz."

Bernice didn't bother to look. *She* was more interesting than Alan Dershowitz any day. Her mother-daughter story was a showstopper. What had gone wrong? She looked perplexed.

"Go say hello," I said to Tracy. "I'm sure he'll know who you are."

"Do you think that's his wife?"

"*Go.*"

Tracy waved and walked away.

I asked Bernice if anything was wrong.

She shook her head and smiled a martyred smile.

"You're not used to people taking the news so casually?"

"What are you talking about?"

"You said, 'April's my daughter!' and Tracy yawned and said, 'Oh, look, there's Alan Dershowitz.' "

"She's a fluff-head. I don't set much store by what Tracy Corcoran says or doesn't say."

"Good." A waitress walked by with a tray of canapés. I took a tiny red potato stuffed with caviar. I could tell the waitress recognized Bernice by the way she lingered a few seconds after the transaction was completed.

"Where's the goddamn champagne?" Bernice asked me.

I pointed. Cash bar.

"C'mon," she said unhappily. There were dozens of people in line for a drink. Bernice stared straight ahead, in no mood to work the crowd. I stood next to her, our shoulders touching at identical heights.

"I started to tell you that I really appreciate your decision about Freddie."

She turned her face and blinked. "So you've decided to believe me?"

"I believed you," I lied.

"You don't trust me."

"That's changing," I said.

"You're still holding back," she said.

"That's just me," I said.

"That's your *parents* and the job they did with you."

"They're Freddie's parents, too. And obviously you don't find him so inscrutable."

Bernice yelped, "Inscrutable! I love it! Did you hear what you said?" The people around us watched and listened. Bernice laughed and leaned on me as if I had said something unbearably amusing. "He was inscrutable all right!" She looked around, pretending to see her audience for the first time. She clapped her mouth shut, hooked her arm around mine, and played the naughty celebrity buttoning her own lip.

I said nothing as we inched toward the glasses of champagne, Bernice basking in her own incorrigibility. Later, in front of a grouping of western Massachusetts realists, I said, "It embarrasses me when you make a scene."

She didn't answer but studied the paintings with uncharacteristic attention. She moved along the wall until there were no more and said suddenly, "How's Dwight?"

"Fine."

"Things are still going well?"

"Yes."

"You never made the big announcement, but I assume you've been sleeping with each other for some time and that's going well?"

"If I say yes, do I have to expound on it?"

"Do you know why I'm asking?"

"You always ask."

"But do you see how this relates to me?"

"Not exactly."

"Your loving him. It's good for me."

"Oh?"

"It shows me what you're capable of. It gives me hope."

"Hope about what?"

She touched her temple with two fingers. "I'm an observer. I see what's happening to us and you do, too."

"What?" I asked.

"Love," she said. "It's softening you. Love—and its physical components of course—expand one's capacity for loving in general. I'm reaping the benefits. Dwight is good for you, for all of us! I see that now, and I'm not jealous."

"He's very fond of you."

She smiled maternally, then moved the knot of my shawl to a more fashionable perch on my shoulders.

And he shouldn't be jealous of me, either, she said. Even though she borrowed me for these nights out. Even though she was my only living blood relative. Even though we were best friends.

TWENTY-SEVEN

Dwight and I were asleep at my place when the phone rang and startled us awake. We flailed in the dark, both reaching in odd directions for the sound. I answered.

"April?" said a woman's voice.

"Yes?" Night panic made my heart pound. It was 2:12 on my digital clock radio.

"I know what you're up to," said the voice.

I slammed down the phone. Dwight moved his legs over mine. The phone rang again. Sitting up now, blinking myopically, Dwight said, "Don't answer it." After a few rings I did. What if I had misunderstood the first time? What if this was the hospital calling about his parents?

"Who is it?" I said as I answered.

"Bernice Graves's real daughter," came the response, "so fuck off."

"Excuse me?" I said. I shrugged at Dwight who was saying, "Hang up the phone. Hang *up* the phone."

"Gabrielle Kerouac," said the caller, "Bernice Graves's daughter."

"Is it obscene?" Dwight asked. "Is it?"

"What do you want?"

"Leave her alone. Just get the fuck away from her," said the voice.

Who, though? Who was doing this; who wanted to fight me for Bernice?

"Don't you dare call here again," I said and hung up.

Dwight said I damn well could call Bernice at 2:15 A.M. over something this important. Maybe this was a dangerous person.

"What if it's true?" I asked. "What if it's all been a mistake?" Was it possible—had Bernice enlisted the real daughter to call me and say there had been an embarrassing error; sorry for the trouble . . . she'd send two complimentary tickets to her show?

"What's her number?" He pushed the buttons and handed me the telephone. She answered after three rings in her hoarse smoker's rasp.

"Bernice. It's me."

"You're up late," she said.

"I just got a threatening phone call." There was a rustle as if she were switching ears and settling in. "From a Gabrielle—I think she said Kerouac."

"Oh, fuck," Bernice muttered.

"She said she was your real daughter."

"Let me get a cigarette," said Bernice.

She was gone for longer than it would have taken to light one from her night-table pack. I yelled her name into the receiver.

"All *right,*" she called back. She returned. I heard the

191

click of her lighter and the sound of her inhaling and exhaling theatrically.

"Tell me what's going on," I said.

"I'm not happy about this," she said.

"Just tell me."

More rustling and inhaling. "She's a liar," said Bernice finally.

"Who is she?"

"A nut case."

"How does she know about me and you?"

Another silence.

What an outrage: Bernice Graves of "Bernice G!"—the woman who made her living stepping on the heels of other people's sentences—at a loss for words.

"Bernice?"

"She found me after that show last summer where I blurted out that I'd had an illegitimate daughter. She came to the station and wouldn't leave until I had seen her. She thought she was the one."

"She said her name was Gabrielle."

"Her name is *not* Gabrielle. It's Sandra Schneider. She calls herself Gabrielle now because she's convinced that she's the one."

"Could she be?"

"No! She is not my daughter. It's not even close. Her birth date is wrong. Nothing about her is right. I talked to her for a while and then Security had to escort her off the grounds. Of course she's not taking no for an answer."

"Why didn't you tell me this before?"

"To what end? Naturally there would have been some feedback. I was bound to hear from some pretenders; a million-five people watch the show. Believe me. You are my daughter. This Saguna is not."

"Saguna?"

192

"That's the name she gave herself. It means something in some spiritual language. She hates Sandra."

"Where did she get Kerouac?"

Bernice didn't answer.

I asked again.

"She's crazy! I don't know where she gets things."

"She got the Gabrielle part right," I said.

"I told you I talked to her. My baby's name slipped out. I always referred to you as Gabrielle. She jumped on it like it was her long-lost identity."

I looked at Dwight, who was following every syllable. I said evenly, "Did you tell this person that your baby's father was Jack Kerouac?"

"Probably! I was trying to get rid of her. I was saying the first thing that came into my head."

I twirled my finger next to my temple as a bulletin for Dwight: cuckoo. "Why do you have to lie about that all the time?" I asked her.

"I wouldn't dream of doing it again, I assure you," she said icily.

"It makes me wonder what else you're lying about—Jack Kennedy, Jack Kerouac, Jack Flynn . . ."

"I was amusing myself! I didn't walk around announcing publicly that I had had an affair with a famous man, now dead. I don't know what made me tell you that story, except self-preservation. It wasn't a case of lying all over again after facing the truth with you. She came along first."

I said I didn't understand. Self-preservation?

"You know," she said. "What I needed to say at that very moment. I trust my instincts. Some call it lying. I see it as a superior intelligence programming your mouth. Things come out which might not make sense at face value, but which your brain directs you to say. 'Jack Kerouac' was one of those things. I didn't fight it."

"That's juvenile," I said. "A lie is a lie."

"This Kerouac thing—that was me being outrageous. I didn't have to give this perfect stranger the time of day. 'Kerouac' came out. I had just seen some clips about some commemorative park they were dedicating in Lowell. It just came out. So naturally, when I talked to you, the same name was on the tip of my tongue."

Dwight was gesturing: wrap it up; this isn't getting anywhere. I nodded and said to Bernice, "I'm too tired to make sense of this tonight."

"Let's just forget she ever called," Bernice said.

"She has my number. She's bound to call again."

"And you'll be prepared! Tell her I've hired a lawyer and we're going after her for harassment. Take your phone off the hook tonight." She sounded confident again, hung up before I said anything more.

Dwight fell back to sleep. I couldn't clear my mind of this three-named pretender. I sneaked out of bed so Dwight could uncurl in his sleep to the diagonal length of the mattress, sat at the kitchen table with a cup of reheated coffee. Bernice was lying to me; she knew more about this Sandra than she could have gleaned from a quick lobby interview. Maybe Sandra was the real child, but she wasn't right for Bernice's purposes. Maybe I was somebody else's baby. Maybe she liked me best after shopping around among newspaper clippings and contestants in her television sweepstakes: adopted baby girls, born April 1952. You could be my daughter! Send pix and vitae!

Win a birth mother for life.

TWENTY-EIGHT

Dear Sonia,

I would very much appreciate your confidence in the matter I'm about to raise. I really need to talk to someone who knows Bernice well and has known her for some time. If you think you could meet with me and at the same time not violate your loyalty to her, please call me. I don't mean to sound mysterious at all. I just need to ask some questions about her life.

Yours sincerely,
April Epner

Sonia called me the afternoon she received the note. "Darling," she said, "don't forget I brought you two together. The least I can do is give you a shoulder to cry on."

"I need to ask you some questions. That's all, really."

"Anything," said Sonia.

I said there was something I had to ask her first: Would she feel it was her duty to report back to Bernice?

"Absolutely not. I consider your confidence sancrosanct. You're the daughter of my oldest and dearest friend."

"Thanks," I said.

"She can interrogate you until you drop, you know."

I said yes, I knew.

"Not a word," Sonia promised.

We met the following Sunday morning over bagels and coffee in Brookline. I was distracted by Sonia's deep magenta lipstick, how it bled onto her cream cheese wherever her lips touched the bagel.

"How long have you known her?" I asked first.

"Since the late sixties; we both worked for Kevin White in his first mayoral race, and then we both got PR jobs in his administration."

I did the arithmetic: Sonia had known Bernice when she was in her early thirties. Younger than I was now. Not a celebrity.

"Was she ever just a regular person?" I asked.

"No," said Sonia, a long "nooo," her lips remaining in a pout for emphasis.

"Ever?"

"I'm not saying it's bad. But she's always been full of herself."

"Why would you be friends with someone like that?" I asked.

Sonia plunked her right elbow on the table and studied the bagel half in her hand at eye level. "Because," she said with finality.

It was a quiz: you define it for me, April. You tell me

what it is about Bernice that makes a person be her friend. We both have felt it. You say it. I've proved myself with twenty years of friendship; you tell me the secret ingredient.

"You feel disloyal to her, don't you?" I asked. "Dissecting her personality?"

"No. I'm not that nice," said Sonia.

"Do you feel sorry for Bernice in a way?"

Sonia barely nodded.

"Like she needs friends, even though she'd be the last person on earth to admit it?"

"Is that what you feel?" Sonia asked.

"There's something about her that does get to you."

"Despite all the crap you have to put up with."

"Despite her wanting you to think you're incredibly lucky to be close to a famous celebrity such as herself?"

We nodded cynically, smiled indulgently. We both drank from our coffee cups. I motioned the waitress for refills. When she had left, after depositing a handful of plastic creamers from her apron pocket, I said, "She lies, you know."

"I know," said Sonia.

"She seems constitutionally incapable of giving straight answers."

"She's a poser," said Sonia, as if that should satisfy us both.

"Did you know she's never given me a straight answer about the man who impregnated her?"

I was watching Sonia closely. I had always thought she had a bit of the Bernice in her, in a paler shade, but this conversation was surprising me. Her reactions seemed almost normal.

"I can't help you there," she said. "Not really."

"Do you know anything at all?"

"Don't forget this part is relatively new—long-lost daughter, unwed mother. That only came out since that show."

"The show," I repeated. "The today-is-the-first-day-of-the-rest-of-your-life episode?"

Sonia put her cup down and leaned closer. "Sometimes I think she was carried away by the moment."

"That's for sure. The cathartic moment."

"That's not what I meant."

I shook my head: What? Tell me.

"That she made it up, right there, with everyone watching."

I processed this slowly, rejecting each of the implications in linear order: made . . . it . . . up. No baby? No illegitimate baby? No baby at all? No Bernice and April? Good television? Finally I said, "I don't think so. Her mother met me. She wouldn't have gone along with a huge lie like that. Besides, look at me. Everyone says I'm hers. *You* said I'm hers."

Sonia put her hand over mine—today's ring was a golf ball of an opal—and squeezed it. I hadn't realized it was in need of steadying. "No, not about her having had you at all," she said.

"What?"

"Maybe I shouldn't, April. It's only a hypothesis."

I released a muted squeal of impatience.

She said quickly, soothingly, "Okay, okay."

"Please—"

"Okay: I think Bernie was married once, when she was really young," said Sonia.

"You *think* or you know?"

"She told me once."

"She was probably lying."

"I don't think so. This was when she didn't lie so much."

"So you think she was married when she got pregnant and he abandoned her?"

Sonia shook her head.

"No?"

"No. She said other things, bits and pieces, that added up to something else."

I stared. Yes. Go on.

"She had a baby. She couldn't take the pressure. She left the baby with him and went off somewhere."

"You know this?"

"She once said so, a long, long time ago. I don't think she even remembers telling me the truth. It all got rewritten with her new identity as a celebrity unwed mother. I think it's hard to keep straight what you've told people when you lie a lot."

I repeated, "She left me with him? And what happened to me?"

"I think he must have turned you over to the authorities. He was just a kid."

"The authorities?"

"He probably couldn't take care of you himself," Sonia said soothingly. "He probably thought he was doing the best thing for you."

"Don't give me that shit. Where did she go? Wouldn't he need her permission before he gave her baby away?"

Sonia winced, hesitated.

"What?" I said.

"He did have her permission," she said softly.

I excused myself, found the ladies' room downstairs, and threw up. I returned to Sonia, thinking I felt calmer. The table had been cleared and Sonia's lipstick was fresh. "How old was I?" I asked.

"Six months? Seven?"

"Not a newborn," I said.

Sonia nodded.

"You must know this for sure. You wouldn't speculate on something this . . ."

"Devastating?"

I nodded.

"She had you for a while; then she gave you up. I know that much. She doesn't think it looks very good. 'Unwed mother' is more . . . sympathetic."

"Six months," I repeated. "Neither one wanted me after that?"

"They were teenagers! They didn't know what else to do."

"Was it Jack Flynn?"

"I think so. I remember her saying 'Jack.' "

I covered my face with my hands and pressed my fingers against my eye sockets to block her out and to think more clearly.

"I shouldn't have told you," Sonia was saying, "but I have divided loyalties. On one hand I say, 'She's my oldest friend.' On the other, 'What kind of person gives her flesh and blood away?' What are my obligations to tell the truth if I know it? And don't I have obligations to you now, too?"

I said through my hands, "She'll kill you."

"What kind of person gives her baby away? I've been asking myself the question for twenty-some-odd years. Wondering. Assuming she had suffered for it, never really allowing myself to blame her . . . but feeling real anger"—Sonia hit her chest with a clenched fist—"especially when the baby appeared and the history got rewritten. . . ."

I shook my head. Took my hands away.

"I'm willing to accept the consequences," said Sonia.

It's all right, I said. I'm fine. It's important to know these things. But I'm all right; I never suffered from being given away, did I? It was better. I'm better. I'll be all right.

The waitress collected her tip, looking annoyed, wondering, I thought, why customers couldn't just leave when they were done.

TWENTY-NINE

 I called in sick Monday morning and came close to telling Anne-Marie the truth: I found things out yesterday. About Bernice. About my adoption.

"What things?"

"Sickening things."

"I'll tell them it's stomach virus," said Anne-Marie. "That'll give you another day. Don't wear any blusher on Wednesday. Have tea and toast for lunch your first day back."

"Thanks," I said.

"It's not about Dwight, is it?"

"No."

"Have you told him what's wrong?"

"No. I don't know if I can talk about it."

"April," she said sharply, "if you blow this with Dwight I'll kill you. Don't fuck this up with your brave-soldier routine."

"Don't start with me," I said, my voice catching and me letting it. "I haven't slept."

"He loves you," she said.

I asked if anyone was in the office.

"No one is in the office. When was the last time you talked to him?"

"Saturday."

"Jesus Christ. So I'm your big confidante? How do you think he'll feel when he finds out you're a mess over something and you didn't go to him with it?"

"I know."

"How?"

"Lousy."

"Right. So don't be a jerk."

"I'm afraid to keep the phone plugged in. Bernice might call."

"So? Give him a time to call and plug it in."

"Could you do that for me?" I asked.

"When?"

"Beginning of fourth period?"

"You got it. Eleven twenty-five. If you don't answer, I send him over."

"Thanks," I said. "Really."

"You bet," said Anne-Marie.

Dwight whistled softly into the receiver and said, "No wonder she's nuts."

I said, "What kind of people give their baby away?"

"Desperate people. Teenagers who weren't supposed to have babies in the first place."

"How many teenagers give their babies away when they've had them for six months?"

Dwight said quietly, "I don't know."

"They couldn't have loved me. You don't give a baby that you love away."

"You don't know that, April."

"Must be a pretty unlovable baby," I said. "Pretty fucking ugly and unlovable."

"I'm coming over," said Dwight.

He held me and let me cry into his neck for what felt like hours. He produced a bubble bath somehow when I didn't even own the stuff. He found a tray and a bud vase and the makings of cinnamon toast. I told him I loved him, and not because I was vulnerable and hysterical and orphaned or because he was acting like a paid companion from the Visiting Nurses Association, but because he left school for me and never mentioned the leaving or the getting back.

"You'd do it for me," he said.

"I hope so."

"You already have." He put his arms around me and rested his cheek on the top of my head.

I have? I asked. I've done something like this for you?

I could feel his shrug. A self-conscious shrug. He'd said more than he'd meant to say.

"Something specific?" I asked.

He kissed the top of my head and put his cheek back down.

"You don't want to say?"

"It's no one big thing."

I knew what he meant: just that we had this now, that he loved me.

There was Bernice to consider. And Saguna. And Jack Flynn, said Dwight, picking up his old refrain. It wasn't really so bad. He said I should give her a chance to tell the truth. Say, "Bernice. I want you to tell me the facts, unembellished. No lies. I found everything out, but I want to hear it from your lips."

" 'I want to hear it from your lips,' " I repeated, savoring the phrase.

"Try to keep her on course. Guide her toward the truth so she won't get herself in deeper."

"Why should I? Let her hang herself. Let her get hoisted with her own petard."

"What's the point of that?" Dwight asked.

What's the *point?* I asked. The point is to let her know that crime doesn't pay.

"No, it's not," said Dwight. "The point is to understand what she did and why. And to salvage this relationship, whatever it is."

"Yuck," I said.

"You want to pay her back, right? Fuck you, Bernice. Fuck you to hell."

"I hate her," I said.

"Now, there's a lie," said Dwight. He took my hand and kissed it front and back.

"You *are* on her side."

"She thinks I'm fascinating."

I laughed the way you do when the doctor setting your broken bones makes a joke—a sob of a pitiful laugh.

"You know you have to talk to her," said Dwight.

We went to Provincetown for the night, first calling Anne-Marie at home and saying, "Think up something that sounds plausible. We'll be in on Wednesday."

"Whose idea was this?" she asked.

"Dwight's."

"Bless his heart," said Anne-Marie.

I tried to say, "He's been so wonderful," but the very formation of the words in my head choked me up so I couldn't talk. Dwight took the phone and promised we'd bring Anne-Marie a tacky souvenir from a stand on Route 6.

"Aren't we spontaneous?" he asked repeatedly as we drove south and then east. "Aren't we the craziest kids?"

"I'm feeling better," I'd answer.

In two hours we were in Provincetown. I had never seen it in winter, never imagined it could look like a New England village instead of carnival grounds when the streets were cleared of tourists. Over dinner at a Portuguese bar I told Dwight that this was the high point of my romantic life so far.

"Eating kale soup is the high point of your romantic life?" He took a spoonful from my bowl and shrugged as if agreeing up to a point.

"Coming here, playing hooky. It's a grand gesture. No one's ever made a gesture on this scale for me."

Dwight frowned at his fried squid appetizer, then at the unlit candle halfway between us. It was set in an ugly red glass ball with plastic netting. He motioned for the waitress to bring a match. She swapped ours for a green ball flickering at a vacant table.

"You were saying something about a grand gesture?" said Dwight after positioning the candle just so.

"This. Running away."

He put his fork and knife down, wrapped his hand around his glass of beer. "I think I can top that. If you don't mind a prepared speech . . ."

What kind of speech? I asked.

He began: Six months is not a long time in the great scheme of things—

"I don't want to talk about that. I'm trying to forget that number. Six months with a little baby—"

"Not that," he said. "I'm sorry. I meant us. Our six months. I meant it's a short time to feel the way I feel." He took a sip of beer. "I had accepted things about my life and didn't think it would happen, didn't think anyone would bring out the things in me that someone might actually find . . . compelling. And then this unbelievable thing happened. This dream, actually."

He found my hand. "I didn't drive you down here to set the scene or create a mood; if anything, I just wanted to get you away from her and from school. But now that we're here, it seems incredibly important that I propose to you."

I tried to answer before I lost my voice. The best I could give him—in return for a speech I was engraving on the soft tissue of my brain for future worship—was limp, ordinary words. I accept. I love you so much. These six months have been . . . I'll be your wife. You knew I would.

On the way home Tuesday we found the same candle, worse in aqua and with "Cape Cod" written on it in glitter, at a drugstore on Commercial Street. We bought it for Anne-Marie and told her she deserved to be the first to know.

THIRTY

"**I** don't want to eat," I said to Bernice. "I'm here to talk."

I had just arrived at her condominium and handed over my winter coat. She held my brown knitted scarf at arm's length and appraised it. "A paisley scarf in a wool challis would be stunning with camel," she said.

"Fine. You can get me that for Valentine's Day."

Bernice's eyes opened wide, her best impression of a child's holiday enchantment. "When *is* Valentine's Day?" she breathed.

"Next week."

She put one arm around me; coat, scarf, hanger, and all. "Our first Valentine's Day together," she said. We walked to the closet this way, and I thought that for once she was telling the truth: born in April and given away in October.

The doorbell rang before Bernice had filled both wineglasses in her black kitchen, before I'd come close to beginning my prepared speech.

"Are you expecting someone?" I asked.

Bernice went right to the door—eagerly, I thought, as if every ring of the doorbell meant the promise of attention and companionship. "Who is it?" she sang.

"April," said the voice.

Bernice scowled and called, "Go away."

"It's April," the voice repeated.

"You're lying."

"How can you be April if I'm standing right here?" I said.

Bernice glared and shushed me.

The voice said calmly, "Bernice, I'd like to come in. It's Gabrielle."

"I'll call the police," said Bernice.

"I have to talk to you."

Here it was, my chance to see the woman who thought she was Bernice's daughter. I nudged Bernice: Why not? It'll be okay.

Bernice touched her head: you've forgotten—she's crazy.

"Who's there?" I asked.

"Sandra Schneider," the voice said politely, as if it were the first announcement.

Bernice was shaking her head no. Absolutely not. No way.

I looked through the peephole. Despite the fish-eye distortion, the woman looked normal—long dark hair, a perplexed expression, an elongated otter face.

"I won't do anything," Sandra said.

"I'd like to get a look at her," I whispered to Bernice.

Bernice unlatched the door petulantly. She walked back to the kitchen and left me to face the intruder.

Sandra Schneider strode across the threshold into Bernice's foyer and whirled to greet me with a karate chop of a handshake. "Thanks," she said. Everything about her was intense. She moved, talked, blinked her eyes, aggressively, purposefully. And she was handsome in a dark, jittery way, like a character actress playing an insane woman.

I looked toward the kitchen. No sign of Bernice. "I'm April Epner," I said.

"No kidding," said Sandra.

"Should I call you Sandra?" I asked.

"I don't care."

Bernice walked elegantly out of the kitchen. "Don't you work nights?" she asked.

Sandra said yes.

"Did you trade with someone to get tonight off?"

"No, I didn't *trade* with anyone to get tonight off."

"What do you do?" I asked.

"I drive a taxi."

"Do you like it?"

"It sucks."

"So don't do it anymore," said Bernice.

"And what should I be doing? Making minimum wage selling Harvard nightshirts at the Coop?"

"Don't yell at her," I said.

Bernice said, "It's okay," meaning: Let her. It proves my point.

Sandra stared at me, our first staring contest. Finally she said, "I know where you're coming from, so don't criticize my manners."

Bernice said, "Excuse me, but I have something on the stove."

"I'll help," I said.

Sandra smirked as if to say, You're just the type.

As soon as we stepped onto the black marble tile, Bernice said, "Don't follow me! You're the one who wanted to ask her in. Go out there before she slashes my upholstery."

"How did she happen to show up tonight? Pretty good timing, I'd say."

Bernice signaled me to be careful. "She asked if she could see me tonight, and I said I had plans. She asked with whom and I said, 'I'm having company.' That was it. She didn't pursue it beyond that."

"How did she know where you lived?"

"How do I know? She's lunatic enough to have trailed me here in that cab she drives."

"Is this the first time she's been here?"

"Of course she's been here! But this is the first time I've been foolish enough to let her in." She had a basket of corn chips in one hand and a bowl of melted cheesy-looking dip in the other. She nodded with her chin for me to leave, to break up the conference and get back to Sandra.

Bernice entered the living room seconds after I did, smiling the refreshed smile that followed commercial breaks on "Bernice G!" "This is hot," she said, holding up the red ceramic bowl.

"Did you two have a nice time whispering about me in the kitchen?" asked Sandra.

Bernice made a classic Bernice face: thoroughly insulted, wrongly accused.

"We were a little surprised to see you," I said.

Sandra glared at me, her lips forming and re-forming silent syllables. Finally she said, "I would think you'd be sympathetic."

"Why?"

"I find it very strange that you wouldn't identify with my problem."

"Which problem is that?" I asked.

Sandra said, "Finding my real mother."

"I'm not your real mother," said Bernice.

"Why do you keep insisting that she is?" I asked.

"I just know it."

"But why?"

"It's the truth! I'm thirty-six years old. I was born in Boston. I look just like her. The part about my father fits so perfectly."

"Why?" I asked.

"Do you know who Jack Kerouac was?"

"Yes—"

"It's perfect, isn't it? I write. I even write like him."

"She doesn't even have the right birthday," said Bernice.

"Now *that* is total bullshit! I happen to know that the social workers assign a birth date so the new family can have a pretty little fantasy of when the birth took place, and so it will be harder for the birth mother to trace the kid."

Bernice looked at me. Her expression was wonderfully ironic and her eyes showed something close to amusement: See. Didn't I tell you?

"Your claims are ridiculous," I said to Sandra. "You can't *will* someone to be your birth mother because you want it that way."

"That's right!" said Bernice.

"Don't you see what she's doing?" Sandra asked me, her voice lowered. "She's picking you over me because you fit the profile. It has nothing to do with biology. It's a popularity contest, and I lost. Period."

"You're *not* my daughter!" Bernice yelled.

"Prove it!" Sandra yelled back.

"And what if I did? Are you going to tell me you'd be satisfied and would leave me alone? And not harass April?"

"It depends what you have."

"What could I possibly tell you that would make you leave here in a civilized manner and drop this . . . campaign of yours?"

Sandra answered in flinches and grimaces. Her stare was off somewhere, darting to either side of our faces as if a sadistic Tinker Bell were demanding eye contact. "Do you think you're dealing with one of the idiots who watches your show?" she asked finally.

Bernice turned to me with manufactured amazement: Did you hear that? How dare she?

"You really have problems, you know that?" I said to Sandra.

Sandra closed her eyes and shook her head violently.

"I think we need a lawyer present," said Bernice. "I think you should leave now."

"I'm not leaving," said Sandra. She sat down on the fawn-colored sofa and folded her arms across her chest. "Give me the proof and I'll leave on my own two feet."

"I have proof," I said.

Bernice looked at me quizzically. What proof? All she had was her *Boston Globe* clipping and her mother's intuition. She stood up and said, "Sandra, will you excuse April and me for a minute?" She headed down the hall toward the bedroom, confident I'd follow. She closed the bedroom door, sat on her queen-size bed, all mauve satin and slippery, and smiled as if she'd caught me in the act of doing something of which she'd long suspected me.

"What are you smiling at?" I asked.

She took one of her bedside cigarettes and lit it, still smiling. She crossed her legs and let one of her snakeskin shoes swing from her bobbing toes.

"I don't like her out there by herself," I said.

"I can see that."

"What did you want?"

Bernice smiled and smoked and bobbed her shoe around. Finally she said, "You're jealous of her, aren't you? Or can't you see what's happening?"

"I'm trying to get rid of her," I said.

"You have no written proof to show her. You want her out of my life for good and you're willing to lie to attain that. You're seeing me through someone else's eyes, aren't you? Someone who desperately wants me for a mother." She smiled prettily: Deny that one, April.

"I want to get rid of her," I repeated.

"But this woman's getting to you, isn't she? I mean, she's hitting a nerve. I've never seen you possessive. I love it!"

"I'm not possessive."

"What do you call it? I've never seen you this hostile, even on one of your bad days. And frankly I'm surprised. I thought you'd be a more gracious winner."

I held up an index finger. Wait one minute. There's more to discuss, but I can't concentrate with her out there.

"Tell her I'll do what I can," said Bernice.

I stopped and asked what that meant.

"I can say a word or two on air, help her find her birth mother. I'll couch it anecdotally—'I have this young friend, et cetera . . .' maybe as a follow-up to my own appeal. Bring you on, too, to talk about our relationship. Tell her that, will you?"

I just stood there frowning. Could we be that far apart in our perceptions of Sandra Schneider's needs? "You can't bring her on the show. You have to end this whole mess, not prolong it."

Bernice said, "But what's it to me—a few words on air? Can't you give her that much, the opportunity to find the woman who could give her the same . . . *sustenance* I give you? An identity?"

I went back to the living room. Sandra was eating corn chips, stabbing them into the dip.

"Bernice isn't feeling well," I said.

"I think she got pregnant as a result of a rape," Sandra announced with a full mouth.

"What are you talking about?"

"My money's on rape."

"I don't think so."

"You wouldn't."

"I'm too stupid, you mean? Not street smart like you?"

"I mean it doesn't fit your fairy tale. On the other hand, it fits for me," said Sandra. "It explains a lot. Maybe everything. My despair, certainly. My being so fucked up about men. I'm the product of a violation." Sandra looked pleased.

"Bernice wouldn't hide that! Just the opposite—she'd do a show on it."

"She did deny it! But I didn't believe one word. She's so full of crap that she's started believing her own pathetic stories."

"She's told me the truth," I said after a long pause. "And I'm sorry, but you're not Gabrielle. I am."

Sandra assessed my statement, squinting and grimacing as if her internal debate teams were presenting their arguments. Finally she said, "How do you know?"

I raised my shoulders apologetically. "Everything's been confirmed through the adoption agency. A blood test. Everything."

"That's a lie," said Sandra.

"I have the documents at home. If you leave us alone, I'll mail you Xerox copies." I retrieved her parka from the couch and gave it to her. "I'll have to call the police if you don't leave," I said quietly.

Sandra took her coat and her knapsack. I turned her toward the door; she took the small, resistant steps of a demonstrator trained in nonviolent protest. She planted herself at the threshold and said, "You don't have my address, though."

"I'll get it from Bernice's lawyer," I said, and shoved.

"Liar," I heard from the other side. "Fucking asshole."

"Is she gone, darling?" Bernice called from the bedroom.

I didn't return to her room. I put the corn chips back in their cellophane bag. I threw the melted Velveeta with chili peppers down the disposal and washed out the red bowl. Bernice appeared and said, "I was calling you."

I said I couldn't hear her with the water running. What had she wanted?

"You're acting strange," she said. Hiding in the kitchen instead of reporting what had happened. Usually I was loaded for bear.

"That's a quaint expression," I said.

"How'd you get rid of Saguna?" she asked, emphasizing each syllable with derision: Sa-goon-a.

"Bodily."

"No!" she said with delight. "C'mon!"

I sponged the lip of the black porcelain sink and fiddled with her gearshift of a faucet until the water stopped. It was time to sit and talk. If I were Trude, I thought, I'd take my apron off now and fold it conscientiously. "Sit down," I said.

Bernice did, intertwining her fingers to feign obedience. I pulled out a kitchen chair and sat down on its squeaky black patent-leather seat.

"This is a switch," said Bernice, "me playing guest and you designing the format."

I paused a moment. "This is serious," I began. "Please don't interrupt until I'm finished." She sat up straighter, crimping her lips.

"I did some research," I said slowly, "and I believe I know the circumstances surrounding my adoption."

Bernice nodded, still neutral: Go on. I'm listening. No nervous squint to her brown eyes.

"I know that you were married—probably to Jack

Flynn—and that you had a daughter whom you gave up for adoption when she was approximately six months old." I stopped there. Bernice's face didn't change.

"Were you married?" I asked gently.

She looked at me then, measuring my tone and expression. What did April want? Would a lie or the truth work best here?

"Please don't make up any stories," I said.

"Is this a test?" she asked.

"I already know the truth. I just want it confirmed."

"Who told you?"

"Sonia," I said.

"Sonia told you that I was married—"

"Just tell me."

She looked around. "I need a cigarette," she said.

"Afterward."

"Is that so? In my house you tell me when I can have a cigarette?" She stood up. I caught her by the wrist and said, "Please." She sat down again with much indignation and smoothing of her clothes.

"Tell me everything," I said.

"His name was Jackie Remuzzi. He looked like us, like you and me. We could have been brother and sister. His father was Italian and his mother Irish, and my parents wouldn't let him in the house. We sneaked around—the usual story. He was a good kid. A cute kid. Went to Brighton High School, didn't get into Latin."

I asked how they met.

"We were neighbors—how's that for exotic? I played with one of his sisters. He was a year older and had a letter sweater from Brighton. He drove us places, complaining all the way. And then he started to notice me when I was about fifteen. His sister was our cover: 'Bye, Ma. Goin' to Brigham's with Frannie!' 'Bye, Ma. Goin' to Cleveland

Circle with Frannie!' Frannie was a good kid, and she thought it was romantic to be our front. Jack would bring along a friend of his for her, and we'd get together like that about once a week.''

"So this was an actual romance," I said. "You dated for a long time.''

"Of course it was a romance! Nice girls didn't go all the way with their boyfriends for *sex*. It had to be for love, and it had to be forever.''

"Where'd you do it?" I asked.

Bernice frowned. "Didn't you sneak around in high school? Couldn't you at least imagine where two kids would do it, or where your students do it now? Are you that unromantic?''

"In his car?" I asked.

She smiled. "We finally did it in my house when my parents took a day trip to Lake Winnipesaukee and I convinced them I had cramps and would be better off at home.'' She smiled grimly. " 'Lake Winnipesaukee' had a special connotation after that. It became our code word for 'You can come over, the coast is clear.' "

"And you got pregnant.''

"Either graduation or prom night, if you can believe I'd do anything that unoriginal.''

"Did your parents make you get married?" I asked.

Bernice discharged a hoot of derisive laughter. "They didn't even know who it was at first. I told them I had been cajoled into sex by an executive at Jordan Marsh—''

I groaned. The first of the Jordan Marsh paternity lies.

"I was a scared kid. Jack wasn't exactly Mr. Maturity. I told my mother and she said, 'Take a hot bath. As hot as you can stand.' As batootzed as she was, it was good to enlist her because she loved a crisis. She wailed and carried on, but she also needed to have secrets from my father and this was a knockout. It was his punishment for sitting there at the dinner table and not talking to us except to bark out his orders. It was a great marriage: he'd scowl and go to bed early; she sat by the telephone and waited for the party line to hang up so she could gossip to her friends. And that's where she began. She called her friends and told them her daughter's cockamamie plan—to leave high school and go study in California! To get a college degree before she even got her diploma! She wouldn't allow it, she told them. She let them argue. Education was important; California was the place for ambitious young people. Jews ran the studios; Bernice was a stunning girl.

" 'But there are colleges in Boston,' Mama complained. 'People come from all over the world to go to school in Boston.' She pretended to let her friends and sisters talk her into it. I listened, and I took notes. She was a genius. 'I called you for sympathy and all I get is arguments,' she would say. She *wept*. 'Are you going to buy her a plane ticket when she's out there, homesick, and wants her mama?'

"She arranged everything. She found a home in Chestnut Hill that took Jewish girls. I had to go in September, even though I was only three months pregnant, because that's when students leave for school. My parents put me in a taxi with my collegiate-looking luggage; I carried a new tennis racket just for the send-off. 'What time is your flight?' the driver asked me as we pulled away. 'You're taking me to Chestnut Hill,' I said. A few minutes later I added that I was going to college in California, skipping my senior year in high school because of my excellent grades; that I hadn't even packed a winter coat.

"I got to Chestnut Hill and I changed my mind. I never even got out of the taxi. I said I was homesick. The cabby drove me back to Oak Square and I called Frannie from a phone booth. Jackie picked me up when he came home from work. He said he'd marry me."

Bernice asked if she had earned a cigarette yet. I said okay. She smoked jerkily, not with her usual elegance. "Pretty pathetic, isn't it?" she asked. "Me and the boy down the block. Both families blaming the other kid, *refusing* to talk to each other; my parents threatening to throw Jack in jail. For what? For embarrassing them?" She blew out a stream of smoke and said, "Ugly. Ugly and ordinary."

"Did you have a wedding?" I asked.

"We did everything on our own—the blood tests and marriage licenses. And we were married at Boston College by a Leo G. Carroll look-alike after I signed the papers saying I'd raise you in the Catholic church. Even Frannie had abandoned ship by then. Our witnesses were two friends of Jack's we had once gone parking with. I don't think we ever saw them again." She sat back in her chair. "And the rest you know."

"No I don't," I said.

She smiled, refusing to be cornered. "Maybe I should just stand here and deliver the eulogy at my own funeral. Nail my own coffin shut, as far as you and I are concerned."

I said there she went again, worrying about herself instead of me. Why couldn't she just come *out* with it instead of—

"*Maybe* if you didn't disapprove of every word I ever said to you," she snapped. "Or of everything I've ever done. Or if I thought you would understand."

I put my forearms and palms flat on the kitchen table— a teacher's garnering of strength, flesh fortified by desk blotter. "Did you love him?" I asked.

Bernice closed her eyes. A few moments later, she covered her face with her hands. I watched carefully, expecting her to peek through her fingers for my reaction. When she put her hands down, her eyes were teary and her makeup had smudged. This was new: not looking for the tally light and setting her lips aquiver, but fighting for control of features that were used to obeying. "I think I did," she said.

"You left him, though."

"Why do you want to hear this? Are you such a masochist?"

"Because when you left him, you left me, too."

She stared at me for a long time with a look that dropped the corners of her mouth beyond retrieval and made her look old.

"I need you to tell me," I said.

She stood up and walked down the hallway in her stocking feet, occasionally touching the wall with her fingertips as if for balance. A minute later, I followed. She was under her satin comforter, curled on her side, still fully dressed. I called her name from the doorway.

She moaned, "What?"

I said, almost in apology, "It happened before I was born. I don't remember any of it. I was too young to know what was happening."

"But now you know," she said into her pillow. "You know what I did and you know what I live with."

I moved closer. After a pause by the side of her bed, I sat down. "Was it just that you couldn't cope?" I asked.

Bernice seized the question, sat up, and put a pillow on her crossed legs. "I couldn't! I wasn't any good at it, and I had no help. I thought it was a mistake, that I should've stayed at the home and signed the papers . . ."

"And not married him?"

"He was a slob," said Bernice. "Do you know what I mean when I say 'slob'? In everything he did."

"He didn't love you?" I asked.

She opened her mouth as if to answer faithfully: Yes.

No. At first—in his own way. We were young. Instead, as if too weary, she said, "I didn't even care."

"But you left me with him."

Bernice covered her ears, then slid her hands upward to pull her hair in frustration. "Not *him*. He had family around—more than mine anyway. His mother raised a bunch of kids, and I thought you'd be with them."

"But you were wrong."

She flounced back down flat on the mattress. "Goyim," she said bitterly.

"What about your parents? They didn't want me either."

"That's right! And I never forgave them!" she said. "I didn't go to my father's funeral and I didn't sit *shiva* for him. Because of *you*. Was that covered in the history of Bernice Graverman that Sonia came up with? Or did you just get the parts that make me look bad?"

I said after a few moments, "I'm the one who looks bad. Not you."

Bernice perked up. "What do you mean, *you?*"

"Aren't you saying I was a pretty sorry baby, a lousy baby who set world records for being unwanted by the highest number of blood relatives?"

"No! It wasn't you at all—it was us. You were good! And a pretty baby. We were no good at it! We thought it was for the best. Like schmucks, we thought it was for the best." She touched my hair, smoothed it, and tucked it behind my ears. "We were all wrong," she said. "And then it was too late."

I let her do it. I let her stroke my hair and murmur endearments. It was new to me, and soothing, Bernice cooing nonsense. There must have been moments like this before she gave me away, I thought, moments when even a miserable seventeen-year-old stands over her sleeping baby with a full heart, and the baby knows.

THIRTY-ONE

She said, "I don't want you driving home in this emotional state. It would be just the kind of poetic justice I've done shows about: you finally accept me for what I am and then you're killed in a car accident." I agreed to sleep over and to share the queen-size bed, borrowing one of Bernice's ridiculous nightgowns. "Don't you have anything with sleeves?" I asked.

"Peignoirs have sleeves," she said.

I wore peach nylon with beige lace trim, her only piece of opaque lingerie. After walking around the bedroom in her black bikini underpants and running bra to show off her fit body, she put on a monogrammed white silk robe. I told her I liked the prizefighter look: now I knew what glamorous television personalities wore to sleep-over parties.

"You must be feeling better," she said sourly.

I called Dwight when she was in the bathroom and told him where I was. He asked if we had talked. I told him that Saguna had shown up, but I had sent her packing; that Bernice had gotten down to the truth as best as she was able.

"Are you okay?" he asked.

"Pretty much."

"How should I read your staying with her tonight. Positively?"

"Yes."

"Is there a reason you're being so cryptic? Is she standing there?"

"Pretty close," I said.

"But you're okay? You reached some kind of understanding?"

"Sort of."

"Did you tell her about us?" he asked.

"Soon," I said. "If not tonight, soon."

Dwight said okay, good; I could tell him everything tomorrow. He said good night. He loved me.

"Me, too," I said.

The faucet stopped running in the bathroom. Bernice yelled, "Say it, for chrissake. Tell the man you love him. What're you afraid of?"

Bernice actually had a vanity table, at which she actually brushed her hair from the roots outward for at least ten minutes. I said I felt as if I had wandered onto the set of "The Loretta Young Show." She also put on cotton gloves after massaging in two coats of hand cream. I asked if she did that when she had male guests. "Absolutely not," she answered with a worried look, as if the very question undermined my own social-sexual judgment.

"What do you sleep in at home?" she asked.

"A nightgown. Or a T-shirt in the summer."

"What about when Dwight's there?"

"Flannel," I said. "Winter and summer. He loves it. The scratchier the better."

Bernice appraised me through half-closed lids. "You're full of shit," she said. "The longer I know you, the worse you get."

"Your influence," I said.

"My *genes*," she said proudly.

When the lights were out she asked contentedly, "Do you think we're going to be okay now that you understand me better?"

I felt a flash of the old anger. "Could you restate that so it doesn't leave the impression that you're the center and object of all experience?"

"Did I say the wrong thing again?" she asked, her voice hard.

It felt late. I was tired and talked out. I wasn't going to reorient Bernice from the center of her universe simply by rewording her sentences. "No," I said. "You didn't."

"Do you think we're going to be all right now?" she repeated.

"What do you think?" I asked.

"I think we're great," said Bernice. "I think we're untouchable."

She got up when I did at 6:15 and made me breakfast in her white silk robe. Frozen blueberry waffles. When I said I had to stop off at my apartment for a change of clothes, she protested. Absolutely unnecessary; certainly *something* in her closet would be appropriate for a day of teaching.

Her closet was a small mirrored and carpeted room of racks, shelves, and wire baskets. "It has to look right with navy flats," she announced, which meant she had silently assessed my shoes the night before. She pulled out a fluffy knit in fuchsia. "Angora," she said. "The color looks marvelous on us."

"Too dressy," I said.

"Try it on."

She arranged the cowl neck just so and added a chain belt from her vast collection. She turned me this way and that in front of the mirror and pronounced me "gorgeous."

"Nice," I said.

"Your students will go gaga."

I ran my hands down the front of my thighs to my knees, checking the length.

"Perfect. In fact, it looks better on you than it does on me. You keep it."

"No," I said.

"*No?*"

"I've got my own clothes. I don't need a makeover."

"Would I do that?" she asked innocently.

I looked back at the mirror. I had seen her in this outfit before, had thought it typically Bernice with its excess of angora fluff and drapes at the neck.

It looked good on me. It felt good, too. I wouldn't have thought so, but it did.

"Come tonight for dinner," she said. "Bring Dwight."

I said no, thanks. Dwight and I needed a night together.

"You're right," said Bernice.

"He's been really wonderful," I said, choking up on the words. "He's the one who insisted I talk to you until we got to the bottom of things."

A look passed over her face, a moment of confusion, as if she had forgotten the night before or hadn't realized there was pain and anger leading up to it. "You could have asked me anything at any time," she said. "You didn't have to wait for Sonia to traumatize you before coming to me. You didn't have to consult Dwight. And even though I feel as if I've sat through a grueling week of congressional testimony, everything is on the record now, and that's good."

"*Veritas vos liberabit?*"

"Truth?" she asked unhappily. "Something about truth?"

"The truth shall make you free."

"Oh, please," said Bernice.

I said there was one thing—Sonia.

"She's supposed to be my friend. I think she betrayed some confidences."

"She helped me a lot. You should thank her instead of blaming her."

Bernice thought about it with her lips set, then said sarcastically, "*Everyone* helped you. Everyone is just so noble I can barely stomach it."

"That's right," I said.

"So is your campaign over? Are you going to stop seeking truth and interviewing my friends behind my back? Or do you and Dwight have a longer agenda."

"We'll talk," I said.

"Not that I have anything more to tell you. You know everything there is to tell."

"What about Jack Remuzzi?" I asked, already picturing Dwight's assault on the phone book.

"What *about* Jack Remuzzi?"

"What if I went looking for him?"

I saw a straightening of her shoulders and a lifting of her head into her public pose as if she were rehearsing their reunion. She raised her eyebrows as if signaling: Well, if it's what you want, I'm certainly not going to stand in your way.

"When was the last time you saw him?" I asked.

"Oh, God. Forever."

"At the divorce?"

"Oh," she said. "Let me think for a second."

"When was that?"

"The divorce?"

"Approximately. I don't need the exact date."

She looked at her nails critically; she twisted her rings into their most advantageous positions.

"Did you get divorced?" I asked.

Bernice challenged me with her eyes, daring me to speak a word of criticism, and said, "Actually, not."

THIRTY-TWO

 I am sitting in the green-room at the station watching Bernice lean toward my biological father and ask him, live, if he's thought about her at all over the last thirty-six years. She tells the audience, twice, "You are seeing our actual reunion. We arranged this appearance by telephone after a researcher tracked Mr. Remuzzi down two weeks ago, but this is unrehearsed. What you are witnessing is the real thing."

I am hiding here where I can't be reached with cameras or microphones or graphics on the screen that announce, "April Epner, their daughter." I want to see it live, but I want to be safe. After this taping I will decide whether to go out and meet Jack Remuzzi. If I agree, Bernice will introduce us; I will be, for the first time since I was six months old, in the presence of both my mother and my father. The city of Quincy has given me the day off.

At fifty-four, he is not handsome, but he is a little

charming. His face is rounder, softer, than mine or Bernice's. His hair is wiry gray, trained to lie crisp and flat; he has sideburns that are a centimeter longer than current fashion. Bernice wants to make him look good—for me, for her show, and for her own vanity. "So, Jack . . ." she says and her voice trails off. She waits for him to speak and, meanwhile, stares like a psychiatrist. The cameramen play psychiatrist, too. Every blink and twitch is reported. Jack Remuzzi's face, his pale lips, the pores on his skin, fill the monitor. We are supposed to think that his discomfort proves Bernice's point. I want to tell them to pull back, to restore some of his privacy.

He has a slow, teasing smile that saves him on close-up. He uses it as a reply when her questions are too precious.

"Did you ever get to college?" Bernice is asking.

"I was drafted in 'fifty-three, and I took some courses courtesy of Uncle Sam when I got out."

"Tell me about your career," she says. "A quick résumé."

"What I do now?"

"Whatever you think our audience would like to know."

"I'm a golf pro at the Ponemah Country Club in southern New Hampshire," he says.

"For those who don't know what a golf pro does . . ." she prompts.

"Everyone knows what a golf pro does."

"You do a lot of travel, on tours?"

"None," says Jack.

Bernice blinks, apparently confused. "What about those golf tournaments people watch on television?"

"That's the big time," says Jack. "I'm the small time. I give lessons and run the pro shop at the club."

Bernice moves quickly on. He lives in Nashua; got out of Taxachusetts—heh, heh, heh—fifteen years ago. What else? He smiles self-consciously—imagine a guy like me getting the third degree on TV.

"What are your regrets?" she asks at the beginning of the next segment.

Jack Remuzzi is not a natural confessor; he cannot play his emotions like Bernice. He shrugs, grins foolishly. This is TV; he knows he's supposed to say the obvious and wring something out of it: I gave my baby away and not a day goes by when I don't pray to God to return her to me. Instead he says, "I suppose I regret the way things turned out."

"Can you be more specific?" she asks confidently.

"Maybe I thought I had all the time in the world to find another girl, get married, have more kids. And then you wake up one morning and you're fifty-one, fifty-two, and you realize maybe you had your shot at it and you screwed it up and you're not getting another. . . ."

"So you're saying you have real regrets?" she asks.

"Sure I do."

"You know that I've found our daughter," she says quietly.

"Yes," says Jack.

"I'm not going to cheapen my show by bringing her on and taping a reunion," says Bernice, who has pleaded with me for weeks to make an appearance. "Our daughter is a private person, a sensitive and keenly intelligent woman. Our daughter went to Radcliffe," she says to the audience, and bobs her head like a keynote speaker expecting applause. They applaud. "She's fluent in Latin and Greek, the two most expressive and difficult languages on earth. After graduating with honors from Radcliffe, she received her master's degree from Wellesley College."

"No kidding!" says Jack.

"How does that make you feel?"

"Jeez," he says. The camera moves in in search of anguish. "I'm smarter than I thought." He laughs and the audience laughs with him. I smile at the face on the TV screen. He's just an ordinary man with a chance to be on a talk show. He reminds me of homeroomfuls of Quincy High School boys whose letter sweaters delay their ordinariness until graduation. He seems nice.

Bernice wants him to cry on her show, like people do for Oprah. "What does Jack Remuzzi really feel when he sees men walking down the street with their daughters . . . when he goes to a wedding where a buddy walks his daughter down the aisle . . . when he passes a card shop around Father's Day? Does he smile like this"—she mimics his goofy joviality—"or does he hurt inside?"

He looks around unhappily. "Yeah. It hurts."

She lets that answer hover in the air before asking, "What went wrong, Jack?"

"Huh?" he asks.

"Other kids make it. We weren't babies. Some marriages last, not many, but some that start that young survive." She looks into the camera and says soulfully, "We'll be right back with more of this extraordinary and very personal show."

Because the commercials will be cut in later, the cameras continue to roll. The monitor fills up with Bernice doing vulnerable. "Jack," she says, addressing him, then pausing as if his name sounds odd in her own voice. She explains her supposed pensiveness: "It's been a long time. . . . Anyway. Your answer to the question 'what went wrong?' "

"You know," he says. "I was a kid. I didn't have any business getting married right out of high school."

"Weren't you doing the *honorable* thing?" Bernice asks. "Giving our child a name."

"I guess so," says Jack.

"Did you really have a choice? We lived two blocks apart. Our lives were intertwined."

"Do you want me to give you a straight answer?" asked Jack.

"Of course I do." She includes the audience with a sweep of her hands. "We all do."

"Getting married wasn't a big romantic thing; it was what you did when you got someone pregnant and you were eighteen and you had half a conscience."

"You're saying—because I want to understand this—it wasn't even a *little* bit romantic? There weren't elements of adventure, of conspiracy, of passion . . . ?"

"Okay," says Jack. "Sure."

"But those have been superseded in your memory by your doing the honorable thing. That's what you're saying?"

"Look—how can I say this? Times were different then, in the early fifties. We didn't have the so-called sexual revolution and we didn't have the Pill. And when you're eighteen, a normal, red-blooded guy—"

"You want it every night and if you're a good Catholic, marriage is the way to go?"

Jack scolds her with a look.

"No?"

"You know why we got married. We got married for one reason and that was because you were pregnant. And that's what guys did if they wanted to do the right thing."

Bernice searches her clipboard for another question. I wonder if she will ultimately cut his treatise on teenage marriage, since it bleaches out any romance from their history. I feel her reaching for a big question to restore her control.

"Tell us about that day," she says quietly.

"What day?" He cups his hand behind his left ear.

"The day you made the phone call and gave our daughter away."

"It wasn't me," says Jack. "My mother called the priest, and the priest called Catholic Charities, and one thing led to another."

"Go on, if you can," says Bernice.

"I was staying with a buddy at Revere Beach over Labor Day, and my mother was taking care of the baby for three, four days—"

Bernice interrupts. "Wait. Let's go back to that time. You are eighteen years—"

"Nineteen."

"Your wife is not there." She nods herself along, does not remind the audience who the wife was, as if that part of the story needn't be illuminated. "So you're getting in one more summer fling—a little dancing, a little football on the beach, a little girl-watching? No place for a baby, right?"

"You had already disappeared," he says.

Bernice continues: "Meanwhile, back in Brighton, Grandma's changing diapers and getting up in the middle of the night with this grandchild she didn't ask for. Thinking, I did this for enough years with my own six; who needs this at, what, forty-five years old?"

"Something like that," says Jack.

"And your sisters say, 'Why should I sit home and baby-sit when he gets to go out and have a good time?'"

"You were the baby's mother. You talk as if you did everything right and I was the heavy."

Bernice folds her hands on her lap as if exercising restraint in the face of such bald insensitivity. Certainly her audience knows her better than to believe him. After a pointed silence she says, "Do you think that's fair? You know I was not coping at that period in my life."

"Oh, excuse me," says Jack. "I must've forgot."

Bernice glares at him. He makes a face.

I smile, and realize I am rooting for him.

The audience gets its turn. It seems that Jack as irresponsible teenage father doesn't bother them as much as Bernice's letting him give her baby away. Women stand up and say, "I was seventeen when I had my first child, and it wasn't easy, and I would rather have been out dancing, too, but I didn't . . . I never could have . . . How could you . . . ?" They frown and squint into the lights, demanding to get the chronology straight. He *asked* you if it was all right? He had to get your signature to do this? You *let* him do this? No postpartum-depression arguments. No walk-a-mile-in-her-shoes defenses. The audience hates what Bernice did. Nothing softens them—not Jack saying "None of you knew my mother," not Bernice saying "She grew up to be smart and happy and successful, didn't she?"

The house lights go down; it is time for Bernice's solo act. She turns to Jack and says, "Before we close, I have a question for you."

He is serious now and steady. He sits up straighter in his upholstered armchair.

Bernice points at the camera and looks directly at me. "If you could say one thing to our daughter, if you thought she was sitting close by, seeing you for the first time, hearing all this"—she gestures to the villains in the audience—"what would you say?"

He finds the right camera and, unwittingly, looks directly at me. His smile is apologetic; I brace myself for some queer, embarrassed words. Instead, he signals me with a quick tilt of his head toward Bernice: She's something, huh?

Then he speaks. Everyone listening hears the words, hears him say he has always loved me and has never for one minute forgotten me. His only child.

But it is her show. The camera returns to her face; tears choke her sign-off. Jack disappears from the screen.

THIRTY-THREE

 There is a knock at the door of the greenroom. I think: one of Bernice's gofers coming to fetch me for the party. I unlock it to find Jack Remuzzi outside.

"Yes?" I say as stiffly as if he were a door-to-door salesman without credentials.

"April?"

I nod.

"I'm your father," he says.

"I know. I saw you." I gesture toward the monitor.

He puts out his hand, the good sportsman, and I shake it.

"How was I?" he asks.

"Good. Quite good."

"Can I come in for a sec?"

I open the door wider and he walks past me. He is shorter than he looked sitting down, maybe five-eight. The makeup gives his face an opaque coppery color. He has loosened his tie, and I can see where the color ends abruptly at his neck.

"Where's Bernice?" I ask.

He waves in the direction of the set—doing whatever she does to end the show, he means. That stuff she does. "She told me you were here, right in the building, watching the whole thing. I wanted to come back and meet you first, without those people of hers around." He steps back. "Let me get a good look at you."

I stand obediently, holding my chin up.

"You do look like her, but not as much as she claims. You're prettier than her."

Good try, I think.

"You don't mind my saying that, do you?"

"No."

"It happens to be the truth."

"Thank you."

He looks around the greenroom as if its props might suggest topics for conversation. He says, "A Latin teacher, is that right?"

"In Quincy," I say.

"And you went to Radcliffe?"

I nod. We both smile and fall into silence. I am waiting; Jack is trying hard to say whatever should come next. He laughs nervously. "What'd you think of the show?"

"What did you think?"

"She put me in the hot seat with those questions of hers."

"Passionate pursuit of the obvious," I murmur.

Jack smiles tentatively. "Kind of phony questions, you mean?"

"Phony's a good word."

"Do people actually like this stuff, listening to what's running through some strange guy's mind?"

"Enough," I say. "Millions."

"They like sticking their nose into other people's business?"

"Are you surprised?"

"Sure I'm surprised. I don't know what women watch at nine o'clock in the morning."

"You never watched her show in all these years?"

"No," says Jack quietly.

"Not even when you knew you were going on?"

"What can I say? I didn't."

"Because of bad memories?"

"Sure, bad memories. Who needs to be reminded of things?"

"I'm surprised you agreed to do it at all."

"You think I shouldn't have?"

"She wanted me on. I refused."

"She pressured me. I didn't feel I had a choice."

"What kind of pressure?"

Jack catches sight of his face in the mirror and ducks to get the full effect. He wipes his cheek with his fingertips and whistles softly. "Cripes," he says. "I look orange."

"How did she pressure you?" I ask again.

"She kind of implied that it would be the only way I'd get to see you. Like she had the key, like she had you in her back pocket."

"That isn't true at all."

"I get that feeling now," says Jack.

"So you didn't really want to do this?"

"Are you kidding? See Bernice for the first time in thirty-five years on the air? Tell the whole world I gave my baby away?" His voice chokes unexpectedly on the last words. He continues with difficulty: "Get up in front of my whole family? People I work with . . ."

"I'm sorry. I didn't know she was using me for leverage."

Jack waves away the notion that I should be sorry.

"Don't," he says, grimacing, as if the words are causing physical pain.

"I'm not at all like her," I say.

His face begins to crumble. There is allegiance to him in my voice that surprises both of us: *And if I'm not like her, I must be more like . . .*

It is more than Jack Remuzzi can bear. He shades his eyes with a shaking hand and turns away.

"A reception for April Epner," it is being called, and the station is paying. There are deli sandwiches and champagne, potato salad and coleslaw, a watermelon basket filled with melon balls, and a platter of two-inch éclairs. Staff people from "Bernice G!" and strangers from Promotion are the guests.

Jack Remuzzi and I enter together to inexplicable applause. Bernice brightens and sweeps over to us. "Well?" she asks him. "Not bad, huh?"

He is composed, but not up to this. "She's a lovely young woman," he says.

Bernice carries a glass of champagne in one hand and an empty paper plate in the other, but encircles my neck with her arms all the same for an approximation of a hug. *I let her do this,* my look says to Jack.

Bernice shifts to stand next to Jack as if posing for a snapshot. She asks what I think.

"What do you mean?"

"Here we are, your parents. All your genes in one room; a complete set."

Bernice is smiling expectantly. Jack looks mortified.

"You're embarrassing him," I say.

Bernice peers at Jack to see if I'm right. "Sorry!" she says. And to me: "He's still shell-shocked."

I ask Jack, "Is this new? Is it possible she's always been like this?"

Bernice loves the question, smiles confidently waiting for his answer.

He looks at me squarely, dolefully. "Always," he answers.

A gofer delivers two plates with a polite sample of each buffet dish. I accept one; Jack refuses his with a shake of his head. "Go on," says Bernice. "We thought everyone would be starved."

"I can't," says Jack. He says he wants to talk to her privately, and I step back.

"What is it?" she asks.

"Is there somewhere we can go?"

Bernice leans closer, inviting him to whisper in her ear. Jack glances at me and I nod. I can't hear the words, but I know the content. He is telling her that he has changed his mind, withdrawing his permission to air the interview.

Bernice's head jerks upright. "That's not your decision," she snaps.

"I think it is," says Jack.

"You gave your permission."

"Under duress," he says, a phrase I have supplied.

Bernice looks at me and I raise my eyebrows innocently: Beats me. I can't hear a word he's saying.

There is a moment's lag where her eyes remain on me while she's speaking to Jack. "What do you object to, specifically?"

"All of it," he answers.

She puts her plate and champagne glass down on the buffet table so she can press her fingertips to her temples. "Am I missing something here? Did we or did we not tape a fabulous show?"

"I think I looked like a horse's ass."

"I wept!" she cried. "How often do you think I end a show in tears?"

"I don't care," Jack says.

Bernice takes a long breath as if employing a relaxation technique. "Look," she says, "you don't know what you're talking about. This is the kind of stuff you win Emmys for. This is the kind of stuff that gets you into syndication."

"This is the kind of stuff that makes your relatives puke when they see you making a goddamn fool of yourself."

Bernice's staff members are glancing our way, and the word spreads: trouble in paradise.

Jack lowers his voice and says, "I'm spoiling April's party. I'm gonna take off."

"You don't have to," I say.

"Which one is your boss?" he asks Bernice.

"Why?"

"Who do I talk to to go over your head?"

She pokes her breastbone. "I make my own creative decisions."

"Her producer's the black woman in the red dress," I say.

"My, my," says Bernice. "Aren't we the helpful daughter?"

"I'll talk to you soon," Jack says to me, and touches my shoulder.

Bernice and I resume eating. I tell her it's a lovely party; so nice of her staff to do this for me.

"Particularly since the taping might be a total loss," she says.

I remind Bernice that the studio audience was hostile toward her. Who needs that kind of exposure?

"Haven't you ever heard of editing?"

"But you can't air the show without his permission, can you?"

"There are ways."

"Just as there were ways to get him *on* the show?"

Bernice assesses this question and decides it's a telling one. "I guess I don't have to inquire as to what you thought of your father."

"He seems pretty straightforward," I say.

She laughs a dry laugh. "How diplomatic."

"Why do you say that?"

"Do you mean 'pretty straightforward' as in 'uncomplicated'? I think I'd agree with you there."

"It was a compliment."

Bernice sets her lips primly and says, "I see."

"What do you see?"

"You connected with him on some level. With very little effort on his part, as far as I can tell. He shows up, gives you a pat on the head, and wins you over, just like that. I strategize for months on how best to approach you and to present myself—"

"Bingo," I say.

Bernice says bitterly, "He's straightforward, as opposed to me. I'm not to be trusted."

I smile and say, "No one ever accused you of being straightforward, Bernice." I even give her shoulders a jiggle until I elicit a pathetic smile. She puts her fingertips to her temples again. "Something in him appeals to you. Something about his . . . pragmatism. I can see it. I really can."

"He just said what he felt."

"Which was less flattering to some of us than to others."

"What do you mean?"

" 'We got married for one reason only and that's because you were pregnant'? That is *crap*. I wouldn't have married him just to make you legitimate. He was nuts about me, not that he'd admit it."

"Do you think he was lying on the show?"

"He put Bernice Graves in her place, didn't he? 'You think you're so unforgettable? Well, all I remember is a positive pregnancy test.' That was clearly his message today. He was nuts about me! Yes, I was pregnant, but he was plenty happy to marry me. No one had to stick a gun to his head. And don't you find it highly significant that he never remarried or had more kids?"

"He wasn't divorced."

"Big deal! Neither was I. That only means something if you want it to."

"Maybe it's painful for him to remember the good times," I say.

Bernice closes her eyes, purses her lips. Shakes her head, No, April. Wrong again.

THIRTY-FOUR

Dwight's parents are in their late sixties, tall and plain like living Shakers. He has told me they won't fuss over me or express gratitude or relief for pairing up with their bachelor son; they didn't realize, he says, that he was past his prime and unloved. He smiles when he says this and I do, too; we both love his rescue version.

"Have you ever brought a woman home to meet them before?" I ask.

"Not like this," says Dwight.

I ask if this means they won't have any basis for comparison. Will they think he fell for the first skirt who got into his pants?

Dwight prods his chest with a macho thumb: he's his own man. He doesn't need his parents' two cents. He picks his own women, baby.

"What if they hate me?" I ask.

"If they hate you . . . they can get someone else to shovel their sidewalk," he answers.

"You'd do that for me?"

"Hell, yes," he says.

We don't kiss hello or good-bye, but we get along fine. Trude and Julius would have greeted Dwight with the same distance. I understand the Willamees' reserve and almost admire it. His sister Lorraine is there to check me out, too, and to give the kind of mock warnings that big sisters are bound by the laws of filial teasing to dispense. I learn that he was called Butch, even Butchie. I rise and say regretfully that I can't marry someone named Butch.

Mr. and Mrs. Willamee look to their children for an explanation. Their hearing is bad. "A joke," Lorraine says, no louder than I had spoken. They hear her, though, and smile wanly.

Mrs. Willamee serves broiled scrod—in case I observe the dietary laws, she says.

"You could have asked me," says Dwight.

I tell her I don't. She tells me her dearest neighbors when they lived in their old house in Watertown were a family named Stern.

"Get it?" says Dwight loudly. "Stern? Jewish."

His parents tsk-tsk him. Lorraine gives Dwight a look of such complex camaraderie—c'mon, you know what they're trying to say; don't make fun of them, they don't get it, don't think it as funny as you and I and April find it—that I want shares in this Willamee-children conspiracy. I ask about the other sister so I can fully picture our team. I know Carleen is older, married, living in New Hampshire, with two children, but I want to hear the collective version.

"Carleen," says Mr. Willamee.

"The good one," says Lorraine under her breath.

"She has children, right?"

"A boy and a girl," everyone says happily. Jason and Lauren.

"How old?" I ask.

"Nine and eleven," says Mrs. Willamee.

"Almost ten and twelve," says Mr. Willamee.

"They're very excited about Dwight getting married," his mother says. She pronounces his name carefully as if she's rehearsed dumping "Butch."

I smile and say the correct thing about their not being the only ones who are excited. It's not really true: I rarely enjoy parties and I never give them. Weddings are for families, and I don't have one. Dwight and I are doing the polite thing.

Mrs. Willamee returns the courtesy of asking about siblings. She understands I have a brother?

"Freddie," I say.

"Older or younger?" Lorraine asks.

"Younger. Twenty-nine."

Mrs. Willamee says, "You're very close in age, then?"

"Seven years."

Her calculations strain the muscles of her face. Hasn't Dwight told her I am thirty-six, old to be their son's bride?

"Is he married?" asks Lorraine.

"No."

"Divorced?"

The Willamees tsk-tsk again. Lorraine apologizes with exaggerated contrition. "Forgive me, April. I know that was a horribly rude question. What must you think of me?"

I smile a smile which I hope is sisterly in its overlapping messages. "No problem," I say.

"Well? Is he?"

"Never been married," I answer.

"A handsome young fellow," says Dwight. "And fond of the ladies. Not unlike myself."

I laugh, the only one. "You'll meet him at the wedding, of course," I say.

"When do you think you'll do it?" Lorraine asks.

"As soon as school gets out."

"What day?" asks Lorraine.

Dwight and I say we haven't pinned it down yet.

Mrs. Willamee instructs her son to bring the calendar from the cellar door. "When does school get out?" she asks, as Dwight complies.

Dwight and I aren't sure. The twenty-first, twenty-third? We'd have to check.

Mrs. Willamee leafs ahead to June, then July, back to June.

"How about Saturday the twenty-fifth? Because the next weekend will run into the holiday."

"Can't," says Dwight.

"Actually," I say, "we could if that's best for everyone."

Dwight tells them I am being overly accommodating. Jews don't get married on Saturday and there isn't any need to catholicize our plans.

"Are you religious?" asks Lorraine.

"No," I say.

"There are five other days to choose from without stepping on anyone's Sabbath," Dwight says.

"Can your people get married on a weekday?" asks his mother.

"Yes," says Dwight. "Her people can. So can my people."

Mrs. Willamee looks at the calendar. It has taken on the complexity of an actuarial table now that Saturdays and Sundays have been eliminated.

"What day do you like?" Dwight asks me, gently transferring the calendar from his mother to me.

"I think it's going to have to be midweek if we want to get a place for the reception. Most of these places are booked a year in advance."

We consult the calendar. Monday, June 27? There shouldn't be much going on that day. He points and I nod my agreement.

A Monday wedding. How nice, they say.

"Who will be officiating?" Mrs. Willamee asks quietly. "A priest and a rabbi?"

"We thought a justice of the peace," I say.

"I suppose that would be the easiest way," she says. After a pause she adds, "That means it won't be a church wedding."

"Correct," says Dwight.

No one asks about my parents. It is a complicated subject for get-acquainted conversation. I raise the topic by saying, "Dwight probably told you that my parents are dead—"

"Yes, dear," says Mrs. Willamee. She reaches for plates and begins scraping them onto hers. Enough of that uncomfortable subject.

"Did he tell you that my birth parents are alive, and will be at the wedding?"

Mrs. Willamee's eyes brighten. "He did tell us. I hope to meet her."

"The woman on TV," says Mr. Willamee.

"Bernice G!" says his wife.

"And my father's name is Jack Remuzzi. Dwight told you they were separated for thirty-five years and that Dwight found my father in two phone calls?"

"I'm looking forward to that show where she has him on," says Mrs. Willamee. "Dwight says they talked about you."

"That may never get aired. Jack doesn't want it to. In

fact they're not speaking to each other because of it." I
realize immediately that I have revealed more than they
want to know, that they don't thrill to the kind of personal
offerings I mete out to Bernice.

"Won't that be a bit awkward at the wedding?" Lorraine
offers.

"No," says Dwight. "They both want things to be right
with April."

"What do *you* want?" Lorraine asks me. I am startled
by the forthrightness of the question. A succinct answer
would be: I want them to be different. I want Bernice to
be more like Jack. I want Jack to be more like my adoptive
father. I want Trude and Julius to be alive; I want no
complicating ghosts of saintly adoptive parents as models.
I want Jack and Bernice to be the only parental package,
so I could be the tolerant daughter of flawed parents—like
you and them.

Instead I say, "I just want them to be guests."

Mr. and Mrs. Willamee listen. They seem to accept it
as if practiced in accepting the bewildering life-style decisions of modern children.

"Whatever is comfortable for April," says Mr. Willamee.

"Do you want your brother involved?" asks Lorraine.

"Sure," I say.

She asks if we are close. I choose the simplest answer
and say that we are.

"So—you're doing a quiet little number, then. Just
immediate family?"

"And some friends," I say, thinking of Anne-Marie and
one or two colleagues.

Lorraine asks what I'll be wearing.

"God only knows," Dwight says dryly.

I explain: I am letting Bernice take me to her favorite

designer who will create my wedding outfit. It is her gift; she has insisted.

"Bernice won't be able to live with herself for the fifteen minutes she'll be watching the ceremony if April's dress doesn't suit her—if it's not exactly what Bernice would wear. So her subtle way of doing things is to say 'I'll take over. I'll design it. I'll pay for it. I'll produce and direct it.' " Dwight finishes his diatribe.

Lorraine and her parents are unmoved. Bernice's actions do not offend them the way they offend me. So? they seem to be thinking. Of course she buys the dress; she's the bride's mother. It's the way of the world.

Dwight says, "April will be a beautiful bride whatever she wears, don't you think?"

The Willamees nod politely. They don't offer any further compliments. Dwight looks worried for me over their lack of enthusiasm. He walks around the table to my chair and bends over to kiss me on the lips. It is seconds longer than a perfunctory public kiss would be. It is a declaration of independence, I think, a contract between us. The Willamees look on. Surely if he's ever brought a woman home, he's never kissed one in front of them. I mouth, "Thanks."

He says aloud, "You're welcome."

THIRTY-FIVE

ernice and I go for consultations on two consecutive Friday afternoons, but we make no progress on my dress. We have talked Lucia out of black silk and out of brown velvet. I keep saying, "I don't understand what's wrong with white."

Lucia with the blond brush cut sets her lips; she is an artist and has no policy about the customer always being right. Bernice believes in her and acts as mediator, unhappy with my white and Lucia's black. She has narrowed her preferences to the swatches labeled "Poppy," "Melon," "Inferno," and "Burpee Big Boy." I say no, no, no, no, to all the reds. Aren't they bothered by the connotations of a red wedding dress?

Bernice says that's exactly why it would be so wonderful—the Latin teacher and the librarian in their singular and quiet devotion to each other saying "fuck you" to the world. She says we're not exactly the Barbie and Ken statues on top of a wedding cake. Why not have fun, tease the guests?

I say, "No reds or oranges. I'm not trying to make a point, especially a half-baked one."

"What do you *want?*" Lucia asks.

"Pastels are nice for early summer," I say.

"Maybe with an Easter bonnet and a little white patent leather pocketbook?" says Bernice.

"What about lavender? That's not too clichéd."

Lucia ponders the suggestion. Finally she chants with her eyes closed, "Gray, maybe, with a suggestion of purple in it. Not bridesmaidy. A smoky gray. Not too pale. A swishy silk. With touches of color hand-painted on it. Subtle but not somber."

"What for flowers?" asks Bernice. "A deep purple?"

"No flowers," says Lucia firmly.

"I want flowers," I say.

"What do you mean, 'no flowers'?" Bernice asks carefully, shushing me.

"I don't do costumes. I don't do veils and trains. I don't do seed pearls and alençon lace. I design dresses that are beautiful enough to carry the day without props."

"This is my wedding, though. Not yours."

Lucia is not accustomed to back talk. She says, "Most clients want to be original. If they want clichés, they go to Filene's or Priscilla's after they've read *Bride's* magazine to see which stores carry the off-the-rack Princess Diana dress that's pictured on the cover."

I say, "My mother got married in a long white dress with all the frills and the flowers."

"Everybody's mother did," says Lucia.

"*I* got married in a peach wool crepe suit with three-quarter sleeves," says Bernice. "I eloped."

"I'm confused," says Lucia.

"Her adopted mother had the frills. I'm her real mother."

"What I meant was that my mother cared enough about tradition that she came out of mourning to get married in white with all the props, as you would put it."

Lucia drags her unhappy gaze over to Bernice for explanation. Bernice says, "They were in concentration camps and their families were wiped out by Hitler. They met in this country after the war and got married."

Lucia is temporarily silenced by this profile.

I add, "They couldn't even have children after what they'd been through."

"That's awful," says the designer.

"You've heard of Auschwitz? They had numbers tattooed on their forearms."

Bernice looks at me, advising caution. I can't stop myself, at least until I've said, "Well, they're dead now." It is their whole story from Bernice's point of view: survived, met, married, adopted, died. I'm perversely feeding it back to her.

Lucia asks if my mother saved this white wedding dress of hers. I answer that I don't know for sure. She was probably too tidy and efficient to keep a dress for forty years.

"Why do you ask?" Bernice interrupts.

Lucia looks hopeful now. Her voice gains some modulation. "I do retros of old wedding gowns. Maybe I could take a look at this one. Or reproduce it from a picture."

"It was probably a *shmatteh*," says Bernice.

"There's definitely a picture. It's on the dining room wall."

"Can you get it?" asks Lucia.

"She hasn't said she wants that," says Bernice. "I don't particularly like the idea of some postwar Andrews Sisters' dress for April. I think it would look kitschy, which is not her look."

"What do you think?" Lucia asks me.

"I doubt whether my mother kept it," I say.

"Still better. I'll modify it. Use some color. Maybe do it in a pale gray satin, heavy satin, ballerina length. How soon can you get the picture?"

"I'll ask my brother to mail it up right away."

"Have it sent to me and I'll get a jump on it."

Bernice huffs. Don't bother to consult *me,* it says. I'm only paying for it.

"What do you think, Bernice?" I ask.

"I think Lucia is a genius," she says obediently.

"You mean that? You'd go along with this idea?"

"It's not my decision."

"Say it like you mean it," I coax.

"Whatever you want is fine."

"It'll be gorgeous," says Lucia. "No matter what the original looks like. I have the artistic license to make it ten times better."

Bernice still looks worried. I ask what it is about the idea that gives her trouble.

"There's just one thing," she says. "No one's going to know it's a copy of Trude's gown. It's not like it's going to register with anyone. It's not like Trude and Julius will ever know, or that it's going to mean anything to anyone there."

I don't answer right away. As always, I measure my need to jump down her throat against the futility of doing so.

Finally she says, "Except you, I meant. And possibly Fred."

"Maybe it's a way of having her at the wedding. Of her seeing me finally get married. A symbol. That's all."

"Like that scene in *Carousel,*" offers Lucia, "where the

dead father is at the daughter's high school graduation, and when she feels his arm around her it makes her stronger and she sings 'You'll Never Walk Alone' in white chiffon?"

"Exactly," I say.

"I hated that movie," says Bernice.

Freddie says why bother to mail the wedding picture when he can hop in his car and be at my apartment in fifty-five minutes. We have not seen each other since he attempted to seduce Bernice, and have only talked once. That time I called to announce my engagement and he said, "To Dwight, the guy I met?"

"Yeah. The same night you met Bernice."

Freddie chuckled nervously.

"Don't worry," I said. "I heard nothing happened. No thanks to you."

"What'd she tell you?"

"She said she didn't think it was seemly to fuck my brother, so she sent you home, despite your willingness to break the incest taboo."

"Incest! She's not my mother. You don't know what would've happened if I'd stuck around."

"Am I wrong? Did you try?"

"I always try," said Freddie solemnly.

"Well, you're a jerk, then."

"I didn't start it. She came on to me."

"And you always take what's offered, regardless? You don't ever set any limits—with women you work with, or friends' girlfriends? Ever just walk away out of loyalty or common sense, or anything? Or do you just fuck whatever's in your path?"

"You're making a bigger deal out of this than you have to. *Nothing happened.*"

"Are you sure?"

"Why would I lie?"

That was true. Freddie didn't have the sexual ethics to recognize when a lie might be prudent. "How are you ever going to meet someone normal?" I asked.

"I meet people all the time."

"I know. But you're infantile. You don't seem to care about establishing a relationship. Do you even like these women you pick up?"

"Sure I do. I see some of them on a repeat basis."

"You should, you know. Because what's cute at twenty-nine can be pathetic at thirty-nine."

"What do you mean?"

"You have to start relating to women on other levels. It's a sign of arrested development to see them only in terms of sex. And you can start with Bernice."

"Look," he said. "You don't know what you're talking about. Guys are different from girls, a *lot* different from some girls—"

"Like me, for instance. You think I don't know which end is up, right?"

"Well, I *assume*—"

"You don't know anything. If you can seduce my mother—"

"Mom was your mother," he said angrily. "Bernice is the one who had you and gave you away."

I said, slowly and distinctly, "I'm the one in the middle. And I'm telling you that I resent your hitting on her, no matter how good your argument is."

Freddie didn't say anything.

"You think I'm wrong, don't you?"

He exhaled a long, misunderstood breath. I waited. Finally he said, "Not every woman views sex as the biggest deal in the world."

"Not like your sister."

"That's right."

"And Bernice is one of those others?"

"Do you disagree?"

"All I know is that at some point Bernice said, 'This is wrong. I shouldn't sleep with my daughter's brother.' "

"Or maybe *I* said that—I shouldn't sleep with my sister's so-called mother."

"Did you?"

"I might have. It didn't reach a point where I had to make any big moral decisions. Okay?"

"You were lucky on this one."

"What do you want me to say, April? I'm sorry?"

"Say you'll smarten up and show some judgment."

I heard him sigh, then recite back, "I'll smarten up. I'll show some judgment. I'll find a nice girl and settle down."

" 'I won't marry a bimbo.' "

"I won't marry a bimbo."

Before we hung up I asked if he was mad at me. "Mad?" he asked cheerfully. Why should he be mad?

Now I tell him that would be great if he'd mail me the wedding portrait. Just wrap it carefully, frame and all. Mail it? he says. Hell, I'll drive it up. Tonight, tomorrow. He asks what I want with it anyway. I tell him that a dressmaker is going to copy Ma's wedding gown for me.

"Whose idea was that?" he asks.

"The dressmaker's."

"Sounds like a lot of trouble."

"I don't mind."

"Look," he says. "About the wedding. Doesn't the bride's family pay for it?"

"Usually, but not always." Particularly if they're dead, I think.

"I'd like to do it," says Freddie. "I think Mom and Dad would want me to, and I don't think you should have to, just because you waited until they had passed away."

"No," I say. "I think that's incredibly nice of you, but you shouldn't spend your money on this."

"Who's going to pay for it if I don't?"

"Me."

"Not her?"

"Bernice? Uh-uh. She wants to, but I won't let her."

"How come?" he asks.

"Because it's my wedding. She'll make it her production, and I don't want her in charge."

"I've got the money. I'd rather spend it on this than take a trip or something."

I am silent for a few moments, and then I say, "We're actually keeping it small and simple."

"Good! I'll get away cheap."

"Are you sure you want to?"

"I really want to."

I tell him there's one thing; and I'm sorry I didn't ask him before he offered to pay for everything, because now he would think that was the reason. Would he do me the honor of giving me away?

"Huh?" says Freddie.

"Walk me down the aisle? Haven't you ever been to a wedding?"

"I'd like that," says Freddie.

"Good. It would mean a lot to me."

He hesitates, then says with difficulty, "It would mean a lot to me, too. Thanks."

"Thank *you.*"

His voice brightens. "So we have a deal all around? You don't have to run it by Dwight?"

I tell him no. It's a bride's prerogative, letting her family pay for the wedding.

"Good! You make whatever arrangements you want and send me the bills, okay? Whatever you want. Prime rib, baked stuffed shrimp. You don't have to ask."

I thank him, then can't help but ask if he thought of this himself.

"You think I'm such a jerk I couldn't come up with this myself?"

I laugh and say, "Yeah."

THIRTY-SIX

Now that our engagement is public, Dwight regularly pops into my homeroom, grinning, to ask ridiculous questions. Should we go to Niagara Falls or the Poconos for our honeymoon? How do I feel about microwave ovens? It escalates into a routine, with each day's question getting goofier. The students love it; they particularly like the variety of endearments he tosses into my room as he passes: "sweet pea," "Tootsie Roll," "lamb chop," "cream puff." I swat Dwight away and wait for the laughter to pass, thrilled actually to see him conspire with the kids. At first I didn't answer; I restored decorum by ignoring him and getting on to homeroom business. Finally one morning, after he'd ducked out, I waited a beat and asked my class, "Whatever happened to 'darling' and 'sweetheart'?"

He is loose now because he knows he's leaving, and

knows he won't have to maintain the act or the good-guyism past this term. On July first he will start his new job as an archivist at the John F. Kennedy Presidential Library. He was hired after one interview, returned with the inevitable tall tale about getting hired because his wife was Jack Kennedy's illegitimate daughter—God, they couldn't believe their ears; they begged him to stay; could he bring my blood, hair, and tissue samples on his first day? When we told Bernice the great news, she said, "I thought you wanted to open a bookstore."

Decided against it, we said: the hours, the bookkeeping, the capital, the public, the details, the racks of Cliff Notes. . . .

"The John F. Kennedy Library is the only place he can go? What about Harvard or M.I.T.? They must need librarians."

"Do you think he did this to get your goat?" I ask.

"Dwight enjoys a joke at my expense."

"I thought you would like the sound of 'my son-in-law the archivist,' " he says.

"It's a great job," I say, "and as far away from a high school library as you can get and still be a librarian."

Bernice thinks it over. "Is it prestigious?" she asks.

"Certainly," says Dwight.

"Are you *the* archivist at the library or are there more?"

"More."

She makes a face: So? What's the big deal?

"It's my dream job," says Dwight. "I get to do interesting work with intelligent people and to look at the ocean while I eat my lunch."

"Is it more money?"

"Much," I say. "He was getting paid less than a teacher in Quincy."

Bernice takes out a cigarette and taps it on the wooden

arm of the living room rocker. I remind her of my no-smoking rule.

"I'm cutting down. I shouldn't let myself slip because I'm agitated."

"About this?" we ask. About Dwight changing careers?

"Not that."

"About the JFK part?" I ask.

"About my divorce," she says. She tells us Jack has filed. She needs a good lawyer and she needs our emotional support.

Dwight and I shift into our humor-Bernice mode. Does Jack's filing surprise her? Hasn't she considered herself a common-law divorcée for thirty-six years? Hasn't she ever considered filing herself?

"Of course I have; every time someone proposed to me I made a mental note to file. Which doesn't mean I have a divorce lawyer on retainer."

"Any lawyer will do for a no-fault divorce as long as he or she can file the right papers and sit with you in court that day," I say. "That's the whole point—it's a routine legal procedure."

"I want the best," says Bernice.

"Why?" asks Dwight. I can hear the annoyance in his voice.

"I have a career, property, investments, reputation—"

"And you think Jack is going to go after you?" I demand.

"His lawyer might!"

"Look," says Dwight. "We watch 'L.A. Law,' too. It's not out of the question, but I would be willing to bet that Jack just wants to make it official and be legally divorced. He probably has some woman up there he wants to marry. He hasn't given anyone the slightest reason to accuse him of going after alimony or a settlement."

"He could have more money than you do!" I said. "We don't know how he lives or what he's got in the bank."

"I'm not taking any chances," says Bernice. "I want a good divorce lawyer representing me and that's that. You don't go out and hire some *schlemiel* just because you think your husband is a nice, simple guy. It's his lawyer you worry about. And you tell me that some divorce lawyer is going to open this file and see 'woman abandons husband and baby and becomes television personality' without seeing dollar signs?"

Okay, we say. Do what you want.

"He started it," she says.

"I'm neutral," I say. "Don't expect any cheerleading. Pretend I'm six years old and you're bending over backwards to protect me from the ugliness of divorce."

"Pick a nice eligible divorce lawyer," says Dwight. "Charm him in your inimitable fashion and kill two birds with one stone."

"You think you're the first one to think of that?" she asks.

"Just make it clean," I say. "I don't want to hear what Jack's doing to you and what you're doing to him."

"I've done more shows on divorce than I care to remember. I know all about children of divorce, and how parents line up the kids on their sides."

"Good," I say. "I think."

"You're being ridiculous, you know," she says.

"I'm getting married. I don't want this aggravation."

"You're right," she says. "I won't mention it ever again."

I am subpoenaed by Bernice's lawyer, Sumner Lebow, to appear at the divorce hearing at Middlesex Superior Court in Cambridge. I call his office and am unable to get past his secretary. She says Mr. Lebow is in court and will

return my call. "Tell him I'm Bernice Graves's daughter,"
I add. He calls back quickly.

"Why do I have to be there?" I ask.

"Just in case we need you."

"What would that be contingent upon?"

"The plaintiff. Just in case he talks about mental anguish, raising you himself, and being deprived of educa-
tional opportunity while fulfilling his role of father."

"He won't do that. You can take it from me."

Attorney Lebow allows himself a condescending
chuckle. "We won't take any chances, though, will we?
We'll have you there to testify to the degree to which your
biological father exercised his paternity."

"I have to do it?"

"You have to do it."

"I asked Bernice to keep me out of it."

"You're a grown woman, Miss Epner. You're not the
object of a custody battle. It's the little ones under twelve
we most worry about when it comes to testifying. I can
assure you that you won't incur any emotional scars at the
hands of the defendant."

"Thanks," I said.

Dwight and I take a personal day and go to the hearing.
Jack is seated in the front row with his lawyer, a fat white-
haired man in a navy blue suit. Jack sprints back to our
row, his face both eager and embarrassed. "Didn't expect
to see you here," he says. I can see he is worried: If I'm
here, it must be at Bernice's invitation. I must be taking
sides.

Dwight says, "Nice to see you, Jack. I'm coming up for
a golf lesson as soon as the ground thaws."

"Just say the word. We'll start at the driving range and
work from there."

"Me, too," I say.

"Great!" says Jack. "It's a great sport for teachers. A lot of our members are teachers. They play late afternoons."

Dwight tells him he's not long for the teaching ranks. Soon he starts his new job at the Kennedy Library.

"No kidding! He was my congressman, you know," says Jack. "He was a personal hero of mine. I didn't go to sleep the night of the election in 'sixty, not until all the votes were counted and I knew he'd won. The Republicans tried to make people think that if a Catholic was president, he'd take his orders from the pope." He smiles as if he's been reminiscing foolishly. "I'd like to see the place myself someday, see the rocking chair and all. They say he would've liked the spot because he was a sailor."

"You and I can go there someday when Dwight's started; we'll have lunch. Maybe Dwight can give us a private tour."

Jack says, "You mean it?"

"Sure."

"It's a date, then. You just say the word." He looks toward the front row where his lawyer is watching us talk. Jack motions he'll be right there. When he takes his seat, the lawyer asks him questions I can't hear. I assume he's being warned about fraternizing with a possible enemy.

"Wonder why he's doing this?" I murmur to Dwight.

"Doing what?"

"Getting divorced now."

"Maybe he wants to get married."

"You keep *saying* that."

"Because I can imagine a scenario where he's been going with a woman for years—she never knew he was married or had a grown daughter—and then Bernice locates him and he's exposed."

I could picture Jack's girlfriend; she wasn't nice enough for him. She would be one of those teachers who golfed; a short, culotted gym teacher, forty-five, with pompons at her heels and overdeveloped calves. Not the stepmother type; not sweet enough for Jack. I ask Dwight if he's sure he doesn't know something I don't know. Have he and Jack had a man-to-man talk?

Dwight says no, he's just exercising his fertile powers of supposition.

"Good," I say.

Doors open in the back of the small hearing room. I know it is Bernice from the citrus blast of Liz Claiborne. She is dressed soberly in a designer cowgirl outfit of navy suede. Sumner Lebow leads. He is small and tanned, starched French cuffs protruding from his pinstripe suit jacket. The strain of representing Bernice is already apparent. She whispers in his ear as soon as they are seated, and he silences her with monosyllables.

"Oyez, oyez," we hear from a man in uniform I hadn't noticed before. The judge rushes in, head down, as if he could do without the ceremonials, and jumps into his chair on the bench. He is a handsome combination of several possibilities, and, because the sign says "Judge Franco Willson" I guess black and Italian.

"Okay!" he says and smiles. "What have we got here?"

The lawyers stand, Attorney Lebow on his feet in seconds, Jack's after smoothing his shiny tie and patting his jacket pockets. They move forward to the bench and confer jovially as if today's business is routine indeed. The lawyers part and look toward their clients.

"Mr. Remuzzi!" the judge booms.

"Yessir?"

"This is your signature on the affidavit?"

Jack looks at his lawyer, who nods. "Yes, sir."

"It says here that your marriage of . . . thirty-*seven* years has suffered an irretrievable breakdown and you seek its dissolution."

Jack nods.

"You've reviewed this with advice of counsel and signed it freely and knowledgeably?"

"Yes."

"You expect me to believe that you've made it this far—thirty-seven years—and you can't go any further?"

Jack's lawyer opens his mouth to direct the judge to the extenuating circumstances, but the judge raises a silencing hand without taking his eyes off Jack.

"Your honah," says Jack, "it's not what you think. We got married thirty-seven years ago, but we didn't stay together more than a couple of months. We've been outta touch for something like thirty-six years. It's not like we're breaking up a home or anything."

Judge Willson shuffles blue-bound papers. "Bernice Graverman?" She waves daintily from the front row. "And do *you* believe that this union has suffered an irretrievable breakdown?"

Bernice ponders the question and the adjective as if it were newly minted for her divorce hearing. She hesitates, then answers as carefully as if it's her round in a spelling bee: "I don't know if I would use the word 'irretrievable.' "

"What word would you use?" asks Judge Willson.

"That seems rather extreme, what you might say if one of us were dead. I might say, 'Unworkable. Impractical.' "

Attorney Lebow asks if he might have a word with his client. He bends over and whispers in her ear. She straightens and says to the bench, "But I do believe our marriage has suffered an irretrievable breakdown. That's what I signed, and that's what I sincerely believe."

Judge Willson glares at Bernice's attorney. "Ms. Graverman can speak for herself, Counselor. She makes her living doing just that." Bernice beams with pleasure. A viewer, possibly a fan. "Let me ask the parties a question: Have they attempted to reconcile their differences or seek marriage counseling?"

Jack's attorney harrumphs noisily.

"You're kidding, right?" answers Bernice.

"I assure you I am not."

"We haven't lived together since we were teenagers! We haven't even talked to each other since we were teenagers."

"Mr. Remuzzi?"

"She's right," says Jack. "It would be like you're ordering two strangers to go and live together, or go into therapy together. We have no relationship to speak of!"

"You have a daughter, I understand." He finds me in the back rows. I nod. Judge Willson smiles as if to say, Thanks, I might need you yet. He reads further and begins to shake his head from side to side, slowly, slowly, so I think I'm hearing the rasping of his neck against his collar.

"May I say something?" Bernice asks.

"Go ahead."

"If you can become someone's common-law wife by living with them for seven years, shouldn't you automatically be granted a divorce if you've lived apart for five times that long?"

"No," says Judge Willson unhappily. He asks her why neither has filed for divorce in all these many years.

"I was busy putting my life together and establishing myself," she says. "It was procrastination. I knew I'd get around to it sooner or later."

"But you didn't. Mr. Remuzzi was the petitioner."

Bernice frowns at his invoking a mere technicality.

The judge reclines on one elbow as if settling in for a long spell. "Mr. Remuzzi? Why haven't you petitioned the court before this time?"

Jack stands and bounces on the balls of his feet. "I'm ashamed to say that I didn't want to go to court and have to hear the story of my life rehashed. I didn't want to see Bernice because that meant bringing up the whole mess of the adoption, and God knows what else. I just wanted to bury the whole damn thing."

"Is there a compelling reason why you did it now?"

Jack grins. "I met my daughter. She's getting married. . . . She's not angry at me. Bernie's life is going good— her show and everything. I thought it was the right thing to do at this point in time."

"What you seem to be telling me is that you took this action now, ironically, because everything's fine—or at least better than it's been for thirty-six years. Some of the pain has been eased with these reconciliations."

"They don't even live in the same state," Jack's lawyer tries.

"This is patently ridiculous," says Attorney Lebow.

Judge Willson stares off somewhere above our heads and squints thoughtfully. He turns to the court stenographer and speaks slowly: "I am denying this writ of divorce and recommending that Mr. and Mrs. Remuzzi seek mediation or counseling for the purpose of further exploring the viability of this marriage. The court is not convinced that this union has suffered an irretrievable breakdown, and until and unless I am convinced, I remand this to the parties.." He touches his gavel to the block of wood and says, "Good luck."

Jack looks to his lawyer to confirm that he's actually heard what he thinks he's heard, that Bernice G. is still Mrs. Jack Remuzzi.

"All rise," says the court officer. Judge Franco Willson steps down and exits.

I hear Bernice's squeal above the angry buzz: "That's it?

That's his decision? Does he think this is going to get his name in the papers?"

Dwight does the sensible thing—he laughs, what I would do, too, if I hadn't just been sentenced. Instinctively, I slip down smaller in my chair to hide, as if an officer of the court will handcuff me and lead me away to a very small cell.

THIRTY-SEVEN

"We go on dates," Bernice tells me. "We go on little dates like we used to when we lived in Oak Square, before you were born. Except we're not sneaking out. Just the opposite—we're going out on fucking *court-ordered* dates. Is that precious or what?"

We are sunbathing at the pool of our new condominium—Dwight's and mine—in Needham. On weekends we clean and paint and move a few cartons around for effect. It is May, the first genuinely warm day of the spring. Bernice has never seen me in a bathing suit. I find her staring from behind her dark lenses when she thinks I'm not looking—a mother deprived of her child's body for all those years of bathing and diapering, now analyzing the finished product. Stripped down this way we look remarkably alike, even though I'm wearing a navy blue tank suit and she's in a white bikini. I laughed when I first saw what she was wearing under her hooded caftan; I pulled the navy blue Lycra away from my own skin and said, "Look. Bathing suit as metaphor."

Now we lie side by side on webbed lounge chairs and I ask her about her dates with Jack. "Are you still attracted to him?" I ask.

"How would I know?"

I repeat her words and say that's a puzzling answer. *Is* she physically attracted to Jack, yes or no?

Bernice sits up in her chair. The skin over her belly droops and forms a fold. "Would you believe that I cannot remember a goddamn thing about us in bed? Nothing. Not his arms, his shoulders, his hands . . ." She lies down again, relaxing the frown so the sun won't record it.

"That's odd," I say.

"Why? It's been a whole lifetime, and a fair number of memorable men in between. I'm not saying it makes sense. I probably blocked it. I have a vague recollection of us groping around in his car. But I've blocked the married sex—you know, in a double bed; kosher."

I adjust the arms of the aluminum chair so I'm lying perfectly flat. "You're still married," I say. "You could refresh your memory. I'm sure Judge Willson would give you his blessing."

"That pervert! He'd be just the one I'd go running to for advice."

I ask if she has any idea what Jack's disposition is on their dating.

"He's not so thrilled. We're not exactly a computer match."

"What do you talk about when you're out?"

"You! What else?"

"Do you talk about your feelings?" I ask after a pause.

"My. Aren't we the little psychiatrist."

"You're saying you don't have things to say to each other about the stuff that happened between you—"

"Which we blame each other for, in case you haven't noticed."

"Well, there's a starting point."

Bernice says matter-of-factly, "Jack, I hate you and you hate me. Let's spend the evening discussing it. April thinks it would be a good idea."

"You don't hate him."

Bernice thinks this over and pouts behind her glasses. Finally she says, "You think every relationship in life is as easy as yours and Dwight's. You meet, you fall in love, you paint your new condo together, you get married. Nothing's that simple. I'm being asked to spend evenings with a man I feel nothing for so I can report back to the counselor and get A's for effort. Period."

I ask how many more dates they have to have to satisfy the counselor. Bernice says it's open-ended.

"Do you want my advice?" I ask.

"Do I have a choice?"

"Maybe you just need to go back to when you were sixteen and seventeen, groping around in the car."

"My, my. A few months of betrothal to an unusually tall man and my daughter thinks everything can be cured by a good stiff one."

I laugh. Another attempt to make me supply the missing statistic in Dwight's physiological equation.

"You know men, though. He'll die of gratitude." She softens the claim with a faint smile.

I laugh and say she might feel a little gratitude herself.

"And how do I broach this with him? Climb into the back seat?"

"It's not so farfetched. Where did you used to go parking?"

"The Rez," she says without hesitation.

"Where?"

"The Chestnut Hill Reservoir."

"Is it still there?"

Bernice says slowly, "I have my own apartment and my own bed and my own French underwear. I'm not going to start jerking men off in the back seat of cars—"

"Not even for a good cause? For therapeutic reasons?"

"I can't believe this is you talking," says Bernice. "Besides, Sumner's refiling as we speak."

"How long will that take?"

"Four months for a hearing. Another two until it's final, providing of course we don't get another day in Judge Willson's kangaroo court."

"He wasn't so far out of line. He's probably presided over thousands of divorces, and he must have seen something worth preserving between you and Jack."

"He wanted to stick it to me. Big-shot television star dumping her childhood husband."

"You didn't file. How was he supposed to have known who was dumping whom?"

Bernice sits up slowly, letting her abdominal muscles do the work. She removes her sunglasses to sting me with her eye contact. "You think he wants to dump me? Is that your assessment of this situation? Jack wants me out of the picture?"

"He's the one who filed."

"He filed because he was testing the waters. He was waiting for me to say, 'But, Jack, everything's all right now. April's happy. You're single. I'm unattached for the moment. Let's see what happens.' "

"I don't think he's that devious. I think he wanted to do the right thing."

"You don't think that *schlumpf* of a lawyer got to Willson and said, 'Don't allow it. He really doesn't want to go through with it. Find some loophole so he can stall for more time'?"

I tell her no, I don't think that.

"You think everything is just the way it appears to be? Jack is content with his quiet celibate life in New Hampshire, getting his jollies by showing women how to wrap themselves around a golf club? I come back into his life—a successful woman, still attractive, still single. The mother of his child. You don't think he's fantasized about us being together, one way or another?"

"I'm sure he has—"

"So what are you campaigning for—'Do it and get pregnant and he'll have to stick by you?' Too late for that, kiddo. You say he's not interested. Good. I'm not interested either. Everyone agrees."

I shrug and roll over on my stomach. "The sun feels wonderful," I say.

"You should have sunglasses on." A few minutes later she asks, "What was that all about?"

"What?"

"Your theory—give him some great sex and everything will work itself out."

I lift my face from my crossed arms and say, "Dwight."

"This is Dwight's idea?"

I put my head back down and mumble, "He thinks you two could end up together."

Bernice forces a scornful laugh. "What does he base this brilliant theory on, other than some after-school special on tricking your divorced parents into reconciliation?"

I say carefully, "Dwight thinks that if you loved each other once, you can feel that way again."

She answers patly with the favorite cliché of television guests discussing their divorces: "Instead of growing up, we grew *apart*, April."

"What about the counseling?" I ask.

"Believe me, our therapist is not so keen on this so-called marriage. He's no Pollyanna."

"Not like me and Dwight, you mean?"

She shrugs and asks for the first time where he is. Not working on a Sunday, is he, in the archives?

He's in New Hampshire, I say, getting lessons on how to wrap himself around a golf club.

Dwight returns for dinner, with Jack. I notice that with the men present, Bernice tosses her head and speaks in brittle phrases, television style. She interviews Dwight on his day's activities: Does he like golf? Will he take up the game? Is his height an asset or a handicap?

"Maybe Jack would like to see the pool?" I ask Dwight pointedly.

He fakes a host's enthusiasm and says, "Great! I'll lend you a suit. We can turn on the Jacuzzi." They take a few minutes to change and enthuse.

As soon as they're out the door, Bernice turns to me, knowing I staged the field trip to gain a private audience. "What did I do *now?*" she asks, rolling her eyes.

"Is this how you charm all those other men?"

"I don't know what you're talking about."

I imitate her well-modulated tones: " 'How was your golf game, Dwight? I understand it can be quite addictive.' "

"I see. This is my problem, then? If I talked some other way you'd be happier and I'd be a better person?"

"You never let your guard down with him. I'm sure he finds it quite intimidating."

"I'm perfectly nice to him. As nice as I am to anyone."

"And that makes you happy? Because sometimes I think I should work at shaping you into a normal person so you'll have friends and you won't be . . . needy."

"In what way am I needy?"

"Not exactly needy—"

She holds up her hand: Wait. No turning back now with this character analysis. Tell me what you were thinking; tell me what it is I need to know.

I search for a phrase that will suit us both and pronounce it softly: "It's lonely at the top, I bet."

Bernice nods sadly. I sit down on an unpacked carton, and she does the same a few moments later. She speaks first. "I'm taking your criticism very well, don't you think?"

"Yes," I say. "Yes, I do."

"When did you first see me as needy?"

I don't answer but think, Always.

"It's very perceptive of you to see it."

"Thank you."

"I hide it very well. I fool everyone, but not you." She smiles broadly, prods my shin playfully with the pointed toe of her white, jeweled shoe.

"What?"

"It's because you love me," she says.

When the men return, Bernice and I are telephoning restaurants. I notice her studying Jack's half-naked body, wrapped in a towel. He has a ludicrous golfer's tan, his torso white within the outline of a short-sleeved polo shirt. I laugh and tease him about it. Dwight steps between us, flexing, and says, "You like it like that? I can do it too, baby." Jack rubs the palms of his hands across his muscular chest and down his arms apologetically. Bernice continues to stare most solemnly.

The four of us go to Sally Ling's where Bernice had told me version number one of my conception. She announces that Jack has come a long way from his subgum and sparerib days. He no longer looks for chow mein noodles or attacks his plate with soy sauce.

"Your influence?" asks Dwight.

"He'd never had anything but a combination plate. I gave him his first moo shu pork."

"Was this on one of your dates?" I ask.

Jack's face flushes a shade redder. Bernice says, "They don't have good Chinese in southern New Hampshire. Not like this, at least."

"I didn't even think I liked Chinese food," he adds.

Bernice uses her menu to shield one side of her face, pretending to shut Jack out. "He's still at the cashew-chicken stage. I'm letting him think that's the real thing until I phase in the Szechuan."

"She thinks I'm a yokel," says Jack. "She's showing me life in the big city."

I wait a few seconds and ask, "How's that been?"

He checks Bernice for her reaction, but she is pretending to read the menu. I recognize that look of bland disregard and know she's listening intently. "Like you see us," he says. "She acts like Bernice and I go along for the ride." He raises his voice and asks, "Would you agree with that?"

She raises her eyebrows innocently: Me? Was I supposed to be eavesdropping on your conversation with April?

I humor her by repeating, "Jack was saying that he's been coming down to Boston every so often."

"She has much more interesting dates with her business-men and law professors," says Jack.

"Those are not dates. They're work-related. I've told you that."

"People recognize her, you know. They come up to her, and then they look at me and wonder, Do I know him, too? Is he the guy who does the weather on her channel? Bernice doesn't say, 'I'd like you to meet Jack Remuzzi,' because she might have to say, 'He runs the pro shop at the Ponemah Country Club.' "

"That's ridiculous. One doesn't introduce one's date to *fans.*"

"If you were out with the president of Harvard University—"

"Who's married, by the way."

"He's being hypothetical," I say.

"If you were out with the president of Harvard University and some fan in a fur coat came over and said, 'Oh, Miss Graves, I love your show. I watch it whenever I have a day off from being a doctor at the Mass. General'—tell me you wouldn't say, 'Oh, thank you, Doctor. I'd like you to meet my date, the president of Harvard University.' "

"Don't look now," Dwight coughs into his closed fist.

A middle-aged woman is approaching our table with a fluttery smile. She's in white slacks, girdled, and a crocheted pink shell—the summer version of every woman who has ever approached Bernice in public. The woman takes the last four steps up to our table on tiptoes.

Bernice's voice gets louder; she says with false energy, "Oh, sure. I have dozens of occasions every year to have dinner with the president of Harvard!"

The approaching fan hears, and the smile grows even more reverential. "Bernice," she says in a childlike voice.

Bernice stops in midsyllable as if she hasn't seen the woman coming.

"I know I shouldn't do this—I know you don't remember me—but I was in the audience for your show on foot problems, and I was the one who asked the podiatrist about those jellies that little girls wear . . . ? Anyway, I got phone calls and cards from people I hadn't seen for years who saw me on your show!"

"Did you," says Bernice.

"And I still run into people who saw me, and I just

wanted you to know that more people watch your show than I ever would have believed."

"What's your name?" Bernice asks her suddenly.

"Cissy Panacek."

"Well, Cissy, I'd like to introduce you to some people: my daughter, April, the Latin teacher. Her fiancé, Dwight, who's with the Kennedy Library. And Jack Remuzzi, my escort for the evening."

Cissy practically curtsies, bobbing her head to each of us in turn.

"Jack is a golf pro," Bernice says airily. "Isn't that an interesting line of work?"

"A golf pro. That *is* interesting."

A waiter approaches our table with pen and pad. Bernice says, "So nice to meet you. And give my regards to all those old friends who saw you on the show."

"I will," says Cissy. "You bet I will. And I'm gonna tell them I met you here."

"With my family."

"You bet," says Cissy and backs away. We smile strained smiles of farewell until she's back at her own table.

"We need a few more minutes," Bernice tells the waiter.

"They never come back when you do that," I say.

Bernice waits until we are alone before murmuring, "The high point of Cissy's life."

"Are you serious when you say that?" Jack demands.

"Can't any of you take a joke, ever?"

"What about me? I'm your best audience," says Dwight.

She turns to Jack. "Didn't I do a nice job making you part of the moment?"

"My *escort* for the evening, some guy I met an hour ago. Yeah, that was a thrill."

"That's right! Because it's ridiculous to give a fan the

time of day. I could have been seventy-five percent less charming and she'd still watch. God knows they bother you all the same in restaurants."

"If it wasn't for people like her, you wouldn't be on the air," says Jack.

"You mean 'Lesson One in Famous Broadcasters' School: Be nice to your fans. Where would we be without them?' Because you can become a slave to that."

"It's not such bad advice," says Jack. "I think when you're in the public eye, you have to put yourself out a bit. I'm not saying I'm in the same boat as you, but I know a little bit about being nice to the people whose dues pay my salary. If you don't like getting interrupted at restaurants, you should find another line of work."

"Or eat at home," I say.

Bernice emits a disgusted huff. How could we ever understand the life of a famous person? "Let's change the subject," she says. "What are we eating?"

"It's my treat," says Jack.

"No, it is not," says Bernice.

"We're grown-ups. You don't always have to treat," I say, looking at Dwight.

"You save your money for your mortgage payments," says Jack. "After you're married and you've established some kind of financial schedule you can pick up the check. But I insist this time."

"All *right!*" says Bernice. "This is boring. You pay. I don't care."

"Good. Let's have some moo shu pork with those pancakes. And how about cashew chicken?"

Bernice laughs and says, "For a change."

"Their whole crispy fish is good," I say.

"Too exotic for Jack."

"Do we want a shrimp dish?" asks Dwight. "Shrimp with garlic sauce?"

"Sure. And one more," says Jack.

"Noodles—house special noodles," I say.

"She has my metabolism," says Bernice.

"Jack's pretty svelte," I say.

"That's true," Bernice murmurs without looking up from the menu. We catch the waiter's attention. Bernice recites our list, adding her own adjectives—that marvelous shrimp with garlic sauce, those fabulous house special noodles. After he leaves, Bernice smiles coyly. I detect a self-consciously naughty statement bubbling up inside her. "No," she says to us. "I shouldn't." She takes a sip of her wine and studies the glass.

"What?" I ask.

She shakes her head.

"C'mon," says Dwight.

She leans sideways and says to Jack, "April thinks you and I need to talk."

"Oh, yeah?" he asks.

"She thinks we need to turn back the clock sexually." Bernice stops. "Am I quoting you accurately?"

"I didn't mean for this to be a public forum."

"What?" Jack asks. "What are we talking about here?"

"This is between the two of you," I say.

Bernice blinks at me determinedly. She adds a slight jerk of her head until I get it and say, "Maybe Dwight and I will go for a walk until the food comes."

Jack squints at me, then Bernice. "The food's coming," he tries.

"We'll be right back. Once around the block."

"Is it safe around here?" asks Jack.

I lead Dwight to the front door and out to the sidewalk. I tell him they need time alone.

"So do we." He squeezes my hand.

"I didn't want to be there when she says, 'Jack, have you ever had a total-body massage on satin sheets?'"

" 'A *fabulous* total-body massage—' "

" 'And do you mind if I wear transparent French under-wear while I straddle your body?' " I add.

Dwight fakes a start toward the restaurant. I pull him back.

"I might be missing some classically excruciating question, though," he says. " 'How does Jack Remuzzi *really* feel, in here, inside, about the woman he called Bernie—' "

I put my fingers in my ears, close my eyes, and rattle my tongue noisily to block out hypothetical Bernice questions.

Dwight stops me with a kiss; his face is warm. I remember noticing in the restaurant a touch of sunburn on his cheeks, and I tell him how beautiful he looks, even in the dark.

They leave together after dinner, Jack's van following Bernice's white Mercedes. We are told that she's leading him to 93 North because he gets mixed up on Storrow Drive and ends up at the airport. Dwight and I try to look convinced; we know he can get to 93 North blindfolded. Jack rubs his face during her explanation, leaving the suggestion of a sheepish smile.

We watch them pull away from their parking spots. Bernice honks and signals; the Ponemah Country Club van noses out and they are gone. I wave nonchalantly, as if Jack really needs directions, as if Bernice isn't lying. As if, in my head, I haven't tied old shoes and tin cans to their bumpers.

THIRTY-EIGHT

Two weeks later, Bernice calls me the afternoon of our Thursday dinner date and tells me I should dress up. She feels, well . . . festive! Summer dresses will make us lovely and give us the option of eating elegant or casual. She personally is going to wear her gold silk sheath with the Mandarin collar and cap sleeves. Assuming it meets with my approval?

I wear my new navy blue Laura Ashley dress, long-waisted and vaguely sailorish, selected to complement my engagement ring. It is Trude's diamond. Dwight has had it reset in yellow gold, flanked by triangular sapphires. Bernice hasn't seen it yet, and I won't tell her that the heart of it was my mother's. I want her to fuss over it and play with my hand in the candlelight as if no food or conversation could detract from its glory. The first day I wore the ring to school I thought it would hypnotize my class—that thirty pairs of eyes would follow my newly adorned hand through every gesture. No one said anything. Not one pair of eyes focused on my finger. When I picked up my mail in the main office, I waved to Anne-Marie from across the room. She was on the phone, but pointed to my hand, rocked in her chair, and mimed a scream which, if executed, would have been grounds for psychiatric leave.

When I arrive at Bernice's, she says she is dying for fish. Legal Sea Foods, or that café in Copley Place? She'll call and see which place has the shorter wait. The doorbell rings a minute later as Bernice is looking up a number. "Get that, please," she sings from the kitchen.

Smiling women, faces I know, are standing outside like carolers, each holding a lit silver candle and a wrapped present. They are singing, "I'll be with you in apple blossom time . . . I'll be with you to change your name to mine. . . ." Bernice is at my side suddenly, her arm around my waist. Belatedly they yell "Surprise!" as I stare stupidly, then burst into tears. They file past me into Bernice's living room: Anne-Marie; Dwight's mother and sister Lorraine; Bernice's stylish TV assistants; my high school friends Lizzie and Joan, whom I haven't seen since my mother's funeral; Sheryl Kierstead and Rita Mc-Donald, whose homerooms flank mine at QHS; and finally, Sonia. Yards behind them is the hired help, a handsome young man wearing a T-shirt tuxedo.

"It's a bridal shower, you dope," says Anne-Marie when we are all inside. I begin pointing and introducing the disparate guests, but they drown me out with good-natured groans about how, after hiding out together in a neighbor's apartment for an hour, they're hardly strangers. Bernice's refrigerator, it turns out, is packed with the pot-luck contributions. The Harvard Student Employment worker is immediately on the job pulling off plastic wrap and turning the counter into a buffet table. Exotic flowers are released from their hiding place in Bernice's shower.

"I prayed you wouldn't open the fridge or use the bathroom," Bernice shouts to me over everyone's head.

I tell her it is the nicest surprise ever. The planning, the organizing, the birds of paradise against the black of her kitchen.

"This is what I'm best at," she says. "Didn't I tell you that once? I am made for this role." It is true. Bernice is laughing with every task, working side by side with the student. She participates socially, it seems, by remote control, monitoring conversations in every room and yelling her comments across the kitchen's half-wall, happily, good-naturedly.

Only Sonia is familiar enough to return her loud shouts of laughter. She winks at me when she sees me listening to their badinage.

I walk to her side and say, "I'm awfully glad you're here."

She grabs me for a long hug and tells me I look great. "*And,* lemme look!" She holds my left hand in her open palm and peers at my new ring. "Absolutely gorgeous," she says. "Wear it in good health." We both smile down at it. I return some of her compliments: she is stunning tonight in her taupe jersey dress.

"Do you believe how this has turned out?" she murmurs, wiping her coral lipstick off my cheek. "I never thought I'd hear from her again."

I tell her I'm sorry—Bernice pressed me for the name of my informant and I buckled under. I tell her we should have no regrets, though; just the opposite. Even Bernice would say everything turned out okay.

"About the fatherhood thing? About Jack?"

I nod. "I'm really very fond of him."

"She told me."

"You know they never got divorced?"

Sonia closes her eyes and says, "Unbelievable."

"Did she tell you the whole story—how they went to court but the judge threw them out? Now they date."

"I know. It's ludicrous."

"No, it's not. He's very sweet."

Sonia nods slowly, analytically. "And you think that's what Bernice is compatible with? Sweet?"

I laugh. "Who the hell knows what she's compatible with?"

"You're sweet. *Jack* is sweet. I'm sweet, for chrissakes. Bernice is not sweet. Why push them together and make both of them miserable? She'd eat him alive. Let him divorce her and find some nice little woman to live happily ever after with."

"You think Bernice wants that, too?"

"Sure she wants that. She likes him. . . . She *appreciates* him in her own peculiar way—a nice-looking escort, the father of her child, available at relatively short notice. No demands." She smiles slyly. "Let me amend that—no demands she *objects* to. . . ."

I ask her what she means.

Sonia measures the distance between us and the nearest eavesdropper. "Bernice and I are talking again. Really talking. And I'm not shy about asking questions."

I look over at Bernice, still bustling happily. "She does look happy," I say.

Sonia squints at me. "You think it's that simple—she looks happy because of Jack? Because they *satisfy* each other when it's mutually convenient?"

"No—"

"Because this arrangement of theirs is not a reconciliation. I'm talking about a truce, an understanding, with fringe benefits."

I say maybe Bernice is putting on an act, pretending it's all modern convenience so Sonia won't give her a hard time. Maybe she and Jack actually have something—

"You want everyone to have what you have, which is darling, of course, but it's a fantasy, isn't it? A daughter's wish for two effectively spouseless, maybe desperately lonely people?"

"I'm not the only one. Dwight thinks it's possible."

"Because he's darling, too, sweetie. He wants you to be happy. And he knows you *think* you want them back together. You want an intact family that can just shrink itself down to normal proportions—"

"I want Bernice to have someone besides me."

"Which is lovely. She'd love your saying that. And they are adorable as a squabbling couple. But they don't belong together. As much as you and Dwight belong together, *that's* how much Jack and Bernice don't."

I say I'm not so sure.

She pats my arm and smiles wisely. She turns and asks how all of these people fit into my life. Dwight's mother, she decides, is handsome in a tall, pioneer-woman kind of way. I offer to take her around. "I can do that myself. You mingle."

Before I walk away I ask, "Has Bernice told you explicitly that she and Jack won't get back together?"

Sonia touches my cheek, adjusts the rotation of my head so we are looking directly at each other. I watch her outlined coral lips say "It does not affect you. He is not divorcing his daughter. Repeat after me: I am not going to lose him again."

I mingle. Dwight's mother and sister are being entertained by Anne-Marie. From across the room I hear a lot of *April*s and *Dwight*s in her monologue and know she is telling them her fairy godmother version of us. I join

Bernice's three employees, bunched together and looking uncomfortable. We have never talked about Bernice. I have always imagined her to be a difficult boss, and imagined if we ever exchanged sardonic glances or rolled our eyes just so, we'd be confidantes forever. I thank them for coming tonight and say, "I've never seen Bernice quite like this."

Gwen, the production assistant with the longest tenure, says, "Like what?"

"Happy, having a good time. Not 'on.'"

They laugh nervously. I ask if she was in this good a mood at work today. The three look to Bernice in the kitchen. She is wearing pot holder mitts and a red organdy half-apron over her Chinese silk sheath, arranging casseroles on trivets with cheerful energy. She is actually taking directions from the Harvard butler; after the student speaks, Bernice rearranges the crockery to create space for a large salad bowl. She stands back and admires her work, then turns to accept her next assignment.

"She's probably relieved with the way everything turned out," says Patti, the secretary. "She was real worried that you might cancel your dinner tonight or that you might really hate the idea of a bridal shower."

"Imagine if you hated this," Gwen murmurs. "The party would have been a disaster. All these people would have to be sent home. You'd be angry at her . . . she'd get angry at you. . . ."

"Was she really that worried?"

They all nod as if it's not the first time they've been brought in to worry about that touchy April. I ask if there's something else—has Bernice seen Jack?

"Jack?" says Patti.

"It's not Jack," says Gwen. "It's this—her daughter, her turf, her surprise party. She thinks your friends are saying to themselves, 'Bernice G! I'm the guest of Bernice G!' No one's questioning whether she belongs or what her role is." Gwen speaks quietly. She is reprimanding me. I look at the others. Their mouths are set, as if they agree with Gwen and are glad she had the nerve to speak for them.

"It's all she wants," Patti adds.

After a few moments I say, "I guess you think I've been really hard on her."

Gwen's speech has made them brave. The second p.a. (Donna? Dawn? I'm afraid to ask at this late date) says, "I guess we hear her side of it, and maybe we sometimes wonder, since your adoptive parents have passed away, why you don't . . . I don't know."

"Bernice isn't perfect," Patti interrupts. "But so what? Nobody's mother is."

I know they are repeating what they've discussed among themselves for months. Their comments sound packaged, as if they've been begged rhetorically at staff meetings, What's the big deal? What does April *want?*

I say, "It's nice to see how much you care about her."

Their faces twitch with a need to say "That's right, April. More than you ever will."

I thank them for their counsel and excuse myself to mingle. When I look back at them a few minutes later with a smile that hints of remorse and reform, their circle has tightened and they don't see me.

We eat with plates on our laps. Bernice doesn't even mention the genuine suede upholstery beneath us. Everyone is given credit for her contribution: Anne-Marie the fruit kebabs, Rita the relish tray, Gwen the baked Brie with almonds, Patti the zucchini quiche, Dawn the pasta salad, Mrs. Willamee and Lorraine the spiral-cut ham and baked beans, Lizzie the gigantic tossed salad, Joan all the dips, Sheryl the homemade four-grain bread, Sonia the calamari vinaigrette.

The Harvard student, whose name is Oren, pours the

champagne and the Perrier. Bernice tells him during one refill that the guest of honor and her fiancé are Harvard people as well. When he carries our dirty dishes away, out of earshot, Anne-Marie asks Bernice if the agency puts out an illustrated catalogue or if she just lucked out.

"Do you believe it? All I said was 'a guy, over twenty-one,' and this is what rings my doorbell." We laugh. Dwight's mother smiles pleasantly, vacantly, as if reflecting on how nice for us that Harvard boys are as helpful as they are smart.

"Architecture," Bernice announces quietly. "His fellowship covers almost nothing. He took the subway here."

"Can we ask him to bring in the presents now?" asks Mrs. Willamee.

Anne-Marie has been to countless showers and knows the rituals. She insists we save the bows for incorporation into a loopy bouquet threaded through a paper plate. Bernice is supposed to be recording names for thank-you notes, but she lengthily expounds on each gift, neglecting her job. Oren takes over, producing a numbered list in the beautiful alphabet of architects.

"This isn't a theme shower," Anne-Marie tells me.

"It's not?" I ask.

"You know—kitchen, lingerie, cash—"

"It's eclectic," says Lorraine.

The first present is a joint gift from Sheryl and Rita: a clock radio. I say it is wonderful—neither Dwight nor I have a decent enough alarm to bring into the new condo. Anne-Marie tells me not to rip the paper and to please hand her each bow with as much ribbon attached as possible.

Sonia's is next: a gift certificate for a facial, manicure, massage, and pedicure at Elizabeth Arden. "Nothing for Dwight," she apologizes.

"Except a gorgeous bride," Bernice yells.

I thank Sonia and tell her I've never had even *one* of these things done to me by someone else, that I can't wait. I'll make my appointment the next day.

Anne-Marie's gift wrapping includes a pair of silver doves in a pipe-cleaner cage. The paper is lacy white; the silver and gold bow, superfluous. "The inside's not tacky," she announces.

And she is right. It is a framed black-and-white photograph: an icy wind across the sands of Race Point. Provincetown in winter. I press the frame to me and smile above it at Anne-Marie. A clamor goes up from the guests. I explain, my voice suddenly choking, "Dwight proposed to me in Provincetown."

They insist I pass it around. Sonia squints at the penciled signature and asks if it's a Joel Meyerowitz. Anne-Marie says maybe; it came from a real gallery. They helped her choose the frame.

"Hand her the next one," Bernice orders.

It is from Dwight's mother and sister—a corkscrew, an electric coffee grinder (large capacity), and espresso cups. "Dwight gave us the idea," his mother says apologetically.

I tell her I need all of these things, that I wanted them badly, that I will think of her and Mr. Willamee and Lorraine every morning, with every use.

A carton is next—Lizzie and Joan's joint gift, nesting saucepans with Silverstone linings. They are sleek and long-handled. Everyone has a word of advice: season them with olive oil, use those Melomac spatulas so they won't scratch, hang them from the ceiling, don't put them in the dishwasher. "Gorgeous," Bernice exudes. "Fabulous present."

The staff of "Bernice G!" gives me a wardrobe of stationery engraved with "April Willamee," soft gray on pale pink; the notes pale gray with pink edging. "It's beautiful. And a lifetime supply." I say aloud, "April Willamee," and everyone repeats it after me as if declining a new noun.

There is one gift left, a flat dress box, Bernice's. I prepare myself for ostrich feathers and transparent chiffon, for pretending to like a honeymoon fantasy outfit. I open the box slowly. Tissue paper swathes something white, something crisper than nylon or silk. I see and feel white handkerchief linen, a long nightgown and a matching robe, exquisitely beautiful. Tiny embroidered knots of pale blue flowers touch the yoke, but everything else is plain. It looks like the work of French nuns; it looks like what Maria would have worn on her wedding night with Captain von Trapp. It is not what Bernice would want me to wear, certainly never anything she'd wear herself. But she picked it for me. It is *my* dream lingerie, *my* idea of what is beautiful. And she knew it.

Lizzie and Joan, with the ride back to Providence ahead of them, are the first to leave. Everyone offers to stay and help, but it is a formality: Oren has washed dishes and packaged leftovers by the time the guests ask. He's wiped the kitchen with Formula 409, removed the leaves from the table, and is now casually drinking Perrier, awaiting further orders. "He's a whiz," says Anne-Marie. "I'm definitely getting him for my next party."

"Maybe you can give him a lift to the T," I suggest.

"We have to take care of the business end of things," says Bernice sharply. "And there's actually more straightening up to do." She calls him into the foyer to help me carry the gifts. In two trips down to the building's garage, Oren and I pack the car. I repeat Anne-Marie's offer— does he need a ride to the T?

Oren smooths back his dark, close curls with a confident hand and says, "No, thanks."

We wait for the elevator back up. "Your sister tells me you went to Harvard," says Oren.

"Bernice?"

"Yeah."

"I did. A long time ago. Before you were there." Before you were *born,* I think. I ask him how old he is.

He smiles and says with assurance, "Twenty-five. I took a couple of years off after college."

We ride up in silence. "One of the nicer showers I've done," he says.

Bernice is sitting on the sofa, holding the bouquet of bows coquettishly.

"Thank you so much," I tell her. "I'll never forget a moment of this."

"I'm giddy!" she shrieks. "I am so relieved I'm giddy! It was fabulous, wasn't it? I throw a great bridal shower."

I kiss her, and she kisses me back in spunky, sisterly fashion. "I'll call you tomorrow," she says.

I say good night and thanks again; I call her Sis.

"Drive carefully," says Bernice. She throws the bouquet at me.

"Nice meeting you, Oren. Thanks for everything," I say, backing out.

"Have a nice wedding," calls the dark and handsome Oren.

THIRTY-NINE

My dress is a pearly gray satin, just as Lucia imagined in her vision. She has deepened and widened the V neck of the original and given me long sleeves, which she pushes up to just below my elbows. The skirt is full—two and seven-eighths yards of satin. There is a crinoline sewn into the waist, just like the party dresses of my childhood. Bernice's pearls are around my neck, ostensibly the "something borrowed"; later she will insist I keep them.

Jack sits next to Bernice in the front row, two seats in from the aisle. After Freddie walks me to Dwight, he joins them, takes the first chair. My back is to them now, but I imagine Bernice welcoming Freddie to the row with a quivering smile. There is my family, three abreast, Freddie, Bernice, and Jack.

They cry during the ceremony. At least I attribute the sniffling from the front row to be the work of all three. Judge Baskin raises his voice to be heard above them. Jack

honks into what I imagine is a big white golfer's handkerchief. He is tanned already, only days after summer arrives
at the Ponemah Country Club.

Dwight and I exchange the civil vows, our hands on his
mother's ancient missal. Lorraine comes forward to read
from the New Testament and Freddie, my only candidate,
in a yarmulke, says a Hebrew blessing. Bernice, in a polka-
dot taffeta suit, reads salient stanzas of Tennyson's "De-
meter and Persephone" as if she's spotlit on a blackened
stage:

> *Me, Me, the desolate mother! "Where?"—and turned,*
> *And fled by many a waste, forlorn of man,*
> *And grieved for man through all my grief for thee—*

She reads endlessly and sits down. There is an embarrassed shifting by guests who expected a poem of love and
celebration. Judge Baskin smiles like an emcee moving on
to the next talent and asks the guests to indulge him in a
civil benediction. Dwight and I relax our stance and listen
with our fingers entwined over our new gold rings. He
says a judge's work makes him cynical and pessimistic,
even sad and angry. He sees the dark side of human nature,
of people, and wonders if that evil has eclipsed all that is
good and bright, if love can take root and flourish. But
when there are forces in this world that bring together
people like April and Dwight . . . well . . . how bad can
things be? No couple seems better suited; no marriage he's
performed has made him happier. He winks at me and
says he is going to show off his Latin for the occasion,
then booms out, *"O si sic omnia!"* Oh, if all were thus. . . .

Then he says, "On to business. By the power vested in
me by the Commonwealth of Massachusetts, I now pronounce you husband and wife." Dwight wraps his long
arms around me for a serious kiss, and I reach up to circle

his neck. Here the photographer begins the candid shots;
this first one—Dwight calls it "Woman Marries Giraffe in
Civil Ceremony!"—will be framed and hung, like religious art, on the wall above our headboard.

There are too few of us for dancing, so we eat and drink
champagne. Freddie wants everyone eating and happy.
Guests with empty plates are led laughing and protesting
to the table where a chef custom-carves the hotel's most
expensive cut of beef.

Bernice holds herself in check, playing guest instead of
mother. She circulates; talks for a long time, I notice, with
Anne-Marie in strapless emerald green. I drift their way
and ask, "What are you two conspiring over?"

"Men," says Anne-Marie.

"I'm fixing her up with Tony from the station, the
traffic reporter."

"The one in the helicopter," says Anne-Marie.

"Does he know?" I ask.

"I'll tell him!" Bernice says. She turns to Anne-Marie.
"I'd steer him toward dinner at a place like Jasper's and
wear what you have on now."

"I'd wait and see what Tony said first," I suggest.

Bernice pats my cheek. She and Anne-Marie exchange
smiles. "We know you would, darling," says Bernice.

She says she must circulate and will be calling Anne-
Marie at home. When we're alone, Anne-Marie says she
has been watching the famous Freddie, noticing his *extreme*
politeness and respect for all, *despite* reports to the con-
trary. Most attractive, too, she's noticed, the lack of
formal introductions *notwithstanding*.

"He's on his best behavior—under strict instructions not
to hit on Bernice, you, or Dwight's sisters."

"How thoughtful," she says sourly. She adds that she

feels sorry for Bernice's date. "He looks like a lost soul. I felt like telling her to stop ignoring him."

I look over at Jack, who is stretching the acceptance of an hors d'oeuvre into conversation with a waitress. I watch silently and say, "He's not her date. That's my father."

Anne-Marie raps my midriff with the back of her hand and hisses, "Your *father's* here, you asshole? And you just happened to forget to tell me?"

"I'm sorry. I thought you knew."

Anne-Marie hands me her empty champagne glass. The sighting of Jack Remuzzi evidently requires her full concentration. "God! He must be mortified knowing everyone's checking him out and thinking, So *he's* the one. . . . And your brother running the show, giving you away and all, like you have no father."

I hand the empty glass to a passing waitress and tell Anne-Marie I will introduce her.

"To Freddie?"

"C'mon."

I lead her to Jack. He smiles gratefully when he sees us approaching. "Jack," I say, "this is Anne-Marie Nardello. She runs the office at my school and is a close friend of mine and Dwight's." He nods, just enough to be polite. I can see he wants to talk to me and has little inclination to chat with a determined small-talker. Anne-Marie senses this and says congratulations, it's lovely to make his acquaintance. Will we excuse her?

Freddie intercepts her immediately as if she is the very buffet customer he's been waiting for. He guides her to the plates and silverware, an ambitious hand on her strapless back, whispering something that makes her smile.

Jack moves me a foot farther away from the milling guests and says, "Honey, I've got to take off."

"Why?"

He jiggles his feet like a runner before a race. His shoulders shrug sheepishly. "You know," he says.

"Are you having a terrible time?"

"I don't know anyone. I feel kinda foolish, neither fish nor fowl."

"Then you stay with me. I'll introduce you to everyone."

"Bernice took care of that, more or less. Ike introduced me to his family."

"Dwight."

"Yeah. He said, 'This is Jack Remuzzi, April's newly discovered dad.' I thought that was nice. Like I was good news instead of a lizard that crawled out from under a rock."

"You *are* good news. I thought you knew that."

He quickly looks down at the floor, and I don't press him for an answer. In a few moments he whispers, his voice cracking, "All I can say is, I give those people credit, God rest their souls."

I know who he means, but I ask anyway. "People?"

"Your people. The Epners. Whatever they did"—he breaks off—"that you could be raised and not hate . . . the person—"

I put my hand on his sleeve and leave it there, hoping he'll be able to finish the tribute.

"You don't think ninety-nine out of a hundred kids would hate the people who did what we did?" He shakes his head in amazement. "They must have made you feel very secure, and loved. That's the reason you're the way you are now. That's their doing. I wish they were here right now. I'd walk over and say, 'Thank you, Brother Epner; thank you for what you did for my little girl. Whatever you did, I take my hat off to you!' "

"I wish they were here, too," I say after a shaky silence.

"And I wish Bernice had heard what you said about them."

"She's jealous," Jack says. "She wants to close the gap and pretend she never lost you, that no one else ever stepped in."

I hold out the full width of my skirt. "This is my mother's wedding dress. We copied the original from a picture."

"It's a knockout. You look beautiful."

"Then you don't think it's a morbid thing to do—wear the dress of your dead mother?"

"Hell, no. I think it's nice."

"It's a way to have her be a part of the wedding."

He says, "Sure; that makes sense."

"I have to work at it, to preserve her, because Bernice is right there, stepping on her heels, halfway into her shoes. It's like losing a baby and having a replacement right away, even calling her by the same name, as if the first one didn't count."

Jack chews on his lower lip for a few seconds, thinking it over. "But maybe Bernie thinks *she* was the original, and she got totally forgotten. You got a new mother and never looked back."

"I don't think she automatically becomes 'Mother' because Trude's dead. It's something I have to feel."

Jack raises his shoulders apologetically. "Maybe it's just a matter of time."

I say I don't know. Bernice would die of happiness if I were to call her Mom. You'd think I'd be able to push myself to do it, wouldn't you? Sometimes I want to, but once it slipped out, there would be no turning back. "Do you and she talk?" I ask.

"Sure."

"Do you talk about me?"

"Of course! What else do we have to talk about?"

"Your marriage," I say carefully.

"Jesus," says Jack. "You call this a marriage?"

"Technically."

"Look—" he says, then hesitates. After all, it's my wedding day. No time for an argument, not the time to say, It won't work out, not the way you think it should.

"Are you fighting?"

He shrugs. "We're polite. She brought me around to meet a few people."

"I should've asked you to bring a date or something so you wouldn't feel alone."

He shakes his head. "No, no, I wouldn't have. I thought Bernice and I would be in the same boat, sit together at the reception. Have our private toast for you; have a good cry. Mother and father of the bride, without the papers. But she has her friends here and we're on our own."

I ask if he's sorry he came.

He says I've got to be joking. Miss my wedding? All he's been saying to himself, a hundred times a day, is "How lucky can a guy get—his daughter doesn't get married at twenty-one, twenty-two, like a lot of girls do, but waits until her father can be there." He looks worried suddenly. "I didn't mean you were waiting on purpose for me to show up. I just meant it was a lucky coincidence for me that you met Dwight later and got married now instead of then."

"Worth the wait on all counts, I'd say."

"That's for damn sure. I like this husband of yours. He makes you smile, and that's when I think you look like my side of the family."

We grin at each other self-consciously. I motion to Dwight to join us. "Jack's leaving now," I tell him, slipping my arm around Dwight's waist.

"So soon? Before the cake?"

Jack puts his hand on his stomach and says he couldn't eat another bite. Great food. A feast.

"He's got a long ride back," I say.

Dwight shakes Jack's hand and says, "I can't thank you enough for coming."

"Me, too," I say, and cut myself off. The lump in my throat allows nothing more. Jack hears it in my voice and can't answer either. I sniffle, and he blows his nose into his handkerchief.

"What a pair," says Dwight.

I go into the powder room and within seconds Bernice is by my side. "I saw you having a heart-to-heart with your father," she says, watching me in the mirror.

Instead of answering, I trace my lips with my pinkie as if it has cosmetic properties.

"Do I get to hear what you were talking about?"

When I still don't answer, she says, "You looked upset when you were talking to him."

"No, I wasn't."

She hesitates, then says, "I thought he said something that made you cry."

"I guess you were watching pretty closely."

"Am I right?"

I say carefully, "He said some lovely things to me. I got a little weepy, that's all. We both did. It's my wedding day."

Bernice says, "Oh," and clamps her mouth shut. She's not interested in tears of joy.

"Don't do this," I say.

She purses her lips and says, "Don't do what?"

I turn to speak to her directly instead of to her image in the mirror. "He understands about Trude and Julius. He was saying that if they were here today he'd walk over to them and shake their hands and say 'Thank you for taking care of April. You did a great job.' He's not jealous of them."

"And I am, of course. Is that a given?"

"You've never said anything like that, something as basic as 'Thanks for taking care of her when I couldn't.' "

"They're dead! Was I supposed to stage a séance?"

"You never said anything like that to me—about your being grateful."

"But I think that!" she protests. "Of course I think that. Who wouldn't? And I let you get this dress as your monument to her, didn't I? I thought that was the same thing. I just didn't say it in so many words."

I ask myself, and repeat the question aloud: "Then why do you make me feel guilty about loving them?"

She flinches.

"You shouldn't be jealous of them. They loved me . . . they were my parents. Children love their parents."

"Like you love Jack?" she asks petulantly.

"Should I apologize for that?"

"You hardly know him. He walks onto the scene and does everything right. Instant father. Love at first sight."

"Why? Is there something I should know about him, another deep secret you've forgotten to tell me, that should turn me against him? Something I'm too blind to see myself?"

"No," she says.

"I just shouldn't like him so much, because you say so, or because he's not your type?"

"Don't put words in my mouth. What I'm saying is, what's so great about Jackie Remuzzi? What marvelous attribute does he have that I don't have?"

I weigh the consequences of telling the truth, that there's just something right between us, but say instead, "I feel sorry for him. He seems so sad."

"And I don't?"

"He always looks lost. It makes me want to rescue him."

"Because he lives in the sticks and sells golf clubs, is that why? While I'm too successful to seem vulnerable? I don't appear to need rescuing?"

"Maybe."

"Well, I do! I wouldn't have put myself through all this if I didn't need you. And what you're saying about wanting to rescue Jack is that you don't love me. In all this time you don't feel for me what you felt for him in the first five minutes. So what do I do now? Wait around and work harder, or just accept the inevitable?"

I turn back to my reflection. Trude's dress in the mirror brings Trude forth. I hear whining complaints from the small April: *You love Freddie more than you love me. I was here first, so you should love me more.*

I see myself, the child, scowling; I remember Trude drawing me toward her, soothing me until I gave up the fight and let myself be hugged; the not-very-long arms and the small hands soothing me, telling me a truth I finally believed after she was gone, the answer I now give Bernice: "How can you even think that? I love you both the same."

Without dancing, the reception is short. It is, after all, a Monday night, so the guests line up eagerly for the final ceremonial act, the cutting of the cake. Bernice pushes my sleeves up to my elbows and poufs my skirt to its maximum volume. She says, "I told the photographer not to take that idiotic shot of stuffing cake into each other's mouth. You'll never use it." She steps back into the ranks. The cake is lemon poppy seed, frosted, with dozens of reed-thin candles crowning the third tier. They are lit expertly by the pastry chef, who signals to someone to dim the lights. Our formal cake-cutting posture relaxes, waiting for the knife and the hotel's next special effect. Dwight stands behind me, circles me with his arms. I lean back against him and move only to let his lips slide to new spots on my neck. The knife arrives and we separate reluctantly. The pastry chef makes the first incision, steps back to let us finish the job. One photogenic piece slips onto a small plate. After the guests realize we're not feeding it to each other, they step forward, forming a ragged line. We cut a second piece, then a third. The pastry chef steps in to take over: enough amateur surgery and enough photo opportunities.

Dwight and I stand there, jobless, until we direct the serving. "Mom?" says Dwight, reaching around the others to honor Mrs. Willamee with the first slice.

"Give Bernice the next one," I whisper to Dwight.

"You give it to her."

I hold it out above the others' heads, reserving the second slice until I spot her against the back wall.

"There," says Dwight, but I've already found her.

She's moving, suggesting the sways and dips of a solo cha-cha as faint music seeps in from the partitioned room next door. A passing stranger in a tux—a waiter? a stray guest from another function?—allows her one pirouette, then walks away.

I call her name; she smiles and waves. Her elbows resume their rhythmic pumping.

"Cake," I say, holding the plate higher. Then, more softly, "Mothers first."

She points to her own chest: Me? You're calling me?

"C'mon."

It's a long walk, a long performance—Freddie has rented a grand and spacious room. She makes her way toward us, taffeta rustling. She tortures me with one playful cha-cha-cha en route.

One by one the guests turn back to the bride and groom and to the business of the wedding: isn't it time to toast these two and leave?

Only Dwight and I wait. We watch, almost patiently; we smile for other reasons. We let her dance.